I0618218

Where the Honeybells Grow

RUTHIE LENOR

Where the Honeybells Grow Copyright © 2020 by
Ruthie Lenor

All rights reserved. No part of this book may be
reproduced in any form or by any electronic or
mechanical means, including information storage and
retrieval systems, without written permission from the
author, except in the case of a reviewer, who may quote
brief passages embodied in critical articles or in a
review.

This is a work of fiction. Names, characters, places,
and incidents either are the product of the author's
imagination or are used fictitiously, and any
resemblance to actual persons, living or dead, events,
or locales is entirely coincidental.

ruthielenor.com

Published by Honeybells Publishing
Edited by A.K Edits
Cover Art by Ruthie Lenor

ISBN: 978-0-578-69705-5

First Edition

TO THE LADIES IN THE CHAT WHO KEPT ME
DISTRACTED WHEN I SHOULD HAVE BEEN WRITING.

Where the Honeybells Grow

CONTENT WARNINGS

MENTIONS OF MISCARRIAGE, CANCER, AND SUICIDE
DEATH OF A FAMILY MEMBER

Chapter ONE

"**W**eren't you supposed to have this shit done already, Charles?"

"Quit complaining. It's not like you had anything better to do today."

"I can think of six more things I'd rather be doing than riding around in this hot ass truck of yours. Is it always this hot in April?"

"Quinn, you live in Kansas, the heat's not that different." Quinn cut him a look instead of answering, then adjusted the air vent for the fourth time as he watched the passing landscape. He'd wrestled with coming back home a few years after leaving but never felt the pull to return like he did the one to leave, so he stayed away. He wasn't even sure if he would have come back now, but layoffs at work and his best friend's wedding decided for him. A few days ago, he loaded up his truck to drive the five hundred miles it took to get to East Rock County, a small ranching and farming town about forty miles south of

Fort Worth. He'd been back for a few days, and between his uncle Quincy and Charles, he hadn't been able to dwell on the way his life had been flipped upside down in the last month.

"Where are we going?" Quinn asked. The tall mirrored buildings of downtown gleamed against the morning sun, making Quinn pull his cap down a little further to shield his eyes from the glare.

"I have to pick up the cufflinks and the shoeshine. Y'all's asses can't stand up with me in dusty ass boots."

"Shoeshine, Charles? Since when are you too good for a spit shine?" Quinn looked down at his worn brown boots, thinking about the last time they'd been cleaned. It'd been a while.

"Man, Jordyn will kick my ass if we do that tomorrow. Store-bought shoeshine only." He looked over at Quinn, keeping one eye on the road. "And it's gotta be brand new, not old dried out shit you put water on like we used to do." Quinn laughed, remembering the 'hard times.' "You hear me?"

"It's your wedding," Quinn surrendered. "Are you wearing the dress too?"

"Shut the fuck up." They both laughed, then focused their attention back on the road and their surroundings. The green of the county had long been replaced with the grey concrete of the city.

Ten minutes later, they were pulling into the back of a small jewelry store with lush green climbing vines all over the red brick of the building. Walking around to the front, they opened the heavy front door and walked into the air-conditioned shop, standing at the entrance for a few minutes, happy to have a reprieve from the heat.

"Welcome in, may I help you?" a slim woman asked from behind the counter she leaned on without looking up. She flipped through a magazine while sitting on a wooden stool with her legs crossed at the knee. The tight, low-cut pink dress she wore highlighted her small push-up bra-enhanced breasts and complimented her caramel brown skin well. After looking up and finally noticing Charles and Quinn, she hopped off her stool and looked over both men appreciatively. She settled her eyes on Quinn, impressed by his sweat-sheened brown skin and the way he fit in his jeans.

"I need to pick up some cufflinks." When a few moments went by without her acknowledging he'd said anything, Charles stepped in front of Quinn to block the woman's view then repeated himself.

"Cufflinks."

"I'm sorry," she stammered, shifting her gaze to Charles. "Picking up or picking out?"

"Picking up," Charles repeated slowly, keeping eye contact with her. "Charles Harris."

"I'm Stephanie," she grinned, leaning her head to the left, talking to Quinn. "I'll be right back." She turned and walked through an open doorway to go to the back, leaving Charles to glare and chuckle at Quinn.

"I should have left your ass at the ranch." Quinn gave him a look telling him that would have been appreciated.

"Not my fault I'm the better-looking one." Quinn scratched his chest through the faded PVU tee-shirt he wore then shrugged. "If you wanted undivided attention, you should've brought Greg's ugly ass." They were both laughing when Stephanie came back.

"I have your cufflinks right here, Mr. Harris." She

placed five black wooden boxes on the glass countertop, opening each of them for him to inspect. Each pair of circular wooden cufflinks had been engraved with the initials of a groomsman. Charles picked one up to test the weight, making sure the promised stainless steel and mahogany wood he ordered was what he was getting. "What do you think?" Stephanie asked. Charles was paying too much attention to his purchase to see her looking at Quinn again. Quinn dropped his eyes from hers to the counter, hoping Charles would hurry up.

"I'm guessing this one is yours?" Quinn lifted the cap off his head a little to get a better look then pointed to the pair inlaid with small white diamonds.

"You'd be correct. Looks good, don't it?" Charles took one out of the box and placed it up against his wrist.

"If you have no issues, just sign and date here." Stephanie slid an invoice to Charles, indicating with her well-manicured fingers where he should sign. Quinn wondered if she purposely used her left hand so he could see she wasn't wearing a ring. After signing and having each box placed in its own silver and black gift bag, Stephanie handed them all to Charles and then turned to Quinn with a flirtatious glint in her eyes. She handed him her card, then said, "Call me if I can help you with anything." With a short nod, Quinn took the glossy magenta card with her name centered across the top in bold cursive letters and stuffed it in his pocket before turning to leave.

"Thanks, Stephanie," Charles said, readjusting the bag handles in his grip before following Quinn through the door.

Before the door closed behind them, they heard her

say, "Bye, thanks for coming in."

"I can't take your ass anywhere," Charles told him. "You've only been back four days, and already, the women are throwing their panties at you."

"All I was doing was standing there." Charles cut his eyes at Quinn's typical act of innocence but shrugged it off since that was actually all he'd been doing. No matter how flashy Charles was, Quinn always caught the ladies' eyes.

"You gonna call her?"

"Nah, she's not really my type."

"Since when is pretty, single female not your type?"

"Since I've decided I'm getting too old for all that shit."

"Oh, yeah. Thinking of settling down in your old age, are you?" Quinn glared at Charles. Settling down wasn't on his radar, but dealing with the bullshit that came with his previous relationship wasn't, either. "Hey, it's cool with me if you are. It's about time."

"Don't hold your breath." Quinn dated Paula for over a year; longer than any relationship he'd been in before. What started out as a casual 'call when you're back in town' thing blossomed into a full-fledged relationship. She made him think about being more than just someone's boyfriend. It all ended four months ago when Paula decided she liked her job better than him and accepted a position in D.C. He never told Charles, but it broke his heart, and he didn't want to go through it again. Not wanting to think about it anymore, he pulled his cap back down, feeling the heat of the day on his skin. "Can we go get a drink? It's hot as hell out here."

"We're headed back to Bellbush now. Anthony's supposed to meet us at The Shop, you know we can't keep him waiting."

"The Shop is still open? I thought Ms. Gloria died." When they were growing up, The Shop was a staple in Bellbush. The small nondescript building served up the best breakfast and lunch in the county. When the owner, Ms. Gloria, died, so did the diner. It closed for two years before it opened back up.

"She did," Charles confirmed, pulling onto the interstate. He adjusted the air to get it blowing faster. "Someone else runs the place now. Jordyn got her to do our boutonnieres."

"She turned it into a flower shop?"

"No. She's a baker with a garden in her backyard."

Thinking about what Charles said, Quinn turned and asked, "So she doesn't serve food, just cakes, and shit? I need food, Charles. This is Texas. I need beef in large quantities and a beer or three."

Forty-five minutes later, they were pulling into a gravel drive up to a peach-colored house with a few umbrella-covered picnic tables in the front and a large rectangular sign on the roof. Painted lime green with the name The Shop printed in hot pink, it made the place easy to spot from the road.

"It's about time." Cora fussed her hand on her hip trying to sound stern as they walked through the door. "We close in an hour." She raised her arm to look at the imaginary watch on her wrist, then tapped her foot on the floor.

"Sorry, sis, we had stuff to do." Charles gave his little sister a kiss on the cheek and his best 'please forgive me' face.

"Yeah, yeah," she waved him off. "Anthony's over there talking to Mr. Miller." Both Charles and Quinn grimaced, looking over at Anthony. They'd both been on the receiving end of one of Mr. Miller's long-winded tales of the old days, and neither would wish that fate on anyone. Charles walked off to rescue him. "How you doing, Quinn?" Cora asked, giving him a hug. "It's so good to see you. It's been so long since you've been back." She held him at arm's length to give him a once-over. "Did we do you so bad you had to leave for twenty years?" She was overshooting his absence by a few years, but his staying away was right.

Quinn smiled, returning her gaze, looking her over too. "You look good, girl," he chuckled. Cora had always been the baby, and time had treated her well. Her short natural hair, bleached blonde, suited her perfectly along with the large gold hoops she wore, matching her fiery personality. He'd forgotten she liked to ask back-to-back questions. "It hasn't been twenty years." Quinn looked around the small space with its white-speckled granite countertops and black metal barstools. There were tall potted plants in every corner of the space sitting atop black and white square tiles. He spotted a long stick of incense in the dirt of one plant, filling the room with the scent of jasmine.

"Seems like it," Cora rolled her eyes. "You still look the same." Lifting her hand, she touched the top of his head. "Need a haircut."

Quinn ran his hands through his hair and put his cap back on. "It'll be edged up for the wedding." He paused under her scrutinizing gaze. "And it had nothing to do with y'all—you know how life goes."

"Well, we missed you."

"Missed you too, Cora Belle." Quinn thumped her lightly on the shoulder like he always did when they were younger.

"Ugh!" She shook her head with a smile. "That you remember, but you can't remember to call me." He'd started calling her Cora Belle as a joke when they were growing up, but it had somehow stuck and worked to annoy the hell out of her.

"I'll do better."

"Good." She took his right arm in her hand and started looking at all his tattoos. They covered his arm from his shoulder to his wrist. Everything from metal gears to hammers and wrenches. "Very industrial. I'm impressed. You planning on adding any more?" She turned his wrist from side to side to see if any space was left.

"Might get a wild hair and have another one put somewhere. Can I have my arm back?" He loved his tattoos, but he'd never enjoyed being gawked at because of them.

Cora pushed his arm away. "You've always been annoying, you know. Go have a seat, and I'll bring y'all something to eat." Cora walked away before Quinn could protest. He shook his head at her typical 'ask for forgiveness before permission' behavior.

"Say, Quinn," Anthony pointed to the man beside him, "you remember Mr. Miller, don't you?" Quinn gave the older man a firm handshake.

"It's good to see you." The massive older man looked exactly as Quinn remembered, wearing his ever-present big-brimmed straw hat and oversized jeans with thick white suspenders. "You sure have grown up to be a big man, the spitting image of Quincy. I remember you leaving here a scrawny little thing." Mr. Miller seemed in disbelief. "Damnedest thing."

Charles and Anthony laughed. "No, sir, wasn't me. You must be thinking of Greg." Quinn couldn't remember the word scrawny ever being used to describe him.

"That's right. He was the runt of y'all's group, wasn't he? He coming in for the wedding too?"

"He'll be here later on this evening," Charles answered. "Kenneth's coming in with him. They both live in Florida now."

"So far away? You were the only one that stayed, weren't you, Charles?" Charles nodded his answer. "I guess I need to warn the county folk the gang's back in town. Tell them to tie up their goats." Anthony laughed far too loud for Quinn and Charles' liking. Mr. Miller stood up. "Well, I gotta be getting back home before Vera thinks I've run away. This is what marriage is about. Gotta check in, even as a grown adult. You sure you're ready for this, Charles?"

"Yes, sir, I am," Charles replied with a big grin.

"Alright, I'll see you boys...men, tomorrow." They watched him leave, then looked up when plates of German chocolate cake were set down in front of them.

"Here ya go. There's only two slices left, so you'll have to draw straws to see who gets it." Charles dug right in, already knowing how good it would taste, but Anthony and Quinn took their time forking into the three layers of chocolate and coconut. Anthony hummed his approval then immediately went for a second bite.

"Damn, this is good. You made this?" Anthony asked,

his front teeth gleaming with bits of chocolate cake. Cora set down glasses of ice water, then wiped her hands on the striped apron she wore.

"I just serve, honey. This is all Gerti." The name alone made Quinn think no way anyone under the age of sixty knew how to make cake taste so good. It tasted of experience and the stuff warm bosom hugs were made of. Cora handed Charles a napkin from her apron to take care of the coconut on his chin. His sweet tooth was legendary, and the fact he'd never had a cavity astonished everyone.

"Are there any of those pralines left?" Cora shook her head no as her brother looked around for the glass jars of candy Gerti made.

"Sorry." She pointed her thumb towards Quinn, who looked confused. "Garland Landscaping came by and got what was left."

"She's always spoiling those begging ass boys." Garland Landscaping, owned and operated by Quinn's uncle Quincy, stopped by at least twice a week. Gerti always treated his crew to some of her homemade candy for all their hard work. "They're like little babies," Charles whined.

"Stop it, she's being nice. Like she's being nice by not charging you for the boutonnieres she made." They all stopped as a big black rottweiler came trotting in from behind the counter. Anthony grabbed up his plate and placed his foot on his chair, preparing to stand on it.

"Chill, Anthony. He's big, but he's all bark. Let him sniff you for a bit." Charles gave the dog a scratch behind his ears and received a contented sigh. "How you doing, Joe? Go easy on ole scary-ass Anthony." Anthony shot him a look, then gingerly sat back down stiffly. He was still as stone while Joe walked around him, sniffing his shoes and pants until he was satisfied, then moved on to Quinn and did the same thing to his boots and jeans.

"Leave them alone, Joe," they heard a voice say from behind them. Turning, they saw a woman standing behind the counter, her dark brown skin glowing from the sun and her locs tied up beneath a headscarf, a few loose ones hanging down from the side. "Hey, Charles, sorry you had to wait. I got your order in the fridge when you're ready."

"I'm ready now. Rehearsal's coming up, and I gotta feed this one before he wastes away." Charles pointed to Quinn, then got up, carrying his plate with him, and followed the woman into the back.

"Who is she?" Anthony asked Cora, his eyes still on the door.

"That's Gerti," Cora answered. Joe huffed out a breath before turning on his back in his favorite spot under the window. Quinn, shocked by her appearance, ran her features through his mind again. He'd expected wrinkles and a head full of grey hair, not the smooth brown skin and plump lips he saw.

Chapter TWO

"Shit, who the hell let you drink so much last night, Quinn? I'm gonna kill Greg."

"It wasn't his fault. I'll be fine, Charles." Quinn shook out two, then three aspirin into his hand and swallowed them down with a room temperature bottle of water he found on the table. "I'll be fine," Quinn whispered against the pounding of his head. "Just give me thirty minutes, and I'll be fine." Charles looked over, wondering if Quinn knew what he was saying. He'd said, "I'll be fine," three times in the last few minutes, but by the looks of him, he was anything but. Quinn, wearing his sunglasses to hide the redness of his eyes, closed them, then placed his head in his hands, regretting his decisions from the night before.

As a favor to the bride, they'd had Charles' bachelor party a week ago when Quinn got in so he wouldn't be too hungover to walk down the aisle. But last night, the groomsmen had their own party after the rehearsal dinner since they hadn't all made the bachelor party. Greg supplied the room, and everyone else provided the cigars and alcohol, welcoming Quinn back to town after being away for twelve years. There were lots of stories and lies told and liquor consumed as the old friends reminisced about growing up in the small ranch town in Texas as kids.

"I'ma kill every last one of y'all if you ruin my wedding." Quinn groaned, waiting for the aspirin to kick in. "One by one," Charles added menacingly before opening the balcony door. Quinn turned his head to the right to see Charles lighting a cigarette, then the glass door closed slowly, clicking shut as an exasperated "fuck" rang out into the air.

Quinn got up cautiously, hands on his knees, rolling his body to a standing position, saying a quick prayer he didn't fall over when he stood all the way up. He took a few tentative steps to check his balance, exhaling and breathing in through his nose to stay focused on getting to the balcony door. Sliding it open, he stepped out onto the concrete, squinting his eyes behind his dark shades at the bright sun overhead.

"Look, man, you know I'd never fuck this up for you. You and Jordyn have been meant to be since the sixth grade. You're gonna marry her in," Quinn looked down at his watch, then brought it closer to his face so he could see, "three hours. It'll be the wedding of her dreams. A long time coming, if you ask me." Quinn felt his headache ease up, so he opened his eyes wider and watched Charles take a long drag of his cigarette then blow out the smoke with it still clamped between his lips while he unbuttoned the top button of his stark white dress shirt. "You got another one of those?" Quinn asked, feeling anxious and slightly guilty for his best friend's nervousness. Charles motioned with his head to where the pack sat on one of the balcony chairs next to Quinn.

"Thought you quit," Charles said, finally more comfortable with the button undone. He exhaled again and watched as the white smoke broke up into different directions before disappearing altogether.

"Hmm." Quinn tapped out a cigarette then lit it, taking a long deep drag to calm himself.

"I've always known I'd marry Jordyn," Charles started saying, looking out onto the hotel parking lot below them. "Since the day I saw her walk into..."

"Mr. Stevenson's homeroom," Quinn finished. He and Charles had been best friends since they were in the third grade, and the story of how Charles and Jordyn met had been uttered out of Charles' mouth so many times, Quinn knew it by heart. "Nothing's stopping her from becoming Mrs. Charles Fleetwood Harris."

"Damn, my whole name, huh?" Charles chuckled, feeling a little less irritated. His dad, Lonnie, had always been a big history buff, and Negro League baseball was still one of his favorite subjects. When it came time for his firstborn son to be named, Lonnie and his wife chose Charles as a first name after her father, and Fleetwood after Moses Fleetwood Walker, who'd played catcher for the Toledo Blue Stockings. It was a great compromise for both proud parents, but Charles had never liked it. He always complained there were too many letters in his full name. "Jordyn Harris. It's got a nice ring to it, don't it?"

"Yes, it does," Quinn smiled in agreement. He could see Charles's mood lifting. He took one last drag of his cigarette before dropping it on the ground to step on it with his boot-covered feet. Looking at his watch to gauge the time, he sighed. He hated getting dressed up. Jeans, tee-shirts, and his old cowboy boots or work boots were what he was used to. Now, he stood out on the balcony in his dark grey slacks and white undershirt, glad he didn't have to put on narrow dress shoes too. Jordyn had graciously allowed them to wear their cowboy boots, so at least his feet would be comfortable. "Let's finish getting dressed so we're not late, can't start your big day with Jordyn fussing at us." A knock at the door had Charles shaking his head as Quinn went to answer it.

"He mad?" Anthony asked Quinn as quietly as his hungover brain could, trying to look around Quinn to see Charles. Quinn nodded his head in answer, widening the door so they could enter. Anthony walked into the room first, followed by Kenneth and Greg. All three of their tired half-smiles as they trudged into the room conveyed their apologies.

"He'll be alright," Quinn said, closing the door. He walked over to the dresser and picked up the bottle of aspirin he had earlier, tossing it to Greg, who caught it gratefully. "I already told him we wouldn't ruin his day."

"Yeah, we all like living," Kenneth chuckled, taking his turn with the aspirin. "I'm a lot more afraid of your wife than I am of you. I'll be on my best behavior." He gulped down two, then sat in a nearby chair to tie his shoes.

"She's not my wife yet," Charles said, looking for his cufflinks. "You better hope she is at the end of today, though."

"Calm down, Charles." Quinn pressed an ice-cold beer in his hand. "Drink it, it'll calm your nerves a bit." He held up another bottle to ask the other guys if they wanted one. They all shook their heads no.

"I'm not nervous," Charles insisted.

"Yeah, your hand shakes like that all the time," Anthony said, laughing. Charles looked down at his hand wrapped around the dark brown beer bottle, noticing its slight tremble. Quickly bringing the bottle to his lips, he closed his eyes, hoping the hops would slow down his racing heart.

"Damn, Charles, I haven't seen you this nervous since you asked her out to the Spring Dance in the eighth grade." Standing to imitate a shy thirteen-year-old Charles, Greg pitched his voice high and spoke. "I was just, I was...wondering... I wanted to know...you know if you ain't doing nothing..."

Anthony took over the retelling. "Maybe we can meet up. I mean go to the dance...you and me. The two of us, together. What...what do you think?"

"I did not sound like that." Charles took another swig of his beer, trying to hide his embarrassment. He sounded just like that in eighth grade, and still did every now and then. To this day, looking at Jordyn made him stumble over his words, he was that much in love. "Will y'all get dressed so we can go?" Laughing, the guys ignored their headaches and finished getting dressed. It took them another hour to finish. Ties had to be straightened, shoes shined, and hair brushed just right. All the attention to detail helped Charles relax a bit and gave the guys a way to distract him from his nerves.

Quinn placed the ring in Charles' hand then watched him slide the diamond band on Jordyn's third finger. Her glossy eyes and radiant smile conveyed how much love she had for his best friend, now her husband. Quinn felt truly happy for them.

When he'd first arrived at his uncle Quincy's doorstep, he wasn't sure what to think about anything. At eight years old, he'd been left by his mother, Tracie, to be raised by her brother. She didn't even stick around to find out if he would. Only told him to stand on the porch, and she'd be right back. He remembered her short brown bob bouncing on her way down the steps and the quick wave of her red-polished fingernails. By the time he realized that wave was one of goodbye, his mother had been long gone, not even the dust from the driveway remained. That was the last time he saw his mother. Quinn met Charles a few weeks after his world turned upside down. He became the first person he trusted with his secrets, no matter how dark they were.

That was nearly twenty-five years ago. Now, he stood as his best man. The never-wavering friend with his definite conviction to loving Jordyn. Even way back then, he knew. Quinn had thought he had that once, but it turns out it only works when both sides share the same feelings.

He vaguely heard laughter, followed by the pastor telling the happy couple their journey won't always be smooth, rocks were to be expected, but together they can level the road. Then with a broad grin, he said, "You may kiss the bride." Charles wasted no time leaning down and placing his lips to Jordyn's, kissing her like no one was watching. Quinn, knowing what it took for the two of them to make it to this moment, clapped and whistled with the rest of the groomsmen and guests until he noticed Charles' hand creeping indecently lower down Jordyn's sparkly white dress. Quinn placed a hand on his shoulder to stop the descent, giving it a squeeze, hoping to remind him they were in a room full of people who were all watching with wide eyes and held breath.

"Ladies and gentlemen, it's my pleasure to introduce to you Mr. and Mrs. Charles Fleetwood Harris," Pastor Thomas announced, breaking off the kiss to everyone's relief. Smiling at each other, the newlyweds reluctantly broke eye contact and faced the crowd, accepting their congratulations as they made their way back down the aisle.

"Did you taste this cake? It's like pouring sugar straight into your mouth." Shelbi Lynn set the fork with the half-eaten bite of cake still on it back down on the clear glass dessert plate then washed her mouth out with the water from the light blue goblet in front of her.

"Was just about to," Quinn answered dryly. He sliced off a piece and smiled as the flavors filled his mouth. He took another bite, nodding his head appreciatively. He'd always had a sweet tooth, and the chocolate bourbon cake with caramel filling and frosting hit the spot and tasted much better than the four-tiered upscale wedding cake the couple had ordered from some downtown bakery.

"How can you eat that? It's way too sweet. Tastes like

they used two too many cups of sugar. I'll have to run three extra miles to work off the little bit I tried to eat." Shelbi Lynn ran her hand over her flat stomach then looked around at the other guests. By the scowl on her face, Quinn could tell she was judging the other women as they passed by, picking apart their hair, makeup, figures, and outfits. He watched her lips moving as he finished the cake but stopped listening after she said 'extra miles'. It was typical of Shelbi Lynn to brag about things no one else did. To her, everything seemed like a competition. Running didn't impress Quinn. The thought of it made him tired.

"I'm gonna grab another piece. You want...anything?" Standing up, Quinn grabbed his plate and turned around, not waiting for an answer. Shelbi Lynn wasn't who he'd expected to be sitting next to at the reception, but somehow, he ended up in this seat after bumping into her while he walked through the dining hall, talking to people he hadn't seen in years. He'd looked for his boys for an out, but as luck would have it, they'd all found someone to keep them too busy to rescue Quinn.

"Umph," Cora huffed as Quinn accidentally ran into her.

"Sorry." Quinn held out his free hand to stop Cora from falling over. "You alright, Cora Belle?"

"Yeah," she answered. "I wish you wouldn't call me that." She smoothed out the bottom of her dress and made sure the jeweled clip in her hair was still where she left it. "Where you off to in such a hurry, anyway?"

"Another piece of cake." He held up his empty plate.

"Oh, you liked it? Charles is a sucker for that cake. I'm surprised he's not in a sugar coma." They both looked to the dancefloor as Jordyn swayed her way across the floor. Her afro bobbed side to side, making her tiara look like a halo. She'd changed into a short dress for the reception and replaced her heels with a pair of sparkly white Vans. When she got to Charles, they started a slow grind to a fast song, making Quinn laugh.

"Those two are in their own little world."

"He's had three pieces already," Cora said, focusing her eyes on the table where Shelbi Lynn sat, waiting patiently for Quinn to return. "Hey, Shel," Cora waved, faking a smile. She looked her over, noting the shimmer on her face from her makeup and the thick look of her long lashes. Looking down at her manicured hands, she saw the blush pink polish of her acrylic nails matched perfectly with the short, pink lace sheath dress and pumps she wore. "Your dress is beautiful." Cora didn't expect her to get up, but she did, and she immediately regretted being nice to her.

"This old thing?" Shelbi Lynn uttered, turning from side to side, the new smell of the dress wafting through the air. "I didn't know anything about the color scheme, so I prayed I wouldn't clash, but it looks like they used a few of them, so I had nothing to worry about." Shelbi Lynn gave a short laugh then pressed her lips together to quiet herself. Jordyn had insisted her bridesmaids wear their favorite color in the style that made them feel the most comfortable. After looking through dozens of bridal magazines, she'd become so overwhelmed she ditched the traditional color schemes and ended up with four different colors from her bridesmaids; emerald green, sky blue, tangerine, and daffodil. From a dress a little too short to a pantsuit fit to perfection, it was more than she could have asked for, and it turned out exactly how she pictured it.

"Shelbi Lynn didn't like the cake," Quinn told Cora. "Said it's too sweet." Cora stilled her face before it said something she was trying not to, as Shelbi Lynn looked away for a few seconds.

"It really was. Did Gerti make it?" Shelbi Lynn asked.

"Yeah, she did...at Jordyn's request. She also made the cookies."

"Oh," she replied with a sneer. "Interesting choice." Shelbi Lynn looked over Cora's shoulder at the desserts sitting atop the white cloth-covered table, piled with trays of chocolate chip pecan cookies. "Those aren't made with liquor too, are they?" she sighed, already knowing the answer.

"They are." Cora bit down on the inside of her cheek to keep from saying what she really wanted. On her list of people she could do without, Shelbi Lynn was top three. They'd never had a pleasant conversation that Cora could remember.

"Well, I can't wait to taste them," Shelbi Lynn lied. Cora nodded and walked off with Quinn to the dessert table.

"Quincy, are you trying to wrangle more cookies off this table?" Cora asked, walking up to the table where he stood with a cookie in each hand. She'd been trying to get him away from the sweets for over half an hour.

"These are the last ones, I promise. I'm cutting myself off after I eat these." Quincy, Quinn's uncle, had been posted up at the dessert table for the last hour, swearing each cookie would be the last one. In his grey dress shirt and black vest, Cora thought he looked handsome. She helped him out by brushing away some cookie crumbs from his beard. Standing next to Quinn, Cora smiled at the strong family resemblance. Not only did their beards match, but their broad noses and dark eyes, the color of rich vanilla, were exactly the same as well.

"Sure, Badge," Quinn chuckled, not believing him at all. Walking up to the table, he gave his plate to the lady in the black coat in charge of slicing and handing out the cake. "Where are you sitting?"

"Over there in the old man section." Quincy pointed a finger to a group of tables near the window filled with white-haired and no-haired men. Most of the faces looked familiar to Quinn, but he couldn't be sure from the distance he was standing.

"Come on, I'll walk you back." Quinn knew leaving would be the only way to get Quincy away from the cookies. With his cake in hand, he turned and saw Shelbi Lynn standing in front of him. He'd forgotten she was waiting. "I'll be back," he told her as he and Quincy stepped around her to get to Quincy's table.

In a sympathetic move, Cora said, "Come on, girl." She hooked her arm through Shelbi Lynn's to walk her in the opposite direction. "Let's go see what Ms. Edith is gossiping about."

Three hours passed before Quinn saw Shelbi Lynn again. She walked up to him while he was talking to Greg and Kenneth and gently eased him away, telling him she needed an escort back to her room. Being a gentleman, he wasn't going to let her walk by herself through the hotel, but he had no intention of coming inside like she kept hinting at.

"You sure you can't come in?"

"Yeah, I gotta get back downstairs and make sure Badge hasn't overdosed on the cookies. Have a good night, Shelbi Lynn." Quinn stepped back to leave, but she caught his hand, hoping to get him to stay. She smoothed her hand down the front of his vest, letting it rest on his belt.

"It'd be a lot better if I got to spend it with you." She smiled and opened the door wide to invite him in. Quinn gave her a small smile and then took one booted step closer, but instead of going inside, he left her with a kiss on her forehead and turned to leave.

Chapter THREE

Quinn sat on the old porch looking out over all the trees and flat land of Honeybells Ranch. Out of all the places he'd been, the ranch had always been the greenest and most lush place he'd ever seen. He closed his eyes as the yellows and oranges in the sky changed to dark purple then black as the sun set. It was his favorite part of the day; when things seemed to slow down and usher in the night.

The ranch hadn't changed much since he'd left years ago. His uncle had added a fancy front gate at the end of the long dirt driveway, but that was all. It remained the same ranch he grew up on after being dropped off at eight years old to a man and woman he'd never met. It was the same place he'd run away from the week after he graduated high school; no plan in place, just wanting to be as far away from Honeybells Ranch as he could be. Now he was back, slowly sipping a glass of Quincy's whiskey, wondering what to do next. He never liked being antsy, anxious, or bored, so he didn't know how much longer he could go without a plan.

"I got a job for you," Quincy said, walking out onto the porch, his brown boots sounding loudly on the wide wooden planks. Quinn chuckled at the old well-worn pair of boots that seemed to never be anywhere but on his uncle's feet.

"What?" Quinn asked, raising his eyebrows in question. He looked over the brim of his Royals cap and took a drag of his cigarette.

"It's been two weeks, and you need something else to do besides mucking out the stables and feeding the horses. And eating my food and drinking all my damn whiskey don't count. Might as well put some money in your pocket while you're here." Quincy shoved his hands in his pockets and leaned against the porch railing, giving Quinn a look that meant things weren't up for discussion.

"Badge..." The nickname had been given to him by his late wife WillaMae and had been the name Quinn called him since he was nine years old. WillaMae had told Quincy that when it came to his nephew and his safety, he was like a mean old honey badger. After a while, it shortened to Badge, and the name had stuck ever since. Today, though, calling his uncle Badge wasn't going to sway him in the least.

"I can't have some grown ass man sitting around my house, broke, doing nothing." Quinn hid his smile. His Uncle was old-school all the way, so not going to work meant not having any money, no matter how much you had in the bank.

"Okay," Quinn relented, "what you got for me?" Being

raised by Quincy, he knew arguing wouldn't do any good.

"Need a landscaper for a few jobs Monday and Tuesday." Quinn smiled. He should have known.

"Where're your normal guys?" Quinn flicked his cigarette out into the yard and placed his elbows on his knees.

"Ronnie's got other jobs to do. I'm trying to drum up more business. There's a retirement home opening in a few months, I'm trying to get the contract for that." Quincy's confidence and hopefulness made Quinn smile.

"How far away is it, this job you want me to do?"

"Just off the FM road up there. I'll leave the addresses on the counter. You do remember how to mow, don't you?" Quinn let his laughter ring out across the yard. He was sure there were birds flying away scared somewhere. Garland Landscaping had been in business for almost thirty years, started by Quincy when he got tired of punching a clock for someone else. With only one truck, him, and a push mower, he'd started door-to-door in the closest city, asking homeowners if they needed their yard mowed. Now, he had three different crews, and a fleet of trucks painted bright yellow so people wouldn't miss the Garland Landscaping logo or the phone number doors. As soon as Quincy deemed him strong enough to push a mower, he had Quinn on one of his crews.

"Make sure you do a good job." Quinn looked at him, not believing he'd say that. After all the grass he'd cut and lawns he'd edged, he could do a good job in his sleep. "She's used to one of the other guys, but you'll have to do. Make sure she doesn't notice. I'm off to play poker."

"Don't do anything I wouldn't do," he told Quincy on his way down the steps. He waved goodbye then watched as he drove down the long driveway. Quinn sat on the wooden porch for another hour, watching the fireflies come out to light the night. He lit a candle to keep the mosquitoes away, and the flickering flame kept his attention for longer than it should have. He finally went into the house when the bottle of Maker's Mark he was drinking looked half-empty. It wasn't his favorite, an Old Fashioned, but tonight, liquor straight from the bottle seemed a good substitute.

The next morning, Quinn woke to the sound of birds chirping and someone's rooster crowing in the distance. The sun beamed through the drapes he forgot to close last night, making him miss his blackout curtains in Kansas. Sighing loudly, he rolled over onto his back and threw his arm over his eyes. Then he sat up, looking down at his clothes. He'd had one too many drinks to even take them off before falling into the bed. He listened for any sounds coming from inside the house and heard the loud snoring of his uncle from down the hall. Getting up, he padded barefoot to the bathroom, where he relieved himself, then hopped in the shower to start his day.

Gerti squinted at the bright sun as she hung the last of her sheets on the clothesline in her backyard. She loved the smell of freshly washed sheets and seeing them hung on a line, waving with the breeze. It always took her back to her time as a child when she had a lot less to deal with. Even though she had a washer and dryer, she preferred the feel of sun-dried linens when she crawled into bed at night. Sunday was a washday, a day of relaxation. She'd wash a week's worth of sheets and curtains for The Shop, and every other Sunday, like today, she washed her locs too. Being waist-length, the whole process took all day when you included drying time. She used the day to unwind and pamper herself the way she couldn't during the week, but most of all, it was a day to be all by herself. No asking what people wanted to order or refilling glasses with tea or coffee. She only had to answer to Gerti.

Sitting down in the white rocking chair on her back patio, she picked up the glass of tea from the table and sipped some down. The late spring temperature rose earlier this year, and even though this was Texas and she should be used to the erratic weather, she was never fully prepared for the heat. It was great for drying her sheets and her locs, but hell on her skin. She used a paper towel to dab at the drops of sweat making their way down the space between her breasts. Sighing, she gave Joe a scratch on his head then picked up the honeydew-colored nail polish bottle next to her. She kicked off her flip-flops and rested her feet on the small wooden footstool to paint her toenails.

The second coat of polish was still drying when she saw Joe's ears perk up. She heard the distinctive sound of a trailer gate being let down, then five minutes later, a lawnmower started up. Knowing Ronnie wasn't supposed to mow until tomorrow, she got up, with Joe keeping in step with her as she hurried as fast as she could with wet polish on her toes to the front of the house. Gerti stood behind the screen door and watched as a stranger in a dusty black cowboy hat mowed her yard, wearing the standard long-sleeved Garland Landscaping shirt in bright yellow. Her position behind the screen kept whoever was mowing from noticing her standing there with her arms crossed over her chest and a look of complete annoyance on her face. Dusty black cowboy hat was ruining, among other things, her peaceful Sunday. Joe sat at her feet, staring at the stranger and barking every few seconds, begging her to open the door so he could go say hello.

Once Quinn noticed Gerti standing in front of her fuchsia-colored front door, he stopped the mower and gingerly walked towards her. By her posture, she wasn't in a good mood. He raised his hat to wipe the sweat from his forehead with the sleeve of his shirt, then chanced looking directly at her face. "I hope I didn't..." He stopped and held his breath when Joe growled, making his presence as protector known. When the dog trotted over to him, Quinn stood still and let Joe lick his hand, allowing him to remember his scent from the other day. "I...uh, I hope I didn't disturb you. My uncle gave me your address, and I came by to mow."

Recognizing who he was, Gerti asked, "Did your uncle tell you my yard gets mowed on Mondays?"

"He did," Quinn answered, looking down at his boots before looking up apologetically. He hoped he hid his amusement at her angry, yet oh so intriguing face.

"Do you know what today is...?" His eyes bounced

between her angry face and the large dog next to him,
wagging his whole butt since his tail was clipped. He
patted Joe on the head to appease him, realizing Gerti
was more dangerous.

"Quinn, the name's Quinn Garland," he reminded her.
"It's Sunday, ma'am...last I checked."

"Why are you here on a Sunday, Quinn Garland?" Joe
kept pushing his head under Quinn's hand for more
scratches, and he obliged.

"I just wanted to..." Looking over at the big Rottweiler,
now licking his hand, Quinn forgot what he was trying
to say.

"He doesn't bite."

"Not worried about that." Quinn knelt down in front
of Joe and gave him a good scratch under his chin, which
seemed to satisfy him because he plopped down at his
feet. Standing back up, he asked, "You want me to come
back tomorrow?" Her hands moved to her hips, making
the hem of the pale pink cotton wrap dress she wore
rise slightly above her knees. Letting his eyes lead, he
scanned her from the curve of her hips down to her
shapely brown calves until they reached her feet, and
he noticed she was barefoot.

"How's that gonna help? You already started."

"Sorry to be taking up your Monday, Gerti, but I want
everything to be perfect."

"No worries, Ms. Edith. It's not every day you turn
seventy-four."

"Ain't that the truth? I'm happy to be turning anything
these days—over, around, or up, as the kids say."

It was Monday afternoon, and Gerti was meeting with Ms. Edith at her shop about her big seventy-fourth birthday party. She had a party every year, and every year, they got bigger, because according to Ms. Edith, you never know if it'll be the last one.

They'd been at it for about an hour, and Gerti's list seemed to get longer by the second. "How many people are you planning on having this year?" Gerti pressed her pen to the paper preparing to write the number. She figured something between thirty-five and fifty but picked the pen back up when the actual number was uttered.

"Eighty or so." Sonny, Joe, and Jack, who were sleeping at Ms. Edith's feet, perked up their ears at the number she threw out.

"Eighty people? In Mr. Garland's barn?"

"I could be overshooting the number a bit, but it's better to have too much than not enough, right?" Ms. Edith tapped on the paper so Gerti could write down the number. She bumped it up to a hundred, knowing a party in Bellbush brought out more than the ones invited. The renovated space could easily hold double, so the size of the barn wasn't a concern, but the number of cakes she would have to make worried her.

"So, enough cakes to serve eighty or so people?" Gerti jotted down the number two, then crossed it out to write four.

"And a mess of those cookies I like. I want a whole table for desserts."

"Who's doing the food for all these people?"

"Quincy told me if I brought him the meat, he'd smoke it for me. Isn't that nice of him?" Gerti nodded, thinking about the huge custom-built smoker Quincy had made a few years ago.

"Y'all have been friends for a long time. It's very considerate of him." She started writing the ingredients she'd need on another sheet of paper. "A lot more than I can say about that nephew of his."

"Quinn? You met him?"

"He came by with Charles before the wedding, and then he came by to mow my yard yesterday."

"On your Sunday?" Ms. Edith asked, surprised. Everyone knew a Gerti Sunday was sacred. You either saved what you were doing until Monday, or you didn't really need it.

"Yes, ma'am. I was this close to siccing Joe on him." They both laughed, then stopped when all three dogs lifted their heads at sounds coming from the front of The Shop.

"Who could that be?" Gerti sighed, then walked to the window to move the white lace curtain aside. Outside, she saw a bright yellow Garland Landscaping truck, and a man in a dusty black cowboy hat, better known as Quinn Garland, was unlatching the gate on the utility trailer that held the mower. "I can't believe him."

"Who is it?"

"Quinn Garland," Gerti answered, annoyed. "Mowing on the wrong day again."

"Give him a break, child," Ms. Edith cautioned. Gerti watched him back the mower down the ramp then turn to the left to start on the grass in her yard. "Come back over here so we can get this worked out." Ms. Edith tapped on the paper again until Gerti sat back down. "How many pecans do you think you'll need for my cookies? I can get some from Henry. He's got all those pecan trees, and he owes me." Gerti didn't want to get into why Henry might owe Ms. Edith for anything, so she closed her eyes to visualize the number of cookies she'd have to make while trying to ignore the sound of the mower coming from outside.

It took another thirty minutes, but when all the plans for the cakes, cookies, and an added homemade ice cream order had been finalized, Ms. Edith thanked Gerti then got up to leave. Standing in front of The Shop, all three dogs sat and watched intently as Quinn walked to them cautiously. His steps faltered slightly when he noticed Gerti standing there.

"Well, look at you, Quinn. I knew I'd be an old woman by the time you came back."

"Ms. Edith, there's never been anything old about you. How have you been?" He moved to embrace her in a hug, but Sonny's growl stopped him short.

"Hush, Sonny, he's a friend." Quinn looked to Gerti, who shrugged her shoulders and gave him an emotionless smile. Sonny was the mean one of the bunch, and that wasn't saying much since all he did was growl more than the others.

"These your dogs too?" Quinn asked Gerti.

"These two are mine," Ms. Edith answered. "I hear you met Joe not too long ago." Pointing at her dogs, she said, "This one's Sonny, and this is Jack." She looked over at Gerti, who was scowling at Quinn. "Did you meet this young lady too?" Ms. Edith already knew the answer but asked anyway to get to Gerti.

"We met a few weeks ago." He kept his eyes on Gerti as he answered.

"Quinn Garland, this is Gertrude Gordon." Ms. Edith

inclined her head toward Gerti, making her uncross her arms and fix her face if only for a bit. "Sometimes it's good to start over." Understanding what she was trying to do, Gerti reluctantly played along.

"Everyone calls me Gerti. Nice to meet you...again." Quinn didn't believe her at all but decided he'd play nice if she could. He noticed she looked different today, wearing a green dress the same length as the one the day before. This one didn't wrap but showed off her shape just as good. The sandals she wore showed off her newly-painted toes, and he hid the smile the sight of them brought on. "I see you haven't learned the days of the week yet," Gerti chided. Bringing his eyes to her face, he saw her locs were pulled into a bun, and she had a ring of white flowers surrounding it.

"Plan on looking into calendars tomorrow." He scratched his beard to keep his smile at bay.

"I've got one you can have." Ms. Edith dug around in her purse until she pulled out a small pocket-sized calendar with a verse of Psalms printed on the front. She handed it over to Quinn, who shoved it into his back pocket. He'd forgotten her purse always had everything you needed.

"I just wanted to tell you I'm finished here." He watched as Gerti looked across the yard, trying to figure out what she was thinking. "If you approve, I'll be heading on home." Quinn lifted his cowboy hat then wiped away the sweat covering his forehead before placing it back on his head. He then challenged Gerti by looking straight into her eyes.

"You did a good job." She was impressed, but she wasn't going to give him anything more.

"Quinn, why don't you carry us home, so we don't have to walk today?" Ms. Edith asked, taking a few steps forward with Sonny and Jack following behind her.

"I can do that. Let me put the mower on the trailer, and I'll be ready to take you ladies home." Digging in her purse again and pulling out a butterscotch, Ms. Edith said to Gerti, "Why don't you get him some tea? It's always so refreshing."

"Ms. Edith."

"Go, child," was her only response.

By the time Gerti made it back outside with a lidded foam cup in her hand, Quinn was waiting on the porch, leaning against the pillar, smoking a cigarette and laughing at something Ms. Edith was saying. She handed him the tea with a tight smile.

"She thought you might like this." Cautiously taking it from her, Quinn took a small sip through the clear straw to taste it, then a bigger one around a smile.

"Thank you, Miss Gordon."

"Gerti, it's just Gerti."

"Okay, Gerti. You ready?" he asked, noticing she wasn't carrying a purse or keys.

"I don't need a ride home."

"Oh, she's fine," Ms. Edith told him. "I was talking about me and the dogs." Quinn looked at Sonny and Jack, who were wagging their backsides at the prospect of getting to ride back home instead of walking.

"How are you getting home?" he asked Gerti with a hint of concern in his voice.

"I don't live far. Joe makes sure I get home safe."

"That's why I leave him here with her," Ms. Edith said. She started walking towards the bright yellow truck, followed by Jack and Sonny.

"Alright. Thanks for the tea." He tipped his hat in real cowboy fashion. Gerti offered him a slight smile but said nothing in response. He turned to leave as Sonny and Jack jumped into the back seat.

"They don't like riding in the beds of trucks," Ms. Edith explained. Quinn looked back to Gerti and caught her smile. This time, it was a genuine smile, showing off the sexiest pair of dimples he'd ever seen.

Chapter FOUR

"**W**hat is it?"

"It's a jukebox," Gerti answered, looking at the side of Cora's face to understand why she couldn't have figured it out herself. "What do you think it is?"

"I think it's a jukebox, but why is it here? It's huge."

When Gerti got to The Shop that morning, Quinn was waiting for her with the jukebox and a message from Ms. Edith. She told her to let him put it against the wall, and she'd tell them more later. Quinn didn't look too happy having to wheel the heavy thing into place at such an early hour, but with orders from Ms. Edith, there wasn't much he could have done about it. Gerti offered him some coffee, but he declined, saying he'd be back later after he did a couple of jobs for Quincy. That was a total lie, but as he watched her take a sip from a white mug with purple flowers all over it, he was zeroed in on the way her lips wrapped around the ceramic rim, and he couldn't think straight enough to come up with another excuse. He had to put a few miles between them to clear his head and calm his body down.

"Ms. Edith made Quinn deliver it this morning."

"Does it work?" Cora asked, running her finger down the green neon curve of the top to see how thick the dust was. "Where the hell did she find this thing?" Without giving an answer, Gerti walked to the tip jar, digging out a quarter to test it out. They both laughed when they heard the thud of the quarter hit the bottom and then nothing.

"Y'all know it's not plugged in, right?" Cora and Gerti looked at Mr. Huddleson, who was sipping his coffee with one of those smug, all-knowing looks in his eyes. Sighing, they both walked away, not wanting to bother with the ancient-looking thing anymore. They definitely didn't want to chance plugging it in and having all the electrical wiring in The Shop short out. Cora went towards the coffee pot, and Gerti walked to the back to grab another tray of cinnamon rolls out of the oven.

Gerti was wiping down tables when Quinn walked in, looking refreshed and more good-looking than anyone had the right to be in the morning. He pulled his cap off his head and stuffed it in his back pocket while his eyes adjusted to the new light. When he could focus on Gerti, he gave her a faint smile with the nod of his head then turned his attention to Mr. Huddleson, who was standing beside him to greet him.

"I didn't think you'd still be in town. How are you?" Quinn looked around and saw a handful of familiar faces sitting at the tables having breakfast, fueling up to start their day, men and women who were friends of his aunt and uncle, who he saw almost every day growing up.

Sitting by the window was Mr. Trudy, who had a pig farm nearby. Tom Wheeler, who taught him how to change the oil in his car, was on the other side of the room. And then there was Ms. Billie, who was a good friend of his late Aunt WillaMae's. She'd always had a switch handy whenever he and his friends got out of line.

"Doing good, Mr. Huddleson." He gave him a firm handshake, looking into his aged but still smooth brown-skinned face. "It's been a long time. You still hauling debris?"

"Oh, yeah. Hoping to retire one of these days." Mr. Huddleson drove around an old beat-up truck covered in political stickers. Every day, he'd drive through different neighborhoods, picking up things people left on the curb, or he'd scavenge behind businesses, jumping into their dumpsters to find what he could fix and sell. His resale store had always been quite successful, and he enjoyed working at his own pace. "You come for some coffee? Come have a seat." He pulled the empty chair next to him out so Quinn could sit down.

"I can spare a few minutes." Looking around, he didn't see Ms. Edith, who'd told him she'd meet him there to explain the jukebox. He lifted his hand and motioned for Cora, who was standing on the other side of the room.

"What can I do for you, Mr. Huddleson? Morning, Quinn." He nodded as a reply.

"Coffee." He looked to Quinn to confirm he wanted some too. "Two cups, please."

"Anything to eat?" Cora asked, pulling out her small notebook from the pocket of her apron. Having not eaten that morning, the mention of food suddenly had Quinn's stomach wanting to be filled. He looked around for a menu but came up empty. "Specials are on the wall," Cora told him.

Looking to the left, he saw a chalkboard hanging from the wall with the specials of the day written in pink chalk. There were four things to choose from. He raised a questioning eyebrow to Cora, who only smiled in response. "What do you recommend?" he asked.

"For you? The cinnamon rolls." Quinn looked at the chalkboard at what the other options were. "They have bacon in them," Cora added. Quinn wasn't sure of the flavor combination, but his growling stomach was telling him to give it a go.

"It'll be the best thing you put in your mouth today," Cora said with a wide grin, making Mr. Huddleson's round brown cheeks flush.

"Then I guess I'll try it." She turned to Mr. Huddleson, who wouldn't meet her eyes as he declined any food, then she left to go fill their order.

"How long you gonna be in town?"

"I don't know yet," Quinn answered. "I guess until they call me back, if they do." His voice trailed off a bit when Gerti walked through the steel door separating the kitchen from the dining area. She looked over some papers on the counter, then picked up a coffee carafe to refill cups for the people sitting at the countertop. When she was done, she poured her own cup, mixing creamer and more sugar than he thought was necessary. He watched as she brought her lips to the rim and blew gently to cool it down. He imagined he could have sat there all day and watched her blow in her coffee cup, but when Cora came back, setting down two pink mugs in front of Mr. Huddleson and himself, his attention was abruptly brought back to the present.

"Gerti will bring out that cinnamon roll in a bit. Can I get y'all anything else?"

"No. This is good," Mr. Huddleson said, pouring sugar into his mug. "Thank you, Cora. Tell your brother to come by sometime."

"Will do, but he's still in honeymoon mode, so I don't know if he will." With a laugh, Mr. Huddleson raised his mug and started on his coffee.

"I remember those days. When I first got married, I had two things on my mind, and my wife counted for one and a half of 'em." Quinn chuckled, then took a sip of his coffee. Surprised by the taste, he took another sip, this time with a smile. It tasted nothing like what he was used to or what he'd been drinking at his uncle's house. He didn't even know coffee could be improved on, but somehow, Gerti had. "It's good, huh? I don't know what she does, but I'm here every morning. What brings you around?"

"Ms. Edith."

"Edith, that feisty old woman?" Mr. Huddleson chuckled, his big belly moving up and down as he did. "Don't tell her I said that. You meet those dogs of hers yet?"

"Yeah, gave them all a ride home yesterday. They were gracious enough to let me have dinner with her."

Pointing to the corner of The Shop, Mr. Huddleson smiled and said, "He's the only one I like. Joe's the most even-tempered of the bunch. That's not saying much since they're all just overgrown puppies, but Joe seems to have the most sense."

It was during the ride to take her home that Quinn learned how Ms. Edith ended up with three ferocious-looking rottweilers. She had asked her grandson for a scary-looking dog, and he brought her three. They were so cute, she couldn't decide on only one, so she kept all of them, and now had three big ass rottweilers—well, two now—who followed her wherever she went.

"One bacon cinnamon roll." Gerti set the extra-large roll down in front of Quinn, who was shocked by the size. "Enjoy."

"Wow." He splayed his large hand over the top of it to measure the size. It surprised him that they were the same. Gerti set a wrapped fork down next to the plate, then turned to walk away. "Um... Gerti," Quinn said before she got too far. She turned to face him, the hem of her skirt swinging around her knees. She said nothing but looked at him to continue as she wiped her hands on the apron she had tied around her waist. "Do you...do you know what Ms. Edith wants me to do with that?" He pointed to the wall where the jukebox was.

"I wish I did. She didn't tell me anything except she'd talk to us about it later." Quinn wasn't sure, but the way Gerti said us instead of me or you made him feel warm inside. He wasn't sure how to respond, so he nodded once, then picked up his fork. "Eat before it gets cold." As she spoke, her dimples showed in her cheeks, not as prominent as when she smiled the day before, but he imagined they were always there no matter what her face was doing. He didn't mean to watch her walk away, but the sway of her hips wouldn't let him look anywhere else.

"You better eat like she said." Mr. Huddleson gave him a knowing smile and a slow shake of his head.

An hour later, and the empty plate was sitting on the table. His coffee had been refilled twice, and now at the table were Mr. Alcott and Mr. Barton. Both men used to be in business together and made their money in the oil fields. They had retired to Bellbush almost thirty-five years ago, bringing with them their families and a desire for a more laid-back lifestyle. They were catching Quinn up on what's been going on around the county and trying to get information out of him about his plans for the future. He couldn't give them much since he wasn't sure what he would do, so he contented himself with listening while the older men talked.

By the time Ms. Edith walked in, he was sitting by himself, and The Shop was empty. Cora had cleared all the dishes from his table, and his coffee had been replaced with ice water. Ms. Edith was followed in by Sonny and Jack, who went immediately to lie next to Joe, who didn't acknowledge them at all.

"I'm sorry I'm late, Quinn. Those dogs of mine had to stop and sniff every rock and blade of grass all the way here."

"I could have come by and got you."

"Oh, no. Walking is good for me. As long as my legs work, I might as well use them." She sat down, looking at Gerti as she did. "Did you eat already?"

"I've been here for a while. Talked to Huddleson a bit. Cora brought me one of those cinnamon rolls." She moved her hands away from the table so Gerti could set her coffee down.

"Sit with us for a while," she told Gerti. "I need to talk to you about something." Not being able to tell her no, Gerti sat down in the empty chair next to Quinn. "Did you like the coffee, Quinn? Gerti makes the best cup I've ever tasted."

"It was pretty good," he lied. He looked over at Gerti, wondering if she could tell how much he loved it. The slight scowl on her face showed she was trying to figure out what he meant by pretty good.

"How do you take yours?" Ms. Edith asked. "I like mine with a lot of cream and a touch of sugar." She dipped her spoon in her mug and stirred. "When my husband was alive, he always said he liked his like he liked his women—Black and full of sugar." She laughed, trying to hide her blush as memories of her husband flooded her mind.

"Not a bad way to drink it," Quinn agreed, looking at Gerti. He noticed her hair was up in a bun again today, this time with small purple flowers throughout. The matching tank top she wore showed off toned arms that he wanted to reach out and touch, and the low scoop of the neckline allowed a peek of her cleavage to show.

"What did you need to talk about, Ms. Edith?" Gerti asked, trying to hurry things along.

"Oh, yeah." She set her mug down and looked between Quinn and Gerti. "I'm giving you that old jukebox."

"You're what?" Gerti asked, shocked that big thing had to stay in her shop.

"It's just been sitting in my garage collecting dust." They heard Cora's muffled laughter from the kitchen. "Figured some music around here might be nice."

"I don't need a jukebox, Ms. Edith," Gerti started, then

closed her mouth quickly when Ms. Edith fixed her with a glare.

Helping her out, Quinn asked, "What do you need me for?" He'd been on the receiving end of one of her looks too many times to count, so he knew what it felt like to be caught in her glare.

"Fix it—because it doesn't work." Quinn looked at Gerti then at Ms. Edith and shook his head. "I've never fixed a jukebox, Ms. Edith." If she had asked him to rebuild a transmission or pull apart a car engine, he wouldn't have batted an eye, he could do it in his sleep. A jukebox was something he'd never even looked at in terms of things that had to be maintained, mostly because he had only seen maybe three in his lifetime. Plus, it plugged into the wall, and aside from turning the volume up, it didn't have enough horsepower to keep his attention. "Don't you need an electrician?"

"How in the world am I supposed to know?" Ms. Edith sipped more of her coffee and looked Quinn in the eyes. "How long have you worked on trains?" He didn't give an answer because he knew she remembered from their ride home last night. "A man who can fix a train surely can get that old thing to work."

"Why'd you have him bring it here? Shouldn't it be in a garage somewhere...with tools, and a floor that's not mine?" Gerti thought about all the parts and pieces inside the jukebox, plus the dust that came along with it.

"You see how big it is? I can't have him lugging it all over the place trying to get it to work." "Ms. Edith, I really don't know if I'll be able to do it. Badge is about to give me a crew, so I won't have much time to commit to fixing it up."

"Oh, a man as smart as you can figure it out." Looking at Quinn, Gerti was certain he was as confused as she was about a jukebox she'd never heard of or seen since she'd known Ms. Edith. "Just come by when you're done. You can work on it after The Shop closes." She had everything figured out, but Gerti could tell she was also up to something. "Plus," Ms. Edith said with a grin. "With Quinn fixing it, it'll give you two a chance to get to know each other."

Chapter FIVE

"Sam comes back in a few days. You think you can handle that?" Cora was talking to Gerti while Quinn sat at the counter drinking tea. He'd been there every day for the past three weeks, coming by after finishing with his landscaping crew. "Sam's sweet on your girl Gerti."

"His girl?" Gerti asked, casting a look at Quinn, who was smiling with a raised brow.

"Sam's asked her out no less than a dozen times. He's still trying to wear her down."

"Where's he been?" Quinn asked.

"He's a truck driver, always on the road," Cora answered.

"Thank God," Gerti whispered, walking around Cora to get to the cake stand. She checked if anyone needed anything, but the few people left in The Shop seemed satisfied to just sit and talk while drinking on the last of the coffee in front of them.

"But when he comes back, he comes here first." Cora

was smiling, amused by Quinn's slightly envious face. "Brings her flowers and little things he's found while on the road." Gerti made a disgusted face then rolled her eyes.

"You don't like flowers?" Quinn asked, hoping to file the answer away for later.

"I have a whole garden out back, Quinn. What do I need with more flowers?"

"I mean, it is kinda cute... kinda," Cora smiled.

"It's annoying," Gerti complained. "I'm being as nice as I can be, but he's not getting it."

"He's not gonna back off until he sees you with a man," Cora pointed out to Gerti with seriousness in her eyes. "As long as you're walking around single, looking like you look," she waved her hand in front of Gerti, "he's gonna think he's got a chance." Quinn had noticed her dress earlier, taking a quick look as she walked around The Shop, but he used Cora's rant to slowly and openly examine it now, and he agreed with her. Today, she was wearing a red A-line dress with nickel-sized buttons running down the front. The top two buttons were left open because they wouldn't stay closed.

"There's no way anyone can resist a chance as long as they think it's an option."

"True. Some guys are thick-headed and need to be shown rather than told," Quinn said to both women.

"Well, I need him to get a clue."

"He'd get a big clue if you walked into the party with someone like Quinn. Big fine man like him would back him off for sure." Cora regretted using Quinn as an example as soon as his name came out of her mouth, but the availability of men their age was slim, especially in The Shop, so he became the default.

"You think I'm fine?" Quinn asked Cora, teasingly. He laughed as she scoffed, then ducked out of the way when a coffee stirrer came flying at his head.

"Shut up. She knows what I mean." Cora gave Gerti a sweet smile to counter the plan she was devising. "Think about it. You show up with Quinn, y'all do a little dancing, a little hand-holding, maybe a kiss or two."

"What are you smiling about?" Gerti asked, looking at Quinn's face. His grin was wider than usual. She surprised herself by letting her mind venture to a place where she was looking into Quinn's eyes as he lowered his mouth to hers.

"Not a bad plan," Quinn answered. He was concentrating on Gerti's bottom lip she was worrying between her teeth. He wondered about how hard she was biting, and at what point the pressure turned into pleasure.

"I bet you think so," Gerti told him, bringing him out of his fantasy.

"I'm talking more about getting over on Franklin," he lied. "I never really liked his ass, anyway."

"So you want to use me to get at him?" Gerti asked, her hand on her hip, feigning offense.

Not missing a beat, he answered, "Seems beneficial for the both of us, actually." His shoulders raised in a shrug as he waited for her to speak again.

"And kissing... is just a bonus," she mused. She wondered if he could feel the heat radiating off of her at the thought of his lips again.

"There is that," he drawled out slowly. His bearded face with its sprinkling of grey hair broadened with his smile.

"No!" she exclaimed as quietly as she could as not to

alarm the other people still in The Shop. She looked around to make sure no one was being nosy. It was a small shop in a small town, and talk of any kind spread like dry tinder on a hot summer day.

"Oh, come on, Gerti, think about it," Cora exclaimed a lot louder than Gerti wished she would. "It's a win-win. Quinn can flaunt you in Sam's face, and you won't have to have him in your face all night."

Gerti was usually open to all of Cora's suggestions, but this idea she wasn't ready to get behind. It wasn't Quinn at all. His rugged good looks and quiet, charming manner should have been enough to make this issue a nonfactor. A confident Gerti without scars would have dove headfirst into a fake date scenario hoping to make it real by the end of the night, but that wasn't her. She was flawed and scared and not going to let herself fall for a man who'd be leaving at the end of the summer. "Why are you pushing this?" Gerti asked Cora quietly, trying to keep her composure.

"Because I'm pushy. And I like to see people happy." Cora stepped closer to Gerti then muttered under her breath, "He'll only have to be your man for a little while."

"A fake one?"

"I'm very real," Quinn said, holding out his arm towards Gerti. "Feel." Gerti looked at his muscled forearm covered in tattoos and tried not to focus on the thick veins that stuck out from under his skin. She looked away without touching him, making Quinn smile.

"No," she said again, before untying the apron from around her waist and walking to the kitchen. Joe followed her.

"It's alright, I can fuck with Sam some other time,"

Quinn said. Cora shook her head, feeling bad about what went down with Gerti. "Is she gonna be alright?" Quinn asked with genuine concern in his eyes.

"Yeah. She just needs to sit by herself for a while."

"I can respect that." Quinn tapped his fingers on the countertop twice before standing. "I gotta get out of here. I'll see y'all later."

Later turned into a week with Quincy keeping his nephew busy with landscaping jobs and managing the different crews, making sure they stayed on track. By the time Quinn got home every day, he was too tired to do anything that didn't involve a long shower, stuffing food into his face quickly and falling into bed. Helping his uncle was becoming more of a job than he'd thought it would be.

"Well, look who it is. Where you been, Quinn? I almost put out an APB on you," Cora joked.

"Funny," Quinn said as he sat on the stool. He held the mug Cora sat in front of him and waited for her to fill it.

"Good morning, Cora," a deep voice said, walking up to the counter.

"Morning, Sam," she responded dryly. "How you doing this morning?"

"Doing pretty good." Cora added a mug for him too and filled them both. "Gertrude around?" Cora looked down at the counter and rolled her eyes, ignoring his question.

"Sam, you remember Quinn, don't you?" Cora asked. She knew their history, so there was no doubt he did. Quinn tried to hide his annoyed sigh but failed. He was tired from restless nights of sleep on the too-quiet ranch. He was counting on the coffee at The Shop to help perk him up a bit, plus he knew setting his eyes on Gerti would have him wide awake, but he was looking at Sam, and Gerti was nowhere in sight.

When they were fifteen, Quinn and Sam spent weeks bickering back and forth about everything from the speed of the GTO to the name of their third-grade teacher. People weren't sure if it was the heat or a test of testosterone, but everyone was ready for it to be over. Quinn had always been a whole head taller and at least twenty pounds heavier than Sam, but when the challenge of who would be the first to kiss Francine Taylor was laid down one day, it all came to a head. After the names were called and fists were thrown, scrawny Sam Franklin had landed a lucky punch to Quinn's nose, staggering him, with blood spurting everywhere. Shocked more than anyone, Sam ran away as quick as he could, leaving Quinn to trek back home on his own with his shirt bunched over his nose. Quinn had never forgiven him or spoken to him since.

"Have you met Gertrude?" Sam asked Quinn. He had a look on his face as if saying her whole name meant he owned the world. Quinn nodded as a response. "That's one fine woman," Sam whispered, for Quinn's ears only. "Still trying to find out about her hair, though. She always keeps it wrapped or in that..." Sam made a circle above his head to show the bun Gerti wore. "Haven't seen it down yet. But I will." Quinn wanted so badly to tell him he knew how long her dark locs fell down her back, but he kept it to himself. Sam didn't deserve to know.

"Looks like Clint over there wants you," Cora alerted

Sam. He looked behind his shoulder and saw Clint looking his way. Cora had no idea if he wanted Sam or not, but she knew she was tired of him taking up space at the counter and wanted him gone.

"How the hell does he look like that?" Quinn asked once Sam was out of earshot. Sam was all muscle and brawn, stretching the arms of his blue cotton shirt to almost bursting. Quinn wasn't a lightweight by any means, but Sam looked like he spent most mornings pushing tractors with his bare hands.

"Two summers after you left, Francine did too," she told the story with a smile of satisfaction. "She was on the arm of some musclehead who drove a cherry red Mustang. Broke Sam up so bad, one day he grabbed an ax and went to work." Quinn's eyes went wide with sinister thoughts. "Not like that," Cora reassured. "I think he chopped down half the trees in the county. Went from house to house getting out his aggression and building muscle while charging people half what your uncle did to do the same thing."

"Why does he call her Gertrude? He's such an ass about it."

"Cause he is an ass. She hates it, too. He thinks it's cute, calling her something no one else does." He smiled at the face she threw at him. He had a special nickname she hated, but he'd been calling her Cora Belle for over twenty years, and he didn't plan on stopping now.

"Where is she today? I've never seen her not here."

"Picking up the supplies for Ms. Edith's party. She's starting on all the baking once we close." Cora refilled coffee for two men who brought their mugs up to the counter.

"Morning, Cora. Let me get..." Mr. Drew looked at the board showing the day's specials, "a slice of pound cake." "Morning, Vince, you sure you need pound cake this morning?"

"I already struggled down Mary's eggs." The older man turned to Quinn and smiled slightly through a shrug. "Been married for almost thirty years, and she's never been able to make decent eggs. How hard is it to make eggs?"

"But you've been eating them for almost thirty years, so I don't see why you're complaining. You could always make your own eggs," Cora responded with an eye roll. The old men around here were all the same. Women in the kitchen and plate ready when they got home from work mentality.

"You modern women are so feisty. Can you believe her?" he asked Quinn. "What I look like standing over a stove?"

"I guess you'd look like you weren't starving, Vince. Here's your cake." She pushed the plate over to him, and he could see the fire starting to burn in her eyes.

Shaking his head, he told Cora, "When a man ties you down, you're gonna give him a mess of fits."

Looking over at Quinn, a grinning Cora replied, "Vince, if a man is ever tying me down, it won't be fits I'm giving him." Embarrassed and blushing, Vince left money on the counter for his cake and coffee, then walked away without his change.

Ten minutes later, Joe trotted in, followed by Gerti. "Sorry I took so long, Cora," she said, slightly out of breath as she tied her floral apron around her waist.

"Oh, no worries, girl. You didn't miss anything." She

handed her a cup of coffee. "Except maybe Sam asking about you." Cora looked in the window's direction where Sam was. He was looking their way and smiling.

"So, nothing important, then." He already annoyed her, and he hadn't even said anything to her.

"Hey," Gerti greeted Quinn. "Not working this morning?"

"I'm about to head out. Gotta check on the crew." He looked down when he felt Joe's heavy head brush against his leg. "Hey, boy," he greeted, giving Joe a scratch behind the ear. Satisfied, he trotted off to his favorite spot by the window.

"Hey, Gertrude. I'm glad I caught you before I had to leave." Sam Franklin had the biggest grin on his face Quinn had ever seen. Too bad it wasn't reciprocated by Gerti.

"Did you need something, Sam?" she asked.

"Just to see you. Are you going to the party tomorrow?"

"I'll be there."

"So will I," Cora chimed in. "Quinn will be there too, right, Quinn?" He laughed at the sad sight of Sam Franklin fawning over Gerti.

"I'll see you there then." He kept his eyes on Gerti, then tapped the countertop with his knuckles before turning around to walk out the door.

"You sure you know what you're doing?"

"No," Quinn said with a laugh looking around at all the parts and pieces at his feet on the floor. "I can't believe I let her talk me into this."

Since The Shop closed at three in the afternoon, it left him plenty of time to tinker with the unfamiliar metal parts he had no idea what to do with. He might have minded if he'd been stuck with anyone else, but lucky for him, he was stuck with Gerti. He was finding getting to know her in the bits and pieces she offered was as much a challenge as figuring out how to put all the pieces back in the jukebox, but he was having a good time trying. "I am better with cars, but this shouldn't be so hard."

"I'm almost done here, so I can help if you need it." He looked her way but couldn't see her face over the counter. It was the first time she'd offered to help.

"You know your way around a screwdriver?"

"Is it anything like a stand mixer?" She threw her head back and laughed. She had tickled herself so much, she didn't realize he had stopped what he was doing and walked to the counter. Looking at her with a straight face, he decided he loved to see the deep set of her dimples when she laughed, and he loved hearing it even more.

"You done?" he asked.

"Yeah, I'm done." She quieted her chuckling as she scooped cookie dough onto cookie sheets.

"What are you making over here, anyway? Smells good."

"The cookies right now. I'll do the cakes later. You going? You never said this morning."

The way she asked amused Quinn. He could tell she was trying not to sound too eager or look at him too long while waiting for his answer. "You think I should?" he asked in a deep quiet voice. She looked at him through her eyelashes, trying to gauge his angle.

"Yes, I do." He smiled, pleased with her answer. "But only because if you don't, you'll have to hear Ms. Edith fuss until next year. She's been planning this for months."

It wasn't the answer he wanted to hear, but he took it anyway.

"Then I'll be there."

"You know you have to dress up?"

"Why? It's in a barn."

"A converted barn." She picked up the cookie sheet and walked it to the oven, shouting on her way back, "It's on your ranch, you know how nice your uncle fixed it up." Opening the door a little, she asked, "Do you have anything to wear besides Garland Landscaping shirts?"

"I might have a shirt or two, smart-ass." She came back carrying a sheet full of warm cookies. Quinn took a deep inhale as she started setting them on a cooling rack. "How are you getting there?"

"Driving myself."

"In that old truck of yours?"

"Don't talk bad about Brownie."

"Brownie?" Quinn said, amused. "You named it Brownie?"

"Yes, I did, and she's sensitive, so be nice." A few years ago, when she decided to buy a new car, she fell in love with a '72 Chevy pickup painted metallic brown. She kept the color but added a new floral bench seat cover. Quinn had seen it earlier in the day and laughed at how girly it was. "But to answer your question, I have to be there early to set up all the cakes and these cookies, that's why I'm driving myself." He tried to hide his disappointment with another question.

"How many cakes you making?"

"A couple." She'd been measuring and mixing for a good two hours, walking back and forth to the kitchen to check doneness and cool the cookies on the racks.

By the looks of things, it was more like a few dozen.

"You need a taste tester?" He reached for a cookie, but she slapped his hand away. "I was gonna let you know if they're good enough."

"They're good enough. Do I look like someone who'd make something not good enough? You don't know me at all, Quinn Garland."

"We should fix that then." They went quiet, staring at each other.

"Quinn..."

"Tell me about these cookies Ms. Edith insisted on you making. Why does she like them so much?"

She knew he was redirecting the conversation, and she silently thanked him for it. Reaching under the counter, she pulled out a bottle of bourbon. "Probably because of this."

"The good stuff," he said, impressed. Taking it from her hand, he examined the label then handed it back to her. She poured some into a tablespoon, dropping it into the bowl with the dough, pecans, and chocolate chips. She did it three more times before mixing it in with a wooden spoon. "That's why I had to drag my uncle away from the dessert table at Charles' wedding."

"You want some?"

"Cookie dough? No, I'll wait until they're baked."

"I'm talking about bourbon." She picked up the bottle and shook it. Quinn nodded his head and watched as she poured a small amount into two glasses.

"So, let's talk about this dance we're supposed to have tomorrow."

"We're not having a dance," Gerti refuted. "Cora talks too much, always one for fairy tales." She handed him the glass, and he held his up to toast.

Smiling, he said, "To slow dancing."

Chapter SIX

"*A*re you sure you don't need my help?"

"I'm positive, Cora. All I have to do is arrange everything on the table." Gerti stopped and took off the gloves she was wearing, then looked at Cora's shimmery white dress. "I would never forgive myself if you got chocolate frosting on your dress."

"I could wear an apron like you. Is this the dress you're wearing tonight?" Cora asked, looking over the drab grey cotton dress Gerti wore under her pink heart apron. "You know this is a dress-up event, right? Ms. Edith is gonna kill you if you walk around in that." Cora pulled on the sleeve of the dress for emphasis.

That morning when she was loading up all the desserts, she'd glanced down at her dress and realized it wasn't the classy dress she wanted to be seen in at the party. It was functional, but not at all pretty. After talking to Ms. Edith and being assured she could use Quincy's house to freshen up and change, she spent another thirty minutes ripping through her closet looking for the perfect dress then chastised herself for doing so. Who was she trying to impress?

"I've got a dress in the truck." Gerti pushed her hand away. "I'll change when I'm done."

"Good." Cora smiled big, showing off most of her teeth.

"What are you smiling about?" Gerti looked over her shoulder to see if she was maybe missing a joke.

"You're wearing orange daisies in your hair."

"I also have purple ones." Gerti pointed to her head where the mix of purple and orange daisies were positioned in her hair. "I have flowers in my hair almost every day."

"Yeah, but Quinn's favorite color is orange." Cora's eyes widened. "Did you know and wear those for him?" Taking a step closer, she studied Gerti's face.

"No, I didn't wear them for him. They match my dress. Why would I know what his favorite color is?" Cora laughed at the way Gerti rambled on.

"You two talk every day," Cora shrugged, feeling amused. "Alone in The Shop after closing. You mean you haven't discussed your favorite things?"

They had, a few times, but favorite colors hadn't come up. "No, we haven't," Gerti lied, pulling on a pair of latex gloves. Then she glared at her. "What are you getting at, Cora?"

"I'm getting at... you and Quinn make a very cute couple. I've seen how he looks at you. He's interested."

"Well, I'm not, so that's settled."

"Why not?" Cora asked again. She refused to give up on them. She felt like she was the only one seeing the forest through the trees and couldn't understand why people wouldn't just do what she said the first time.

"Let's see, he's between jobs, he doesn't live here, and I'm not looking for a relationship."

"But he's here now. Why not have a little fun while he's in town? Let someone look under all those skirts and dresses you wear every day." Gerti smacked her hand when she reached for the hem of her dress.

"Stop. Now, go away. I've got to get this table set up." Tamping down her annoyance, she smiled, hoping it came off genuine. "You look beautiful tonight. I hope the man you wore that dress for notices." Cora smiled back, a hint of embarrassment creeping up her neck.

"He better."

"Gerti, this is lovely!"

"It meets your approval, Ms. Edith?"

It took Gerti an hour to bring in all the cakes and cookies and touch up frosting smudged during the transport. She had to shoo a few people away who were also setting up in the barn, getting all the tables and chairs in place. She'd stepped back to inspect her work when Ms. Edith walked up.

"Child, yes," she beamed. The feathers in her hat waved with the movement of her head as she nodded. Dressed head to toe in silver, her floor-length dress glittered and shone brightly under the overhead lights hung from the ceiling. "You have outdone yourself, Gerti. I don't know how you're gonna top this next year."

Next year. Leave it to Ms. Edith to be thinking about her seventy-fifth birthday party already. "I'm sure you'll think of something for me to do. A naked man jumping out of a giant cake, maybe."

"I had one of those when I turned thirty."

"Of course you did." Peeling her eyes away from the table, Ms. Edith looked at her for what must have been the first time because her smile dropped. "What is it? I've got more cakes if you're worried." She had a few stashed under the table in coolers. She'd wanted to save them for later, but the way Ms. Edith looked at her, bringing them out now might be best. Gerti took a step to get to the table, but Ms. Edith stopped her with a hand to her arm.

"Don't tell me this is what you're wearing to my super special seventy-fourth birthday party? It's grey," she said with a frown as if it was the most hideous color she'd ever seen.

"I'm only wearing it to set up." She looked down at her dress, trying to see what Cora and Ms. Edith saw. She could admit it wasn't the most attractive dress she owned, but when she walked past the mirror earlier, she wasn't repulsed like they seemed to be. "I've got another dress."

"Good. You can't catch a man in that."

"I'm not trying to catch a man. Thought we already discussed this?"

"You've already got a few in your trap, child. All you need to do is close it." Ms. Edith gave Gerti's arm a few motherly pats. "Now go get dressed before anyone else sees you."

Embarrassed, she replied, "Yes, ma'am."

Gerti drove her truck up to the Garland house to change, deciding to throw the grey dress into the burn pile when she got home. When she talked to Quincy earlier while she set up the cakes, he promised the house would be empty for her to use to get dressed. She was thankful for his promise now because as she drove further up the driveway, she realized she'd never set foot in this house and was about to see where Quinn laid his head every night. Not that she cared.

When she got to the door, she wasn't sure if she should knock or turn the knob and go in, so she stood there with her feet on the welcome mat for a few moments trying to work out what to do. The decision was made for her when the door swung open. Quinn stood on the other side, surprised to see her.

"Hey," he greeted, wearing the Honeybells Ranch dress shirt a lot of the men wore to events at the ranch. The crisp white shirt accentuated his dark skin and drew her eyes up to his scruffy beard. She wasn't prepared for him to be standing there looking so good.

"Hi. Your, um... uncle said I can use the house to change." She looked down at her grey dress, finally seeing what Cora and Ms. Edith had.

"Oh yeah, he mentioned someone was coming by." Quinn widened the door so she could step in. "He just didn't say it would be you." The door closed, and he motioned with his head for her to follow him. "You can use my room."

"Thank you."

Gerti walked in and looked around the spacious room with its heavy cast iron bed, messily covered with a handmade red and white quilt. The antique dark walnut dressers were still in good shape despite their age and made the room cozy paired with the wool rug on the floor. She stood by the door, waiting for Quinn to say something since he was standing by the bed.

"There's a bathroom through that door over there." Walking up to her, he took her bag off her shoulder and grabbed her garment bag from her hand, hanging it on the closet door and setting her duffle bag on his bed. "I'll lock up when I leave, then you'll have the house to yourself."

Quinn stood by the bed for a few seconds longer than he should have, looking her over from the orange and purple daisies in her hair down to the drab grey dress she wore. He thought she looked beautiful.

"If you don't leave, I can't get ready, Quinn."

"Oh, yeah." He walked to the door with an embarrassed smile. "I'll see you out there." The door closed with a soft click, leaving her alone to breathe in peace.

Using Quinn's bathroom, it took Gerti forty-five minutes to shower and dress in her papaya orange wrap dress. It fell off of one shoulder and showed off the smooth delicate skin of her neck and decolletage. Her umber skin glowed against the brightness of the dress, rivaling the most beautiful painted works of art. She wore white diamond studs in her ears and a wide gold bangle around her wrist. Simple, but very much her. Taking one last look in the mirror, she dabbed her favorite perfume behind her ears then gathered up all her things and left to join the party already underway.

"Damn, Quinn, who knew your ass could clean up so good?"

"I'm looking a lot better than you are, Charles." With two quick slaps of their hands, they pulled each other into an embrace. "How you doing, Jordyn?" Quinn asked her as she stood next to Charles.

"I'm good." Quinn gave her a kiss on the cheek, and she squeezed his arm, her thin silver bracelets chiming with every move of her hand. "I can't believe Ms. Edith invited all these people."

Looking around at the sea of people in the barn and then to the huge open doors where people were still walking in, Quinn said, "I can. She never did anything by half. Plus, there's nothing else for y'all's country asses to do around here."

"Oh, okay," Charles laughed. "You been back a few weeks, and I can't even tell you left. Who starched this shirt?" Charles poked the arm of Quinn's white denim shirt. His dark jeans were topped by a brown belt with an oversized silver belt buckle. "You look like an old laundry starch ad."

"I'll see y'all later," Jordyn said, walking off when she saw someone else she could talk to. She'd had enough of Quinn and Charles' banter.

"You done ran off my woman." Charles shook his head, but the grin on his face told Quinn he didn't mind her leaving since he got to watch her walk away.

"She's too good for you, anyway."

They stood off to the side as more guests arrived. Charles pointed out faces Quinn hadn't seen since he'd left, then introduced him to a few people considered new to the county. A multitude of single women also approached them, all wanting a closer look at the Quinn, with his broad shoulders and thick thighs that couldn't be hidden under his jeans. He suffered through shaking limp hands and gave non-genuine smiles to almost twelve women while Charles stood by not even trying to suppress his laughter.

"It was nice meeting you, Quinn. You should stop by the boutique some time so we can talk more." The woman, whose name he had already forgotten, slipped a business card in the left pocket of his shirt and gave him a flirtatious smile. Instead of answering, he nodded then sighed when she walked off."That was brutal," Quinn told Charles. "I hope that's all of them." He wiped his hand on the leg of his jeans then started walking towards the restroom to wash his hands.

"Tough price to pay for being one of the few single men in the building under forty. You took it like a champ, though." Quinn didn't answer, too focused on keeping his eyes forward, trying not to look at any of the women he'd seen earlier. "I'll meet you outside. Maybe we can talk your uncle into letting us taste some of his barbeque."

"Quinn!" Quincy yelled out. Walking over to his uncle, flanked by Charles, Quinn stared at the closed top of the smoker, hoping his stomach wasn't growling too loud. "Make sure Ms. Edith gets back inside alright. She's supposed to be in there when the band starts playing." He looked over at her as she took another sip from the red Solo cup in her hand, and the empty in front of her. They both sighed, thinking about the food they weren't going to get to eat until later. "And take away that damn cup. If she don't stop drinking, she'll be too lit to enjoy her own party." Charles laughed and shook his head as he watched her tip the cup back again then swallow.

"You ready to go in, Ms. Edith?" Charles asked, standing to her left while she looked up at Quinn standing on her right. She smiled up at Quinn, and Charles discreetly picked up her cup from the table and poured the brown liquid into the grass.

"I get an escort for my birthday?"

"You get two." Charles put his hand on the back of her chair to help her up. She hooked her arms through both of theirs, and they walked inside the barn as the first strings of a guitar played. Ms. Edith beamed when her guests cheered as she entered. Standing at the edge of the room, she gave a sweet kiss to the leaned-down cheeks of both of her escorts then went to greet her guests.

"Do you feel a little cheap?" Quinn jokingly asked Charles.

"Nothing I've never felt before with Jordyn." Charles moved closer to Quinn and sniffed him.

"What the hell are you doing?"

"Your cheek smells like brisket."

The band got everyone dancing, playing all the old-school jams Quinn remembered Quincy playing on his record player as a kid. Standing off to the side, he watched couples pair off. The men pulled the women in close to start a slow grind to the thrumming of the bass guitar and the steady beat from the snare drum. He spotted Gerti across the room, looking around and smiling at the dancing couples as she stood near the wall. She reminded him of something he couldn't quite name, in her orange dress with coordinating purple and orange flowers in her hair. Then he saw the corners of her mouth turn down as Sam Franklin walked into view towards her. Dressed in white jeans and a dark blue denim shirt, his cognac boots looked too new to be dancing in, but Quinn figured he'd find out soon enough.

He watched intently as Sam talked to Gerti. She plastered on a smile but didn't seem at all interested in anything he had to say. He would have been content with watching Gerti give him the cold shoulder, but when Sam motioned with his thumb towards the dancefloor, his feet were in motion before he knew what he was doing. Even though they were clear across the room, Quinn made it to her in half the time it would usually take. Sam was practically pleading for Gerti to join him when Quinn came up from behind. He placed his right hand over hers at her side and his left hand on the small of her back.

"Looks like they're playing our song." Quinn's deep soothing voice tickled her spine, making her hand involuntarily squeeze against his to keep her upright. He gave her a gentle tug to get her moving then, without warning, whisked her away to the dancefloor, swaying her gently in his arms to the music.

"I'm sure Sam is shooting daggers at your back," Gerti said, even though she was thankful for the rescue.

"Is that your way of saying thank you?" Quinn looked down at her alluring eyes, filled with amusement and a hint of fire.

"I guess it's gonna have to be." She gave him one of her rare smiles, and he pulled her in a little closer.

It had been quite a while since Quinn had held a woman so close, but he was sure no one had ever felt like Gerti. "What did he say to you?" He didn't mean for his question to come off sounding so jealous. He figured he could blame it on the way her hand felt in his, so soft and warm. Unable to control it, he chanced pulling her closer.

"The usual," she whispered. She didn't mean for it to come out that way, but the new closeness of their bodies made her forget her voice. "How it's nice to see me, how pretty I look. How pretty I'd look on his arm."

"You should tell him to fuck off." Quinn watched one of her eyebrows raise at what he'd said. It made him smile.

"Have you ever heard me talk like that?"

"You want me to tell him?" Quinn stopped dancing then started walking towards the direction they'd left Sam in.

Trying not to laugh too hard, she squeezed his hand to keep him right where he stood. "You're not causing any more trouble at this party."

"Fine, but if he says anything else crazy to you, I can't be held responsible for what I might do." Quinn held her hand up to his chest and pulled her in close again.

Confused, she looked up at him. "Calling me pretty is crazy?"

"Calling you pretty is lazy, Gerti." He held her hand above their heads, spinning her around before bringing her body back to his. "You look a lot better than pretty." He searched his mind trying to think of the right words, then finally remembered what she reminded him of. "In this dress, you look like... the sunrise." Stunned, Gerti looked at him, unable to say anything. On the days he came into The Shop, they would talk for hours after closing. It started the way any relationship would; getting the basics out of the way, then diving deeper into the more personal topics. She'd had a hard time telling him everything, carefully picking what she thought he could handle. A sunrise. That seemed to raise the stakes a bit, and Gerti wasn't sure if she could handle it. The song changed, and the band played another slow song, but she was too dazed to hear a single note. "If I'm holding you too close, just let me know."

"No, this is fine," Gerti whispered, adjusting her hand in his, feeling her palm sweat.

"Good, because he's still over there glaring at us." He turned their bodies so she could see without looking too obvious. "Should we put on a show for him?"

"You're supposed to be being good." She felt Quinn's large hand slip an inch lower on her back then felt his mouth by her ear.

"I can be very good," he whispered. The warmth of his breath closed her eyes as a shudder slowly rippled down her body. Caught up in the delicate scent of the perfume behind her ear, he lowered his head and pressed his lips to the smooth brown skin of her exposed shoulder. Straightening back up, he looked into her eyes, not a hint of an apology in his gaze. The song stopped while the band changed lead singers and reset for the next set.

"I have to go," Gerti said, letting go of his hand and backing away from him. Quinn watched her hurry away, then turned his head to see Sam still glaring in his direction while he sipped on a beer. Feeling bold, Quinn nodded with a smile, then turned and walked away.

Chapter SEVEN

"You sure you know what you're doing?"

"Yep," Quinn replied with a muffled chuckle from behind the jukebox. It was his standard answer to Gerti's question. She'd asked him no less than twelve times in the last two weeks. Actually, he didn't know what he was doing, but he wasn't about to say it out loud. Joe barked from the corner where he lay basking in the end of the day sun, knowing the truth. "Hush, Joe," Quinn said to him with a smile.

"You know, it's really not that big of a deal," Gerti said as she filled the sugar dispenser. "I'm sure you have better ways to spend a Friday night. We've never had music before, we don't need any now." At almost five in the evening, The Shop had been closed for a few hours. Gerti and Cora had already cleaned the kitchen and wiped down all the counters, tables, and chairs. The only thing left to do was take inventory to find out what needed to be bought Monday morning. "I don't know what Ms. Edith was thinking."

"Me either, but since she asks me every day how it's going, I'll keep at it." Quinn sighed from his spot on the floor, lifted his cap, then wiped at the thin layer of sweat on his forehead. "Who taught her how to text?" She had made a habit of sending a good morning text to him every morning, and asking him how things were going with the jukebox. "I don't have the heart to tell her it'd be better off on the side of the road."

"I'm sure she appreciates your determination," Cora said, carrying over more dispensers.

"More like stubbornness," Gerti added, walking towards the window.

Quinn looked up from behind the jukebox when her voice sounded closer than before. Gerti was the main reason it was taking Quinn so long to fix the jukebox. From his seat on the floor, he had a perfect view of her bottom half as she walked around The Shop. Her everyday attire of skirts and dresses fell just past her knees and made him wonder what her thighs looked like under the thin material, but since he had no way of knowing, he settled for feasting his eyes on what he could see; her perfectly shaped calves and pretty feet that showed off ten perfectly polished toes. Quinn had to take a deep breath to focus on not making a puddle on the floor, drooling over how good she looked standing on her tiptoes, taking down the white lace drapes that had been hanging in the windows for a few days. He thought he was being sly, but when he turned his head, he saw Cora watching him, seeing right through him with a smile.

"Why don't you let Quinn help you, Gerti?"

"I've got it. He looks pretty comfortable down there

on the floor, anyway." She glanced his way and threw him a heart-quickening wink before releasing the tension on the rod so she could slip the old curtain off.

Groaning to himself, he closed his eyes and asked, "Why do you change those out every few days? Why not leave them up for a couple weeks or something?" He quickly scanned her from head to toe. Today, she wore a light denim skirt with a row of multicolored buttons running down the front and a green shirt tucked in, showing off her waist. Quinn noticed the spots on her shirt; stains from her day at work, despite the apron she always wore. He thought she looked beautiful.

"That's where Mr. Trudy sits," Cora said, pointing to the small round table in front of the window with one chair.

"Haven't seen him in a while." Quinn thought about the last time he saw him. He had been sitting by himself. "He has his own seat here?"

"Comes in after you're gone," Cora answered. "He's a pig farmer who smells terrible," she added. "He needs a seat across the road if you ask me. Gerti's the only one who can stand close enough to him to take his order."

"All he wants when he comes in is a cup of coffee and whatever the special of the day is." Gerti had had this conversation with Cora more times than she cared to say. No matter how hard she tried, she couldn't adopt Cora's thinking they should turn away some people.

"He could call it in, and we can meet him outside at his truck," Cora suggested, wrinkling her nose as if the smell had somehow come in The Shop. Quinn looked towards Cora then to Gerti, who was folding the curtains on the table.

"He offered to sit outside," Gerti told Quinn, looking

down at the floor. "But he shouldn't have to." She walked over to the other window to take that curtain down too.

"So you take the curtains down because?" Quinn asked, moving his head, so she'd look at him and give the answer to his question this time.

"Because..." she started, then stopped to reorganize her thoughts. "Because his smell lingers in the fabric," Gerti mumbled. Quinn understood her reasoning, nodding in awe at her kind heart. Her answer made him wonder about the way he smelled when he came in after working all day. Landscaping all morning in the hot sun, he hoped he wasn't offending anyone with his odor. Quinn figured although Gerti might be too nice to say anything, Cora would have let him know immediately if he needed to take a shower before coming by. He now understood her anger the day he ruined the linens drying on the line. "He likes the scent of the detergent I use."

"I'm glad he only stays for one cup of coffee," Cora said, snidely. Dropping the curtains on a nearby table, Gerti warned Cora to be nice before placing the rod back in the window. "Yes, mother," Cora replied. She didn't like being reprimanded. Gerti walked past her to grab the new curtains from the linen cabinet in the kitchen. After she left, Cora asked Quinn in a whisper,

"What's up with you two?" Giving her a shoulder shrug, he didn't say anything. "I saw y'all dancing at the party. Looked like a little more than pretending to be her man."

To Cora, the party felt like ages ago, but with the feel of Gerti's skin still fresh on his lips, it might as well have been hours for Quinn. Their dance played in his head each night, from the song the band played to the slight tremble he felt from Gerti when he held her closer.

He tried to play it off, sensing Cora working up another plan. "We just danced."

"I danced with a couple guys, and none of them held me the way you were holding her." Cora saw a hint of remembrance in his eyes. "You should ask her out."

"Not planning on staying in Bellbush, so there's no reason to." Playing with someone's feelings wasn't something he wanted to do. He knew that pain and didn't want to be the one causing it.

"So what?" Cora griped. "It'll give you both something to do while you're here." Gerti stepped back in the room, and they both went silent. Cora and Quinn both looked down at the work in front of them to avoid Gerti's gaze as she wondered why the talking stopped.

"Everything alright?"

"Yeah," Cora answered, picking up the yellow notepad on the counter. "I need to go check the pantry, be right back." Practically running away, she disappeared through the kitchen doors, leaving Quinn and Gerti alone.

Quinn cleared his throat, not believing Cora ran away the way she did. "Those are nice," he said about the blue and yellow floral print curtains Gerti had draped over her arm. He tried to fill the silence left by Cora's exit, maybe get Gerti's mind away from what they could have talked about while she'd been gone. They hadn't been alone since the party, always buffered by someone in the room.

After their dance, Gerti busied herself with the desserts, doing everything she could to avoid him. He found it funny that whenever their eyes met, she would quickly look away, but not before he saw the flustered look on her face. He took it to mean the kiss affected her the same way it did him. Her smooth, warm skin made it hard for him to apologize, but he wasn't sure how to bring it up either. The last thing he wanted to do was make her uncomfortable. "Did you enjoy the party?"

"I did." She looked down at the curtains and traced the pattern with her finger then walked over to the first window to hang them up. "Ms. Edith had the most fun out of everybody. Who knew she had all that energy?" Ms. Edith had covered every square inch of the dancefloor. If she wasn't partnered up with someone, being led in a dance, she was yelling for people to get up so she could lead them in a line dance. "She danced more than the band played." He could tell she was avoiding talking about the kiss.

Quinn stood up and walked towards her to hold the rest of the curtains for her. "She danced circles around me, that's for sure. Did you get back out on the dancefloor?"

"I'm not really big on dancing."

"Then I'm honored you gave me the privilege." His smile when she looked up at him made her fingers tingle. She shyly looked down at the floor where he'd been sitting a few moments ago. Small metal pieces lay in a pile by the rusty black toolbox he used. "Look, Gerti—" he started as she spoke.

"You're never gonna... Sorry, go ahead."

"No, what were you saying?" Quinn asked.

She sighed then finished her thought, keeping her eyes on his toolbox. "You're never gonna finish." Her smile brought on a challenging one of his own.

"Oh, I will. You just wait." Feeling emboldened by her

dimpled grin, he let his last sentence lead him into what he wanted to bring up. "When I do, we'll dance to the first song that plays, like we did at the party." He saw the quick way her eyes glanced at him, then back down at the floor. "Look, if I made things awkward between us, I didn't mean to. I guess I—"

"It's okay," she cut him off, apprehensive about the conversation. She was good at avoiding these types of situations and being able to run away, but the way Quinn looked at her, she had nowhere to go. Her feet had planted themselves in place as if they knew better than she did.

"No, let me finish." He set the curtains down on the table, suddenly feeling as if they weighed a ton. "I guess I got caught up with the way you felt in my arms. I know I'm not sticking around for long, and this all started with us wanting to get Sam off your back, but I'd like to get to know you better."

"Quinn..." She wasn't sure what to say. She knew she needed to say something, anything, but before she could think of words to say, a knock sounded on the door. Cora came back right before the knocking stopped with her list in hand, looking at Joe, who got up and barked. She darted her eyes from Gerti to Quinn, then to the front door, when the knocks came again.

"Y'all gonna get the door?" she asked since they were closer to the door than her. Annoyed he had to take his eyes off Gerti, Quinn sighed then went to open the door. Sam Franklin stood on the other side. Turning the door handle, he gave him a bothered glare, then a nod when the door opened. "Sam." He hoped he could hear the exasperation in his voice.

"Quinn," Sam chuckled. "Do you ever leave?"

"What can we do for you, Sam?" Cora asked, not wanting a brawl in the doorway.

"Hello, Gertrude." Stepping past Quinn and ignoring Cora, he walked towards Gerti, who was doing her best to keep calm. "You look lovely today. I brought this for you." He pulled a long-stemmed white tulip from his back pocket and handed it to her. Quinn closed the door with a little more force than needed before walking back over to the jukebox.

"It's pretty," she said dryly. "Thank you." They all looked over at Quinn, who was loudly gathering his tools off the floor. "You didn't have to," she said to Sam once he turned back her way.

"You know it's never a problem." She heard Quinn grumble something from behind her but didn't ask him to repeat it.

"Let me go find something to put this in," Gerti said, wanting to put some distance between her and Sam.

"I'll help you." Cora hastily followed Gerti through the door to the kitchen. Once they were alone, she asked, "You really think we should leave them alone in there?" Gerti put the flower down on the counter and paced back and forth a few times. This was new territory for her. Never had she had two men jockeying for a position in her life. She wasn't even sure if she had space available for anything other than the hollowness it had been made up of for so long.

"Just got back, huh?" Quinn looked over Sam's clothes, noticing they didn't look like he'd been sitting in them for hours. His shirt looked freshly pressed, and he could smell the scent of soap still lingering on his skin.

"Yeah, took a haul up to Colorado. Got back as fast as I could. It's a nice state. You ever been?"

"A few times," Quinn answered. They couldn't see Cora as she walked to the door to put her ear up against it to listen. Gerti followed suit so she wouldn't be left out. "They sent me to some of everywhere with my job."

"Must be hard being laid off. No job, no prospects —living with your uncle to boot."

"Why are you here, Sam?" Quinn asked, not bothering to correct his wrong assumptions. "I've been back for a while and in The Shop for about the same amount of time. Gerti has never brought your name up once, but you still keep coming around." Sam studied Quinn for a bit before answering.

"Remember when we were kids, and we'd read all those mystery books at school? I loved all of those books."

"Get to the point," Quinn warned.

"She's the mystery I'm trying to figure out. I want to know how long her hair falls down her back and how far her legs go up." Quinn thought that was the weakest explanation he'd ever heard. Seeing the look on Sam's face as he thought about Gerti started Quinn seething. Even with no claims on her, he hated that Sam thought of her like that.

>From the other side of the door, Cora's mouth dropped at what Sam said. "Does he not know we're right here?" she whispered. "Go let Quinn pretend to be your man again so he can kick his ass."

"No," Gerti mouthed before listening to Sam speak again.

"So you understand?" Sam asked.

"Yeah," Quinn sneered. "Gerti's the present under your Christmas tree you can't open until the 25th, and the calendar shows it's March 3rd. Why don't you just give up?" Before he could answer, Gerti pushed through the door, to Cora's dismay, with a half-empty water bottle in one hand and the tulip in the other.

"Sorry it took so long. For the life of me, I couldn't find a vase, you'd think I'd have plenty around here." Gerti looked between Quinn and Sam, then Cora's disbelieving face. "What did I miss?"

"Not much," Quinn spoke. "Sam's telling me about his love for the Hardy Boys." Ignoring the glare Sam sent his way, Quinn went back to loudly cleaning up his mess.

"The books?" Cora asked.

"He's a funny guy," Sam countered, giving a fake smile to Quinn's back. "Do you have plans tomorrow evening?" Gerti's eyes widened slightly. Quinn whipped his head around to see what she would say and saw Cora motioning with her eyes for him to save her.

Taking the bait, Quinn walked over to the counter. "We still on for tomorrow night?" he asked loud enough for everyone in the room to hear.

"What?" Gerti asked, confusion on her face.

"Tomorrow night," he repeated slowly. "Dinner at my place, remember?"

"Your uncle's place," Sam tried to correct.

"At Honeybells, remember?" He kept his eyes on hers, knowing she was thinking it over. Cora gave her a gentle nudge with her elbow to get her to answer.

"Yes. Dinner. Yep, we're still on." She missed the way Sam's disappointed eyes fell to the countertop while she stared at Quinn.

"Good." Leaning forward so he could tell her something only she could hear, he waited patiently for her to lean into him too. "You should tell him to fuck off." She smiled and tried not to laugh at the way the hairs of his beard tickled her cheek. Trying not to meet Sam's eyes while Quinn whispered in her ear, she straightened, slightly shaking her head at him. "Hey, one more thing," Quinn said with a smile on his face, knowing how mad Sam must be standing beside him being ignored. Gerti leaned in again to hear what he had to say. "Just wanted to say you smell good." He smiled, then walked out of The Shop to the sound of her giggles.

Chapter EIGHT

Gerti's Monday shopping trips were exhausting. Standing at the back of her truck, she wondered why she didn't go to The Shop first to unload everything. She'd always parked at her house and walked it over. The extra steps never seemed like a problem until today. Grabbing a few bags, she spotted Quinn coming up her driveway in the Garland Landscaping truck. The sound of the diesel engine was hard to ignore. She waited until he got out to speak. He took the bags she carried then a few more from the back of Brownie before greeting her.

"How are you today, Gerti?" The way Quinn said her name made her believe his lips were made for just that. He gave her a smile, sending the black hairs of his beard moving with the rounding of his cheeks. She swore the smattering of grey hair mixed among the black shimmered under the sunlight.

Grateful for the help, she led him through her house to The Shop, cutting through her backyard to follow the path that led right to the back door. She swallowed down a laugh, thinking about how she should have followed behind him. She could have filled her eyes with the way his dark jeans fit over his thighs. Something she did often, but today, she could have let her gaze linger.

"You do this every week?" Quinn asked, setting the bags on the counter. He took his cap off, tucking it into his back pocket.

She bent down to pull a large pot out from under the cabinet and set it on the stove before answering, "Yes. Can't get caught unprepared. I'm gonna get the peach tea ready for tomorrow. Want to help?"

"Sure, what do I do?" She pointed to a bag full of peaches, and they got started, washing, slicing, and filling the pot. His knife-handling skills were impressive. His hands worked in tandem; one gently holding the fruit while the other sliced through it with precision.

"Do you cook?" she asked, while they worked side by side.

Quinn tossed a wrinkled brown pit in a bowl, then answered, "It beats starving. I've lived on my own for twenty years, so I had to learn how." She gave him a smile, then tried to think about what else his hands could do. "You would've found out if you didn't stand me up the other night."

She'd not taken his dinner invitation as the real thing because she'd thought he was saying it to get at Sam, but the way his shoulders slumped slightly, he wasn't. "I'm so sorry." She placed her hand on the back of her head, feeling ashamed. "You didn't go to a lot of trouble, did you?" He gave her a shrug. "You really cooked?"

"Grilled some salmon and potatoes," he said proudly. "Had a nice salad." He smiled his knee-weakening smile, and she regretted not going even more. She wanted to make it up to him.

"A few candles." She couldn't tell if he was masking the real way he felt, but his smile didn't reach his eyes like it usually did.

"I'm not planning on cooking for a few hours, but you're welcome to stay." She handed Quinn a big pitcher and pointed to the sink for him to fill it up. "Let me make it up to you."

"What are you making?"

"Honey pecan chicken." Gerti raised her eyebrows, hoping it sounded like something he'd want to eat.

"Sounds good. I think I will." He would have stayed if she offered peanut butter and jelly. He liked being around her. "Where do you want this?" He poured the water into the pot, and Gerti followed with scoops of sugar. "I came by to mow your yard. I should probably do that." She smiled up at him, remembering he had a job to do. "You know, that smile of yours is why Sam keeps sniffing around you."

"I never smile at Sam Franklin."

"I know. And he hates it." He walked over to Joe and gave him a much-appreciated scratch under his chin. "You want to help me mow, boy? Maybe your mama does?"

"I don't pay Garland Landscaping so I can mow my own grass. Go on and do your job, Quinn Garland. I'll be back at the house when you get done."

"Yes, ma'am." He pulled his cap back on, grabbed a peach, took a bite, then walked out the back door.

An hour and a half later, the yard was done, cut the way Gerti liked and edged to show off the large stones surrounding her flower garden. She stood behind the screen door, watching Quinn load the riding mower back onto the trailer. He walked to the back door of the truck, and whether he knew she was watching, lifted the hem of his shirt to wipe the sweat from his forehead. Gerti couldn't help but watch the movement of his belly as he breathed in and out. She was having trouble controlling her own breath as more of his muscles came into view when he suddenly took off his shirt. He turned his back to her, and she marveled at what she saw.

With the sun beaming down and the layer of sweat from the work he'd done, Quinn Garland was single-handedly putting on a master class of muscle groups with each move he made, from the broad span of his trapezius to the smooth concave of his erector spinae. She laughed to herself, knowing she hadn't thought of those words since anatomy class in high school, but the word 'back' sounded too simple for the remarkable way Quinn was made. As if sensing her eyes on him, he looked over his shoulder and caught her just as she stepped out of view. Shaking his head, he grabbed a clean shirt and pulled it on before closing the door and walking up the steps to her front door. Remembering his manners, he knocked before going in, even though Joe watched him as he lay on the floor chewing his new bone.

"Come on in," Gerti shouted from the kitchen, hoping she didn't sound out of breath from running.

She was pouring tea when he entered the large kitchen. Decorated in black, yellow, and white, there were sunflowers in wine glasses affixed to the wall in groups of three, sunflowers on the kitchen towels that hung from the handle of the oven door, and a sunflower timer on the counter.

"Do you mind if I wash up before I have that tea? I changed shirts, but I'd still like to at least splash some water on my face."

"Sure, go down the hall and you'll run right into the bathroom. Towels are in the cabinet next to the shower. I'll be on the back porch when you get done."

Following her directions, he found the small bathroom and the towels she mentioned. Looking into the mirror, he was glad he washed up. This wasn't the first date dinner he'd envisioned, but he was realizing, with Gerti, he had to take what he could get.

He noticed her before she noticed him when he walked out to the porch. Being nervous wasn't like him, so he tamped it down, chalking it up to the heat. "Having your shop right behind your house must be real convenient," he asked.

"I'm never late for work, if that's what you mean." She handed him a glass, then waited. He smiled after taking a sip.

"This is your peach tea?"

"Yes. You like it?"

"I do. I should have told you the first time I had it, but I didn't think you wanted to hear much from me."

"I didn't. But I got over it."

"You were so mad, I thought for sure you were gonna cuss me out and sic Joe on me."

"Thankfully for you, I'm not a cusser. You interrupted my quiet Sunday."

"My apologies."

"None needed...anymore." She had forgiven him weeks ago. "How's it feel, being back?"

"Fine, I guess," he answered truthfully. "Between my uncle and Ms. Edith, it definitely hasn't been the vacation I thought it would be." He shook his head, then took another sip, deciding Gerti's peach tea might be his favorite thing to drink.

"You really don't have to fix it."

"It's pure principle now. I'm not being bested by a damn jukebox." Gerti's laughter made him look at her. Both her dimples were on full display. "Plus, I get that dance when I do, so I've got an incentive to get the job done."

"So, tell me about this job back in Kansas I keep hearing about." She changed the subject on purpose, even though the feel of being held by him on the dancefloor was still fresh on her mind.

The murmurs started a couple of weeks ago about him getting a new job and leaving soon. Sometimes his uncle Quincy couldn't hold water. He wanted to wait until they offered him the position before alerting the whole county. "Well, after I got laid off, someone put in a good word for me and got me on the list for a trainer position they have opening soon. Got an interview next week."

"Is that what you like to do, teach people?"

"You know, growing up, teaching wasn't even on my radar. I wanted to get as far away from school as I could. Then I started at the railroad, doing grunt work mostly.

The trainers were the ones I'd always see in their tailored suits and sports cars. I decided that's what I wanted to do. Took me a while to get there."

"So, you'd be a teacher of sorts?"

"Yeah, standing in front of a classroom Monday through Friday. No on-call shifts, no working out in the elements, less stress on my body." The mention of his body had Gerti gulping her tea to cool herself down.

"Do you think you'll like that? You being a cowboy and all." She'd never seen him ride a horse, but his cowboy boots and hat were usually never far if not already on his body.

"No idea, but after being laid off, I know doing what I was doing isn't an option. It's not stable enough anymore, even after all the years I did it. They want youth more than knowledge out in the field now."

"You always been good with mechanics?"

"I'm good with my hands, if that's what you're asking." Gerti looked at him with wide eyes, almost choking on her drink, wondering if he could read minds. "I'm kidding," he laughed. "Yeah, mechanics came pretty easy to me."

"So you never have any car troubles, huh?"

"Well, I've got an old '69 Cornet sitting in one of Badge's garages I need to fix up."

"What's keeping you from fixing it?"

"That dance I'm trying to get from you." She couldn't help her smile at the way his deep voice answered her question.

Chuckling, she said, "Let's get you some food, Quinn Garland."

"Damn, girl, you cook like this all the time?"

"You're surprised?"

"I've only had your cakes and cinnamon rolls. Why don't you serve meat at The Shop?"

"Well, I never intended to have The Shop. When I got here, I had a lot of cleaning out to do. I started with the house." Gerti looked around the kitchen, remembering the way it looked when she first got there. "Then I went to the house The Shop is in. Back then, I'd drive my truck around and park out front. One morning while I cleaned up, Mr. Huddleson and a few others stopped by and asked what I was doing. I had a pot of coffee going and a few muffins I'd made the day before. They sat down and ate all my muffins and three pots of coffee. When they left, they dropped some money on the table and said they'd be back the next day." She finished the last bite of her chicken and grinned. "They came back every day after, and a month later, Mr. Huddleson surprised me with a new sign. They put it up before I could see it. They were so proud, I didn't have the heart to tell them they punctuated The Shop wrong."

"I've always wondered about that. Been meaning to ask you, but didn't want you to get mad."

"The people that come in have never asked for bacon and eggs—ever. They're content with whatever I serve," she shrugged. "I like to bake. I like the smell of sugar. Sweet things." She wiped her mouth with her napkin and could feel his eyes on her. "You had one of my maple grilled cheese sandwiches the day of the wedding."

"With the French toast?" Gerti nodded her head. "That was the best sandwich I've ever had."

"I'm glad you liked it." Quinn wiped his mouth, trying

to figure out how he could get her to make him another one.

"So, sweet things, huh?" He looked out into her yard at all the colorful flowers she grew. "That why you have all those flowers out there?"

"Part of the reason," she answered. "I like pretty things, too."

"So do I," Quinn said, holding her eyes with his own. "You need help with these dishes?"

"You do dishes?" Getting up, he walked to the front of the sink and turned on the faucet.

"You're making me dry?" she asked, watching the bubbles fill the sink.

"No, I can wash and dry. You go do whatever you do after dinner."

"I wash the dishes after dinner." Gerti tried to grab the dishrag from his large soapy hands, but he blocked her with his body.

"Then find something else to do, I got this." He knew his Aunt WillaMae would've taken a switch to him if he didn't help with the dishes after someone made a meal for him.

"Fine, I'll put the food up then."

Gerti moved around the kitchen, putting the food away and wiping down the countertops while Quinn washed and dried the dishes. She had to stop herself from watching him as he cleaned the dishes, making sure they were sparkling clean before drying them with the towel. When he was done, and everything was put away, Gerti pulled out a big green ceramic bowl from the refrigerator.

"Cherries?" Quinn asked, seeing the dark red fruit

filling the bowl.

"They're my favorite. Can't eat cake all day." Walking to her, Quinn grabbed the bowl and started walking to the front door. "Go on out there, I'll grab some water, I'm right behind you." Ten minutes later, they were sitting on the front steps sharing a bowl of cherries for dessert.

"You really love your porches, don't you?" Quinn asked, picking a cherry up by its stem. The bowl between them didn't seem to bother either of them since their hands got to brush up against each other when they reached in.

"I grew up in the suburbs where we only had concrete slabs and too much noise from the street to want to sit out there. One day, I'll put fans out on the back, so it's not so hot. It's hard to enjoy the smell of the magnolias when you're sweating up a storm."

"How'd you find this place?"

"My grandmother lived here."

"Ms. Gloria was your grandmother?" He took a moment to look at her to see if he saw any resemblance.

"Yeah, this is where I spent my summers. I either had my hands in the dirt planting flowers or pulling up weeds. I spent most nights sitting on the back porch trying to figure out how to catch lightning bugs and have them be alive in the morning."

"Those holes they said to put in the top of the jars were never enough to keep them going, huh?"

"Nope. I would feel bad pouring the poor things out, but it never stopped me from catching them." Gerti took her shoes off, flexing her toes, and dipped her hand into the bowl to pull out the cherries one by one by their long dark brown stems.

"There's some right there." Quinn pointed to a pair of lightning bugs playing tag in the middle of her front yard. "We'll let them live this time," he said with a smile. "These are good. I can't remember the last time I had a cherry. Where'd you get these?"

"Mr. Whittle at the farmers market sells them. He's got the best ones around." Turning her face from Quinn, she spit the cherry pit as far as she could into the grass. After getting over his shock, he threw his head back in a loud, boisterous laugh. "Sorry, I got tired of spitting them in my hand."

"Don't apologize, I'm impressed."

"Not a big deal. It's something else my grandmother taught me. She'd have an old coffee can out there for us to aim for, though."

"She was quite a woman."

"The best."

Quinn let the silence linger between them before speaking a few moments later. "I should probably get going. Besides The Shop, I've got a few other places to mow tomorrow."

"Can't have you falling asleep on the mower, can we?" They got up, standing on the steps, Gerti on the top one while Quinn stepped down to the step below and turned around.

"No, can't have that." He licked his bottom lip as he looked down at his boots, his jeans tucked into them. "Plus, I really need to take a shower. I tried to wash up as best I could in your bathroom. I hope I don't smell too bad."

"You smell kind of like my garden, actually."

"I smell like a bunch of flowers?" They were looking

eye-to-eye now.

"Like the grass and soil when the wind blows." She laughed at herself. "That sounded a lot more poetic than I intended it to." She closed her eyes, embarrassed by what she'd said. "You smell fine."

"Gerti," Quinn said, looking at her mouth, concentrating his gaze on her lips.

"Yes?" The word fell slowly from her mouth as quick and hasty she was not. She was slow motion, everything around her was. Quinn thought the stars twinkled slower, and the lightning bugs shone longer, all because of her. Time stood still for Gerti, and Quinn was in no hurry.

"I really want to kiss you right now." All the reasons she shouldn't ran through her mind, one after another, but were quickly pushed aside when she got the sudden urge to know how his lips would feel pressed against hers.

"Okay." With her permission, he took her by the waist then leaned in, touching his lips to hers ever so softly before pulling back to make sure she was still with him. It might have been chaste to some, but to him, it was everything. Seeing her small smile and closed eyes, he went in for seconds, this time focusing on her bottom lip before using his tongue to feel his way to her top. Opening her mouth to invite him in, she grabbed two fistfuls of his shirt as the kiss became more heated. He could taste the cherries on her tongue, making him deepen the kiss and pull her closer.

Gerti discovered Quinn's lips were made for more than saying her name. The moan that escaped her lips made him stop. It sounded too good, and she felt too right in his hands. If he didn't stop now, he wasn't sure if he would be able to at all. Pulling away, he rested his forehead on hers while they both caught their breaths.

"You're making it hard to leave, Gerti."

Not wanting their night to end, but knowing it had to before she did something she wasn't ready for, she said, "I'll see you tomorrow, Quinn." Leaning up, he placed a kiss on her forehead and stepped down to walk to his truck.

"Good night, Gerti."

Chapter TEN

"**n**ow, I know you got a job lined up back home, but I appreciate you stepping in to help me out with the crew these past few weeks."

"Well, like you said before, I can't sit around here doing nothing." Quinn took a sip of his coffee, trying to hide his grimace from the bitter taste of his uncle's brew. At five in the morning, it was too early to go to The Shop, where the coffee tasted much better, but his body needed the caffeine. He ran his hand over his beard, scratching at the hair he never allowed to grow as a heavy equipment mechanic. "And the job's not a given. I have to go through interviews like everybody else."

"You had one last week."

"Just the one. They do them in rounds. It's... a process of elimination."

Quincy nodded, remembering the days of having to compete for a job. Even if you knew you were more qualified or the better candidate, the process was always grueling and never guaranteed. "Do you want it?" Quincy asked him.

"Yeah, I do." Quinn's response was enough to convince Quincy, who looked at him proudly. "It's a great position," Quinn added. "My whole life is back in Kansas. Be nice to be gainfully employed again when I go back."

"Sounds important. When's the next interview?"

"They're gonna call this week and set it up." He went to put his cup in the sink. "I'ma make some eggs, you want some?"

"No, got a meeting in a couple hours, I'll eat there."

"This about the retirement community?"

"If we get the contract, it'll be big for Garland Landscaping. Might even have to hire a few more guys." Quinn smiled. Garland Landscaping was a labor of love, and nothing brought his uncle more joy than being able to provide jobs for those in the county needing them. "I'm gonna head to the shower. I wrote down where you need to be today." He pointed to a sheet of lined yellow paper on the counter. "Do The Shop last, by the time you get there, most of the cars will be gone, you can do it by yourself. Send the crew home after the Prichett job. He's got a lot of trees to cut down, so you'll need to keep them in line. They like to get silly sometimes." Quinn nodded once, already knowing how his young crew could be.

The list Quincy left for Quinn forgot to mention how long and frustrating the day would be. His crew comprised five teenagers, eighteen- and nineteen-year-olds who'd graduated high school by the skin of their teeth, but had no plans for anything else. Quincy started hiring the county's young people about six years ago after seeing too many of them walking around 'not doing shit' as he eloquently put it. He would always boast about how they quickly figured out they wanted more out of life and would find a better paying, less strenuous job after working for him, many of them even going off to college. He didn't mind the high turnover though, because he figured he was doing them and society a favor.

"Say, Q, we really have to cut all these trees down, man?"

"I already told you, Terrence, a quarter of the lot has to be cut. He's trying to plant over here and needs the trees gone." Quinn didn't tell him the stump removal would take another two days. "The more you ask, the longer it'll be before we're done."

"Shit, man, I shoulda went on to JC like my mama wanted me to." Terrence looked around the lot, trying to count the trees still needing to be cut down. He stopped after twenty, realizing it might take longer to count than to actually fell them all.

"Junior college will be there for you in the fall. Let's finish this so we can get back. I got things to do." Having never had a younger brother, working with this crew was a change. Quinn felt like he answered too many questions and had to redirect too many times, but luckily, the guys were hard workers once they got started.

"You mean people, right?" Terrence smiled as he watched Quinn replace his earmuffs and start the chainsaw again, ignoring his question. They spent the next four hours felling trees and cutting the logs into transportable pieces. The property owner wanted enough wood left to fill one of his small outbuildings, but said Garland Landscaping could keep the rest.

When lunch came, they grabbed their coolers and found a shady spot to sit. "So, Q," Jay, who'd downed his second bottle of water, said. "What was it like, leaving this place? Big Q says you left on the first thing smoking as soon as you could."

"Yeah, I did." He took a bite of his sandwich and looked out into the distance.

"You weren't scared to leave?" Quinn cut his eyes at Jay, breathing in to prepare for the question-and-answer session that always seemed to happen at lunchtime. "I mean, you'd been here all your life. You weren't scared of the..."

"Unknown," Freddy finished, trailing his hand in the air dramatically, causing Quinn to give them his first smile of the day. Pulling out a bottle of water from the cooler, he took a big gulp before answering.

"A lil' bit, but more afraid of staying around here and not doing anything. Thought it was my only option. I didn't..." He almost said he didn't have Garland Landscaping to make sure he stayed on the straight and narrow, but he did. He had Quincy every day. "Let's get back to work," he told them, suddenly missing Gerti's face. The sooner they were done, the sooner he could see her.

It took two more hours before they finished. All of them were sweaty, tired, and hot, and mostly grateful the job was over for the day.

"Where to now, Q?" Terrence asked with more pep than anyone else had after cutting down so many trees.

"We gotta stop by Bells Blues to drop off some of this

wood."

"What they need it for?" Quinn looked over at Terrence from behind the wheel and shook his head. Questions were his thing, and he always had one. Quinn turned the air up another notch to blast it even though the windows were down. After hours of cutting down and trimming trees, he and his crew were pretty ripe. Even with the heat, he had no intention of being closed in with four sweaty, smelly guys. "You ever been there? All the old dudes talk about it."

"They use it for their smoker, and no, I've never been there."

"You'd probably like it," Terrence told him.

"Because I'm old?"

"Yeah," he answered bluntly.

Waving him off, Quinn looked in the back at the other guys who were half-asleep. "After we drop off the wood, we'll go back to Honeybells and unload the rest, then the truck needs to be washed." "By us?" Quinn looked at Jay out of the corner of his eye, surprised he was listening.

"Don't look so put out, Jay, it's part of the job," Quinn told him.

"Don't we have to go by The Shop? It's Tuesday, right? She always has those peanut clusters for us when we're done." Terrence's hopeful face made Quinn chuckle.

"Yeah, I'll do it by myself."

"Didn't you do it by yourself last time?"

"What's your point, Terrence?" Quinn questioned.

"You're into her, aren't you?" Quinn pressed his lips together to keep the smile from spreading. "She's nice, as far as older women go."

Freddy, up now, joined the conversation. "She gave us these peanut butter brownies once. I almost fell in love."

"Woman like that ain't thinking nothing 'bout you," Leon said, laughing.

"Q, get to know her," Terrence said as if it were some big revelation. "She makes cookies, too."

"Those lemon ones are my favorite," Jay said. Talk of Gerti and her treats had everyone alert now.

"The oatmeal with the chocolate and pecans are my favorite," Terrence added. "Make sure you ask if she has anything for us."

"Yo, Q. Why we wash the truck before you go to The Shop? It's gonna get dirty before you get there." Terrence had shed his yellow Garland Landscaping shirt and had it wrapped around his head to wash the truck.

"All that dirt's gonna mess up the tires I spent so much time shining. Look at 'em," Jay said proudly. "I can almost see my face in the rubber."

Quinn knew they were tired from unloading all the wood and the ride back to Honeybells, but was pleasantly surprised by how much attention to detail they were putting into getting the truck clean. "I'm taking the other truck. I don't need the big one."

"Speaking of rubbers," Terrence said, stuffing his phone in his pocket, "anyone got any? Angel just texted, wants me to stop by." Jay, Leon, and Freddy all patted their pockets and shrugged to show they didn't have any. "Man, y'all asses is sorry. What about you, Q? I know you got one I can have." Terrence's pleading face made

Quinn laugh. "You got any, Q? Come on, man." Feeling sorry for him, Quinn stuck his cigarette between his lips then pulled out his wallet and handed him the sleek black square.

"You always gotta be prepared, Terrence," Quinn warned. "Last thing we need is little Terrences running around here."

"I know, Q. I usually am, but she caught me off guard. I'm not putting you in a bind, am I?" Terrence was being nosy with his question, but Quinn didn't sweat it.

"No, Terrence, I'm good."

"Cool. Let's go, Freddy, I gotta get home and take a shower real quick. I smell like a bag of onions." Terrence sniffed his underarms and made a face. "Thanks, Q. Don't forget to get us some candies."

"See y'all tomorrow." Flicking his butt into the grass, Quinn thought a shower sounded like a good idea. He still needed to mow at The Shop, but a fresh layer of sweat over a clean body seemed considerably better than what his body was covered in now.

When he pulled up to The Shop, there were a few cars on the lot. He parked the truck to the side of The Shop and went on inside to wait out the few stragglers still sitting around talking. Sitting at the counter were Old Man Thomas and Pete Rivers. Old Man Thomas had always been old. His hair, now practically gone except for the few hairs sticking out above his ears, had always been grey, but he refused to get rid of them.

"Quinn," Pete Rivers coughed out after taking a sip

of his tea.

"Sirs. How y'all doing today?"

"I think you're old enough to call me Pete."

"Pete, how are you?" Quinn corrected. He stood between them and shook their hands, then he chanced a glance at Gerti behind the counter cutting pieces of cake. "Gerti." He removed his cap, stuffing it into his back pocket, and gave her a smile. He looked at the menu board on the wall and saw only the red velvet cake left. Everything else had already been crossed out.

The red color of the cake matched her nails; both looked delicious. As she sliced, she got a bit of frosting on her finger. Something she always did, but today, it made Quinn think back to the other night when she allowed him to kiss her. It was everything he'd hoped for, but not nearly enough to satisfy him. He glanced at the frosting on her finger again and swore if he could lick it off, he'd eat nothing but her and that frosting. Shaking himself from his thoughts before his body gave them away, he said, "Hope these guys aren't giving you too many problems."

"No problems today. They're having a very heated discussion about..."

"Moonshine," Thomas finished. "You ever had any?" he asked Quinn.

"I had a couple sips when I turned seventeen. Had me sick as a dog for hours." Hearing the word 'dog' brought Joe to Quinn's feet from under his favorite window. He plopped down on Quinn's boots, huffing out a breath. "Swore I'd never drink it again. I prefer more refined alcohol, that comes with a label you buy from a store."

"Well, when I was twenty-three, someone dared me to drink a whole pint in one sitting..." Pete started laughing, putting a hand to his belly and throwing his head back. "I did it, too. Passed out an hour later and woke up married. Never touched it again."

"Smart decision," Quinn told him, patting him on the back.

"I told Pete whatever he drank couldn't have been moonshine, because the good stuff would have put him on his ass a few sips in. I don't know what he was drinking."

"My cousin made it."

Gerti placed cake in front of both men, then looked at Quinn.

"You want a piece, Quinn?" He did, but not of cake. He shook his head no, then watched her walk away before he turned back to the men who still hadn't decided which one was right.

An hour later, after a few more heated debates over sports, women, and the price of oil, Quinn excused himself to go to the restroom. After washing his hands with fruit-smelling soap and reading the inspirational poster on the wall about the feeling of home, he decided to start mowing. He'd work around the cars outside if he had to.

Walking back to the counter, Quinn found himself alone, except for Joe, who had moved back to the window. "Gerti," he called out.

"I'm in the kitchen. I'll be right out." Looking over at Joe, Quinn took a drink of his tea, smiling at the taste of peaches.

"Hey, sorry. Didn't mean to leave you alone. Did you need something?"

"No, I'm gonna go get to work."

"Oh yeah, sure. Cora kind of bailed on me, so I'll just be here getting ready for the morning." She gathered a few plates on a nearby table. "Umm, will you be coming back in when you're done?"

"I'd like to."

"I'll leave the door unlocked, then."

"Why don't you lock it? I'll knock when I'm ready." He pulled out his cap, tugging it down as he walked down the steps to the trailer. Gerti watched him for a while as he drove the mower around. She studied the way his large hands gripped the steering wheel and the way his forearms and biceps flexed and were highlighted under the setting sun. The gears inked on his arm were a blur from far away, but she'd seen them up close enough times to know how many teeth were on the biggest one. She took a step back when he glanced her way. Not sure if he saw her watching, she walked away to clean The Shop.

Quinn knocked on the front door an hour later, wearing a different shirt and giving her a half-smile through the glass.

"All done?" she asked, opening the door wide to let him in.

"Yeah, you don't have that big of a lot." He heard her lock the door back then felt the air sweep by him as she walked towards the counter again. He caught the faint scent of cream cheese frosting. "Who mows the lot in the back?"

"I do," she answered. "Your uncle sent a crew to do it once." Gerti gave him a small smile. "The very first time they were here, they mowed down half my plants and flowers." Quinn looked at her with raised brows, surprised to hear that. "Yeah, I think I fussed at him for three months. I let him know his services were only needed for whatever he could see from the road."

"He didn't take that well, did he?" Gerti had moved behind the counter to refill the sugar shakers. She shook her head no from side to side. "You need some help?"

"You mind cleaning off the tables?" Quinn walked towards a table where the spray bottle and rag were. "Then can you put the chairs up when you're done? I'll sweep and mop after."

"I can do that."

"Thank you," she said gratefully, "I really appreciate the help. You never told me about your interview."

"It went good. They talked a lot about the position and what would be expected. I had to dress up. Wore a suit and tie."

Tilting her head to the side, she noticed Quinn's facial hair. "You cut your beard?" He ran a hand along the hair on his face, feeling warmer because she had noticed.

"Yeah, thought the shorter look went better with the suit." At the mention of the suit again, Gerti couldn't help picturing him in one. "I'm not used to wearing one, but I gotta for this job." She couldn't imagine him having to cover those tattoos every day. His arms were a work of art all on their own, built up through years of wielding heavy tools and lifting engine parts. She sighed, thinking he'd have to cover them up for eight hours a day. Not that it was of any consequence to her, especially after he left. "You like it?" he asked. She brought her eyes up to his face.

"I, uh, I prefer it longer." She liked the way it felt when it brushed against her cheek.

"Good to know." His tongue darted out and swiped across his bottom lip, leaving it wet and bringing back memories of their kiss. "Where do you want this?" He held up the rag and spray bottle. "I'll start putting the chairs up."

"I'll take it. Let me get the water ready and start sweeping." She walked through the door to the kitchen, straight to the sink where the yellow mop bucket was. She stood at the sink for a few moments, telling herself to stop acting like a teenage girl with a crush. She'd turned on the water when she heard Quinn's boots behind her.

"I thought about you all day." He came and stood next to her. "Having you on my mind made for a very long day." Gerti turned off the water and smiled up at him.

"You should have called," she whispered.

"I...don't have your number." He didn't know why her number wasn't in his phone. Seeing her every day, he didn't really need it, but he'd take about anything that had to do with Gerti Gordon. He handed his phone over to her, saying, "We should fix that." While she had her head down typing her name and number in, he took two steps closer, stopping when the toe of his boot touched the tips of the white sandals she wore. He stood so close she placed the phone on his chest when she was done, but she didn't step away.

"There you go, Quinn Garland."

"Can I kiss you again?"

"Are you always gonna ask?" The question came out a whisper even though they were the only ones in The

Shop. His overwhelming presence in front of her made it hard to breathe, to speak louder.

"Not if you tell me I don't have to," he answered.

"You don't have to." Reaching up on her toes, she placed her lips to his. This kiss was soft as the last one, a gentle peck, followed by another with more pressure, ending with a teasing bite to her lower lip.

"That's good to know."

Chapter ELEVEN

The next few weeks seemed to fly by for Quinn. He got up before dawn every day to lead his crew on multiple landscaping jobs. His days were hot and longer than he wanted them to be, mostly because of Freddy, Terrence, Jay, and Leon. They had questions for days, and Quinn either answered them or yelled at them to get back on track. Luckily, his days ended much better since he spent them at The Shop, fixing the old jukebox, catching up with the locals, and talking to Gerti. Today was especially good because he had great news.

"Hey, Gerti, come here!"

"What? Are you alright?" Rounding the corner, she found Quinn smiling at her. She wiped her hands on her black apron and looked at him with concern. "Did you hurt yourself?"

"I'm fine," he answered, touched by the concern in her voice. "I'm also done." Quinn raised a hand towards the jukebox with a smile. "You've got music, ma'am."

"You did it." She ran her fingers along the smooth neon lights curved around the front of the jukebox, then pressed the small square buttons that selected each song. "Any requests?" She rose to her tiptoes and gave him a kiss. "Thank you." She'd be the first to admit the last thing she needed was a jukebox, but now it worked, and after all the hours Quinn put into fixing it, she couldn't even imagine it not in her shop.

"You're welcome." He held her by the waist and nuzzled his face into the crook of her neck, making her laugh. "This damn thing wore me out, all I want right now is a drink." He hadn't forgotten about their deal of a dance when he finished, but he wanted to be a little more clean when he held her in his arms. "You got anything to make me forget all the headaches this caused trying to get this thing to play?" The pitiful way his eyes begged made her smile, but she shook her head no. "Ok, how about a place where I can buy a six-pack?"

"You hungry?"

"A little." He looked at her as she reached behind her back to untie her apron. "You cooking?

"Not tonight, but how 'bout I buy?"

She didn't give him a chance to say no. He was sure he'd go anywhere she suggested, but he wasn't going to let her pay, no matter what she said. They cleaned up his tools together to the sound of Al Green. Humming quietly to the words, Quinn noticed how dirty his jeans were and the sweat stains on his shirt. Compared to the denim skirt Gerti wore that accentuated her waist like a beckoning call to his eyes, and the yellow shirt, cropped and off the shoulder, showing off just enough skin to drive him wild, he felt way underdressed. He wasn't sure if Gerti should be seen out with him anywhere. Apparently, Gerti didn't have the same misgivings because she threw him her keys and told him to drive.

Fifteen minutes later, they were standing in front of her truck outside of Bells Blues. Gerti grabbed his hand, tugging him along until they got to the front door. Gerti knocked with her right hand after Quinn refused to let go of her left, feeling too soft and warm against his own.

"Password?!" a deep bass of a voice boomed out through a small square cut in the door. They watched a pair of dark eyes, tinted pink from the smoke in the air, dart back and forth between the two of them for a few seconds.

"Let us in, Billy." The eyes focused on Gerti, causing Quinn to wrap his hand tighter around hers. Then there was laughter. The door swung open, revealing a large man in a red suit jacket with a white polyester tank top underneath.

"Gerti! Girl, long time no see. Get in here." Billy opened the door wide along with his arms to encase her in a hug. "It's good to see you." He rocked her gently while Quinn still held onto her hand.

"You know where to find me most days," she muffled out against his big barrel of a chest.

"I don't get up early enough to see you anymore." He held her at arm's length by the shoulders, looking her over in the dim light of the doorway. "You look good." His smile beamed wide and genuine, then fell when he looked over at Quinn. "Who's this?"

"Billy, this is Quinn. Quincy's nephew."

"Quincy Garland?"

"The one and only," Quinn responded dryly, not happy with the way Billy's eyes rested on Gerti.

"If that's the case, then you're welcome on in." Quinn and Gerti took a few steps inside then heard the door close. "Janice is tending tonight. Be warned, Mack and her are on the outs again."

"Again?" He nodded yes, then retook his seat at the barstool in front of the door.

"Thanks for the warning," Gerti told him, leading Quinn over to the bar.

Whenever Janice and her man weren't doing good, she took it out on the drinks. She'd either pour too much alcohol or not enough to get people the buzz they were seeking. It really depended on what she thought about while she poured.

"What can I get you tonight?" The monotone question said only a splash of liquor would be used for whatever they requested. Janice dried glasses with a towel while she waited for them to answer.

"What does she make best?" Quinn asked quietly, not sure what to do.

"Make us your special, Janice," Gerti answered. Quinn glanced at Gerti skeptically with the way Janice twisted the towel around the inside of the glass in her hand as if she was trying to make it pay for Mack's wrongs. "How you been?"

"Been better," Janice said, with a roll of her neck, setting two glass tumblers on the counter. She filled them with ice, then poured a splash of one of the top-shelf whiskeys, topping it off with something that looked like cola, poured from an unlabeled glass bottle. "You running a tab tonight?"

"Yeah." Quinn handed her his credit card then took a sip of his drink, letting out a little cough from the bubbles as they tickled his nose. He brought the drink to his nose to smell it because the sip tasted nothing of alcohol. "If this is Janice and her man on the outs, then I need them to get back together real quick." He watched Gerti take a small sip of hers then set it down with a chuckle. Taking out a cigarette, he lit it, taking a deep inhale before blowing it out and setting it in the glossy brown ashtray next to him.

"The drinks were a lot better the last time I came." Quinn had to lean into her to hear her voice over the band playing, but he didn't mind. He pulled her stool closer, giving her bare shoulder a kiss.

"He must have messed up bad."

"Probably," Gerti whispered, still feeling his lips on her skin. To his surprise, she picked up his cigarette and took a drag.

"Y'all alright?" Janice came up asking.

"Yeah," Quinn answered, never taking his eyes off Gerti and her lips wrapped around the butt of his cigarette.

"Janice, what's Mack got out there?" Gerti blew the smoke over her shoulder away from Quinn.

"The usual, ribs and brisket. He's got chops tonight, too."

"Can you bring us a couple of sandwiches?" Gerti looked over at Quinn, who nodded in agreement.

"Anything else?"

"Give us a shot of..." She looked over at Quinn. "What do you have a taste for?"

Keeping his real answer to himself, he turned to Janice and asked, "What's the strongest bourbon you got?"

"Let me go put in your orders, and I'll get it down for you."

"Bourbon?" Gerti chuckled. "Good thing I'm eating, or I'll be on my ass."

"You use it all the time for those cookies and cakes of yours."

"I use it by the tablespoon. Shots, and this," she circled the rim of her glass with her finger, "I might not be able to get up tomorrow."

"You had a little with me one night." His lips brushed across her shoulder again. "Besides, you're closed anyway. You've earned a day off—completely off." She rolled her eyes playfully at him. She couldn't remember the last time she'd used Monday as an off day. "And you're a much bigger lightweight than I thought if you think this drink is gonna do anything to you."

"Is that why your eyes look all droopy?" Gerti picked up his drink to taste and see if his had more alcohol than hers.

"Help yourself," Quinn joked, a little more than turned on by watching her take a sip.

"Just checking." The drinks were so watered down, getting drunk wasn't going to happen. She figured Janice used a finger's worth of whiskey topped off by East Rock County's best tap water mixed in the cola bottle.

"It'll take a lot more than a shot and whatever this is to get me drunk." Noticing she'd picked up his glass again, Gerti took another sip, letting a small piece of ice slide onto her tongue to suck on. Quinn was so mesmerized watching her drink from his glass and suck on that piece of ice, he really didn't need more drinks. The beauty next to him had him three sheets to the wind and begging for more.

"Here you go." Janice sat down two pork chop sandwich plates, with sides of slaw and hand-snapped green beans. Then she walked to the far end of the bar, reached up, and pulled a bottle of bourbon from the highest shelf. Bringing it back to them, she sat two shot glasses on the bar top and filled them. Raising the bottle, she said, "Bottoms up," before walking away and out the door.

"What are we drinking to, before we turn these up?" Quinn asked, a glint of hopefulness in his eyes.

Thinking about it, she smiled, then said, "To Mondays off." Quinn touched his glass to hers then brought it to his lips, stopping when Gerti opened her mouth, threw back her head, and downed her shot. He followed suit when she squinted her eyes at the burn. "How's that for a drink?" she asked in a whisper, rubbing her chest where it burned.

"It's a lot better than the last one." Gerti picked up her sandwich and started to eat. The small moan she let out at the flavor had Quinn adjusting in his seat. "That good, huh?"

"Yes. Or I'm really hungry. Neither one of us ate earlier, we need something in our stomachs. Can't have you falling down drunk at the pinball machine."

"Pinball?" He looked at her face with her slight smile, telling him he'd be playing a game he hadn't played since elementary school, no matter what he said about it. Gerti took another bite of her sandwich then scooped a forkful of coleslaw into her mouth. "I'm much better at pool, but I guess I can try pinball."

"They've got one in the corner over there," she mumbled around the food in her mouth. Looking over his shoulder at the game against the wall, he turned back to see Gerti chewing on another mouthful of slaw.

"How can you eat that?"

"What, coleslaw? It's good." She licked her lips, and Quinn almost changed his mind about her eating it.

"It's cabbage."

"So?"

"That should be enough. You actually like it?"

"Just eat your food, Quinn Garland." Janice came by and refilled their drinks. Taking a sip, Quinn smiled at the actual taste of alcohol.

"Janice must be feeling better. This drink is good."

"Well, Mack's outside on the smoker. Maybe they kissed and made up." Quinn took a couple of bites of his food, starting to understand why Gerti picked this place.

"You come here a lot?"

"Haven't been here in a while. I used to come with Cora after a few of her breakups to make sure she didn't do anything she'd regret. Now I spend my Sundays thinking about the week ahead while I paint my nails."

"That can't wait until Monday?"

"Monday is when I prepare for what I decided I needed on Sunday. The success of The Shop is all in the preparation."

They spent the next thirty minutes talking, laughing, and eating. Gerti even tried to bribe him into eating his coleslaw, but he wasn't taking the bait, even if the promised kisses made him think about doing it. When they were done, he pushed his plate away, leaving his coleslaw untouched, then he drank down the rest of his drink before picking up the half-smoked cigarette.

"You know what they say, all work and no play..."

"You're one to talk, Mr. Work While I'm Off," Gerti said, about him coming in every afternoon to fix the jukebox.

"I wouldn't call that work."

"Really? You mean all the sweat and cussing you did, getting it to work, was fun for you?" Quinn thought back to the view he had of her legs as he sat on the floor, trying to figure out all the ins and outs of the jukebox, and the effortless conversations they'd had that still made him smile.

"Yes." The way he looked at her with those piercing dark brown eyes, glossy from the smoke in the air but also half-lidded from his drinks, sent a familiar pulse between her thighs. And the way he looked at her shoulder, as it glistened under the low lights with the thin sheen of sweat created by the warm night, made her believe he could feel the pulse too.

"You need a refresher on what fun is." She poked her finger into his muscled arm, then before he could say what she knew he would say, she added, "We both need a refresher."

"That's better. Now, you ready for pinball?" He used his thumb to rub circles on her back. "I haven't played in years, but I'm sure I can beat you."

"We'll see." Standing up from her stool, she went to walk past him, but he stopped her with a gentle hand sliding down her arm. "Don't tell me you're scared, Quinn Garland." She turned around to face him.

"Nothing like that. I just..." Getting his meaning, she

stood between his widespread legs and wrapped her arms around his neck. His seat on the stool made them eye-to-eye, so he wasted no time wrapping his arms around her waist to pull her closer and press his lips against hers.

"We haven't even started, and already, you're not playing fair."

"Never said I would." He leaned down to kiss her neck when Janice came up to them.

"Y'all want another drink?" She started stacking up their dishes, smiling at the glow on Gerti's face.

"Not yet," Gerti answered, trying to suppress her laughter with Quinn nibbling on her skin. "Let me beat him at pinball first."

"You want me to bring it over there?" Looking down at Quinn, Gerti nodded her head yes then pulled him to the pinball machine.

The Star Trek-themed game was probably as old as both of them, but when Gerti dropped a quarter into the slot, all the lights came on, and the pings and dings sounded loudly, letting them know it still worked. Janice came by with their drinks a few minutes later, apologizing for the taste of their earlier drinks, then walked off out the back door to Mack.

"What are we playing for?" Quinn asked, taking a sip of his drink. He hummed at the taste of it.

"It's good?" Gerti asked, raising her eyebrows.

"Damn good. It's an Old Fashioned."

"You like those?"

"It's my favorite drink tied with your tea." He took

another sip, smelling the orange as he swallowed. "Kind of reminds me of you." He watched her hips as they moved each time she tapped her fingers on the buttons on each side of the machine to flip the ball up into play.

Without taking her eyes off the ball, she asked, "How do I remind you of a drink?" He shrugged his shoulders even though she couldn't see him.

"I don't know, you're just kind of simple and old-fashioned, I guess. I mean, you still hang your clothes out on the line. You wear dresses, and... you bake." Her hips were making him lose his train of thought. Setting his glass down, he went to stand behind her. Placing his hands on top of hers, he touched the front of his jeans to the back of her denim skirt. "Then there's the cherries." She tried to play, but his nearness and the deepness of his voice distracted her. She pushed the round white button at the last minute, using her body to help propel it up, which also pushed her back into Quinn, where she could feel how his body reacted to the alcohol and being pressed up against her.

"This is you not being fair again."

"Not my fault you have trouble staying focused, Ole Fashion." The slow grind pressed his obvious erection into her and made Gerti mistime her flip, sending the shiny silver ball into the outlane, losing her turn. "Looks like you lost." Quinn kissed her neck, a sweet peck followed by a seductive sweep of his tongue.

"Dance with me," she said, boldly turning around, still surrounded by his arms. Not waiting for an answer, she grabbed his hand and led him to the small dance area to the side of the stage.

There were a few couples already dancing to the beat

of the music, moving to the slow guitar riff of the blues song the band played. Quinn raised her arm above her head, twirling her before enclosing her in his arms and letting the deep baritone voice of the wide-girthed singer lead them into a slow sensual grind.

The temperature in the room seemed to rise but didn't affect either of them as they only danced closer, unfazed by the added heat on their bodies. They let the other people in the room fall away while they danced, kissing as their legs intertwined and their hands caressed each other's arms and backs.

As one song turned into the next, Quinn realized everything about Gerti captivated him. They'd gone from quiet talks to dancing in blues clubs. "You're incredible, Ole Fashion." A slow, sensuous kiss, tasting of oranges and bourbon, punctuated his loud whispered declaration with a syrupy cherry on top.

He took a step back, needing the space between them to settle down his body since a crowd of people surrounded them. He watched her hips sway to the music, moving left to right. Then as his eyes moved up, he saw a single bead of sweat roll from her neck down to the crease between her breasts. The space he created when he stepped back wasn't helping him at all, so he pulled her back into him, willing to risk it all, crowd be damned, and slowed her grind to a speed just shy of torture so he could feel her hips in his hands and extend their night on the dancefloor together. Quinn's hands ventured lower to palm her ass, filling his hands with what he'd been watching for hours.

He could feel the vibrations in her chest from the moan she let out. Another kiss and more roaming hands had both of their heads spinning. "Let's get out of here?" he whispered loudly in her ear. Agreeing, she gave him one last kiss before she grabbed his hand and led him off the dancefloor.

Chapter TWELVE

The dark two-lane road didn't seem to be a problem for Quinn as he made the long drive back to Gerti's house. Keeping his eyes on the spots of light illuminated by the headlights and his left hand on the wheel, his right hand switched between holding hers and feeling the softness of her left thigh. They didn't do much talking, letting the slow jams on the radio fill the silence as they passed glances from one to the other. Driving past the turn that would take him to The Shop, Quinn drove until he turned into her long gravel drive, throwing the shifter into park as soon as he was close enough to the house to do so.

He turned to her and kissed her lips, opening the door at the same time. With the door opened, he used his hand to pull her body towards him as he stepped out, thankful for her old truck and its bench seat leaving nothing in the way of him getting to her. With a laugh, he wrapped his hand around her ankle and pulled her to the edge of the seat where he stood, impatiently waiting to get her legs wrapped around his waist.

"Tell me now if you don't want to do this, Gerti." The sexy way he said her name, the pleading tone in his voice, plus the way his beard rubbed against her neck as he kissed her sealed her fate. "I'll go take a walk to calm down and see you tomorrow."

"It is tomorrow."

"You know what I mean." His hand on her right knee slowly eased its way up before she stopped it with her own, lifting it away to bring it to her mouth.

Kissing his palm, she said, "I know." Then slowly, she licked his thumb before sucking it into her mouth to give him the answer he wanted. Quinn let out a low, strained yet relieved groan.

They fumbled into the house, making sure not to trip over Joe, who seemed a bit put out they'd disturbed his sleep and loud snoring. He felt even more put out when he wasn't invited into the bedroom with them. His sad whimpers went ignored when the door closed before he could get his nose in to stop it.

"Lights?" Quinn asked as the toe of his boot hit the leg of her heavy brass bed. He would have ended up on the floor if Gerti hadn't reacted quickly to push his body towards the bed, where he landed with a quiet, shocked grunt at her reflexes. Changing his mind about the lights because it meant she would have to step away from him to turn them on, he brought her close, lifting her knee so she could straddle his waist. "Never mind, can't have you going too far."

"Can't have..." she whispered, but was cut off by a kiss. A soft, purposeful kiss. Quinn's hands found her waist under the yellow shirt she wore, causing him to hum into her mouth at the warm feel of her skin.

Quinn's response gave her a sense of relief but didn't fully quell her anxiety. She was by no means a virgin, but she couldn't remember the last time anyone saw her naked. Even with the lights off and Quinn's eager hands roaming over her skin, she had to remind herself to stay in the moment and not let past experiences and embarrassment about her body stop her from enjoying what was about to happen.

Pushing down her fears, she boldly pulled off her shirt, smiling at the disappointed groan Quinn let slip past his lips at the separation. A hungry moan quickly replaced it as his lips found the rounded tops of her breasts. His tongue came out to play too, licking his way up her neck to the underside of her ear then back down to her jaw. She braced herself by gripping his biceps, feeling the muscles of his arms flex under her hand. He pulled down her bra, happy she'd worn a shirt that required her to go strapless. His hand on her ass pushed her forward to rub her center against him and relieve a little of the ache his erection had started to throb with.

Another moan from Quinn made Gerti laugh. "What's so funny, Ole Fashion?"

"That moan of yours is very sexy, Quinn Garland." Her hips swayed side to side so she could hear him make the sound again.

"Now who's not being fair?" Gerti felt the hot, rough skin of his palm move from her skirt-covered hip, up her side and around to her left breast, her nipple hardening under his touch. She sighed, then again deeper when his fingers pinched and played until she made sounds even she didn't recognize.

She kissed him, hoping his mouth would muffle her moans, but Quinn wasn't having any of it. "Oh no, Ole Fashion, I don't play the quiet game. If it feels good, you better let me know. I want to hear it." Gerti wouldn't call herself loud, but the way Quinn made her feel when they weren't even naked yet, she knew she'd be hoarse in the morning.

Before she knew it, she felt his hand under her skirt, rubbing the front of her panties, coaxing her clit to make an appearance. When he felt her wetness seep through the cotton fabric, his fingers dipped inside, rubbing against her short shaved hair to feel the slick goodness she'd made for him. "Damn," he whispered, not having any other words for how wet she felt. Gerti laughed again, stunned at his loss for words. The rumble in her chest from her laughter only made him harder.

"You're gonna stop laughing at me," he spoke against her neck, his breath warming her skin.

"I would never—" When she felt her nipple being covered in something warm and wet, she realized it was Quinn's thumb he'd had in her panties, and she forgot how to finish sentences. He worked slowly as his tongue took the scenic route, swirling around her areola before licking his way to the hardened center that felt so good in his hand but even better in his mouth. "Damn," she whispered, growing wetter and impatient since Quinn still had his clothes on. She couldn't believe they were here.

As hard as she had fought against a relationship with Quinn, it had happened anyway. Cora's words about having fun for the summer ran through her head. After tonight, whether she was pressed up against him on the dancefloor or talking to him on her front porch at night, fun with Quinn was what she wanted. At least for as long as she could get it.

"I knew I could knock that smile off your face. Lay down for me." He was glad she had lace covering her windows to let in the moonlight, giving him a faint view of the outline of her body.

"You're wearing too many clothes, Quinn Garland."

"I can fix that, but let's get rid of these first." With deft hands, her skirt was undone, her panties pulled down her legs. Running his hands up her smooth, thick thighs, his fingers touched a long, raised scar on her right leg that ran above the side of her knee to her hip. He almost asked about it, but Gerti opened her legs, and his focus shifted to the prize of her creamy center. Moving his hands to the inside of her thighs, he glided them down her smooth skin until his fingers were dipping and dancing within her folds, moving in and out within her tightness. His fingers were wet, and he was harder than he ever remembered being. "Tell me it feels good," he rasped out, not satisfied with her soft moans.

"It feels, oh... yes."

Moving up to his knees, he leaned over her to get to her mouth. "Tell me," he said against her lips but didn't give her a chance to say anything before he licked at her top lip, nibbling at her bottom lip and tasting her tongue, sucking it into his mouth, making her moans grow louder. Moving his sucking and licking to her breasts, he continued to play inside her wetness with his fingers, attempting to coax out her first orgasm of the night. He wanted it as much as she did and was excited when he felt her squeeze his arm at the same time her walls tightened around his fingers. "That's it, baby, tell me."

"Ahh, Quinn." Her back arched off the bed, her head dug into the mattress, and Quinn desperately wished for more light so he could watch her face to memorize how she came undone. See if she opened her mouth or bit her lip. See how tightly she squeezed her eyes shut or if they rolled to the back. He wanted to know everything.

He could feel her trying to close her legs, trying to trap the delicious throbbing, but Quinn stopped her. Using his hand on her knee to keep her open to him, his thumb made lazy circles on her clit as she came down. When he felt her loosen, he slowly pulled out his fingers, licking them clean so he could get at the condom in his wallet.

The thud of his boots sounded against the rug beneath the bed, followed by the slow sound of the teeth of his zipper disengaging. The mattress dipped and moved while Gerti laughed, imagining Quinn struggling to get out of his clothes with one hand because he refused to take his hand off of her knee.

"Laughing again, are you?"

"I'm sorry," she giggled. "Chalk it up to nerves." She felt him go still, and the hand on her knee dropped in temperature.

"We don't have to do this." Even though he was past the point of no return, if she wasn't into it anymore, then he'd stop. He'd recite the name of every player on the

'94 Cowboys team and pray it worked to settle him down. Even though she couldn't see him in the darkness of her room, he aimed his most pleading eyes in her direction. She laughed again, but this time her amusement mixed with a sliver of trepidation Quinn could hear.

"I haven't done this in a while," she said, sitting up in the bed. "But I don't think laughing is part of foreplay. I'm sorry." She pressed her lips to his, and he accepted her apology.

"Am I making you nervous?"

"Little bit."

He smiled; the feeling was mutual. She had him petrified. Since the first day they'd met, he'd known she wasn't easily impressed. Even with all his slick talk and smooth ways, he worried about being able to back it up. He chuckled low to himself, then louder as he thought about how silly worrying was. He had Gerti naked in bed with him. All he had to do was shed his clothes, but he laughed harder.

"Maybe laughing's not that bad," he said with a rumble that shook the bed. She kissed him, feeling his teeth on her lips as he quieted down.

"Do you want some help taking your clothes off?"

Her question sobered him up, leaving him smiling in the dark room. "No, I got it. Just..." He grabbed her hand and placed it over her heat. "Keep it warm while I get situated." She hummed out a pleasing sigh when the tip of her middle finger circled her clit, bringing her hips up off the bed.

"Shit, Gerti. Don't make it sound so good."

"You'll feel better." She felt the bed move again as he got into position, placing both hands on her knees then widening her thighs with his hips as he touched his tip to her warm wetness, pushing his way inside with a satisfied grunt. "Fuck," she moaned as he stretched her so deliciously.

He pulled out to gather himself after hearing her choice of cuss words. "I swear, woman..." He fisted himself, taking a deep breath. "Now you want to say that word?" Slowly, he inched his way back inside of her, concentrating on how long it took him to be fully encased in her tightness. He tried not to focus on the vibrations coming from her chest as she moaned and sighed with pleasure. Kissing her seemed to help him set a steady pace, letting her lips melt into his as his hips rocked back and forth, the tip of his length reaching that magic spot deep inside her. "Say it again."

"Quinn." His mouth, on her neck, kissed and sucked. His hand, on her breast, teased, feeling the beat of her heart.

"Say it. Tell me how good it feels." Gerti didn't know if she could. Being filled and stretched so deliciously made her legs tremble. The steady rhythm of the sound they were creating, bringing her closer to where he wanted her to be. "Tell me."

She clutched his back, bracing herself for what her body desperately yearned for. "You feel... you feel so good." Quinn picked up his pace when he felt her tighten around him, her red nails digging into his back, then her hand wrapped around his arm as she fell over the edge, crying out his name before whispering a drawn-out "fuck."

"That's it, baby. That's what I like to hear." He moved inside her, not letting up, not slowing down, stroking her through her orgasm, making sure she felt every inch of him and knew he wasn't stopping until she got enough. She let go of his arms and let hers fall above her head, relinquishing control of her body to him, not because he was the man nestled between her smooth brown thighs but because he knew what he was doing. He was making her tingle and shiver all over. Making her feel weak and powerful at the same time. Raising her to heights she'd never imagined she could go.

"Fuck. Oh God, Quinn... Fuck." A few minutes later, she came again, gripping him within her, drenching him with her wetness. It was all he needed for his own release, growling her name against her neck as he gripped her hip and pumped into her until he was empty, and they were both spent, sweaty, and satisfied.

Chapter THIRTEEN

Quinn woke the next morning to the sound of rain and distant thunder. When he opened his eyes, he could see the sheets of rain through the clear panes of the lace-covered windows in Gerti's room. Letting his mind replay the night before, he couldn't help but smile thinking about how good she felt underneath him and around him. He had no idea of the time, but he knew her soft warm body wasn't next to him when he reached for her. He let out a disappointed groan, then lifted his head to listen for her sounds, but came up with nothing. Swinging his feet to the floor, he stood up, stretching his arms high to work out the kinks in his back, then walked nude to the bathroom.

He vaguely remembered using it last night, too much in a rush to get back to Gerti and fit his body behind hers. Now, in the light of day, he could see the different shades of blues she decorated with. The walls were painted an ocean blue, and the shower curtain and rugs were the color of the sky. Everything else was stark white, including the toilet and tub. She had one of those big oval tubs that would easily fit him and served as the shower too. He stared at it, picturing Gerti sharing a bath with him, the tub filled with bubbles and lots of slippery wet skin. He turned to the mirror and looked at his face while he washed his hands, then smiled when he saw the boxed toothbrush on the counter.

He spotted his clothes on the floor and bent down to pick up his jeans, not bothering with his shirt or boxers, leaving them in a pile next to Gerti's skirt and yellow shirt. While he buckled his belt, he noticed Gerti out on the back porch through the window, sitting in her white wicker chair and sipping her morning coffee while she watched the rain. He hurried to leave the room to be near her, stopping to pick up the two black foil wrappers on the floor and tossing them in the trash as he walked out the door.

"Morning," he greeted, the last bit of sleep still coating his throat. He coughed to clear it away then took a sip of the coffee he'd brought out with him. Gerti looked over at him and smiled with her lips still on the rim of her mug. Quinn leaned against the wooden railing of the porch and set his coffee down on the ledge to light a cigarette. Gerti took a cleansing breath in, looking at him without a shirt while he scratched at the scruff on his face as he smoked his morning cigarette. With the grey sky, he looked like a cozy warm blanket on a cool rainy day she wanted to be wrapped in. "Good morning," she returned. "I see you found the coffee." He filled his eyes with the sight of her, wearing a lavender silk floral robe that fell past her knees; so her, the pattern should have been named Gerti. "Are you hungry?" Before he could answer, he noticed Joe running across the grass. He looked up at him but continued to nip at the fat raindrops falling from the sky, trying to catch them in his mouth.

Quinn smiled at the playfulness of the overprotective dog then took another look at Gerti, who was watching him. "No, coffee's enough." He took a sip and another drag, blowing the smoke out before taking his coffee and going to sit in the chair next to Gerti. "You left me to wake up by myself, huh?"

"Joe needed to go out, and you were dead to the world."

"Come here." He flicked his cigarette into the gravel of her flower bed then patted his thigh, ready to receive her. She took her spot on his lap, giggling when his lips pressed to her neck then quieting when his lips pressed to hers. "That's better." He waited for her laughing to stop before asking. "So, we're really doing this?" Last night had been great, and he wanted to know if it might happen again. It wasn't just the sex; it was being with her, laughing, talking, and touching. He wanted it all.

"Looks like it," she answered. "At least for the time being." She wouldn't kid herself. She knew it would all come to an end.

"You start all your mornings out here?"

"My Sunday mornings. It's peaceful." Her hand caressed his back, letting the pads of her fingers enjoy the smooth feel of his muscles.

"I don't have a lot of quiet mornings. The city doesn't sleep much."

"Do you miss the noise?"

"A little." He placed his hand on her hip, squeezing a bit to feel the fleshiness of it. "After a while, you use the noise like a clock. A truck honks twice before it pulls off the curb at 4:45 every morning, and a plane flies by at 5:15. If I'm still in bed when the brakes of the buses start squeaking, then I know I've probably slept in. I keep my room dark, not like yours, so I don't know what time it is unless I set my alarm. I miss a lot of sunrises."

"I like seeing the start of a new day. My grandmother wasn't one to waste the day away, as she'd say. So we were up before it got too hot."

Placing a kiss to her collarbone then lower to the center of her chest, he asked against her skin, "Didn't like the heat?"

"She said you got more done because your body hadn't realized it was hot as hell yet. I grew up in the suburbs with central air, so coming out here for the summers was... different."

"You didn't grow up here?" A few locs fell in front of her face when she shook her head no. He tucked them back behind her ear. "You seem cut from Bellbush cloth. I didn't know you weren't from here."

"My mom grew up here. She left as soon as she could, though. Went off to college in the East and never looked back. She loved being able to go down the street to the store or walk to a movie theater. She left Bellbush and didn't look back. She doesn't even visit; she hates the quiet." Gerti looked off into the distance for a bit, watching the rain become sprinkles before continuing. "But she'd stay long enough to drop us off at the beginning of each summer and pick us up the weekend before school started." Quinn didn't miss the 'us' in her sentence, but thought he'd save that question for later. He enjoyed hearing her talk.

"And your dad?" She adjusted on his lap, suddenly feeling heavy.

"I feel like I'm crushing your legs." Quinn felt her nails rake along the back of his neck. He closed his eyes at the soothing sensation and shook his head slowly from side to side.

"Not at all. You... are crushing all the right places." Opening his eyes to look at her, he saw her sweet dimpled smile and leaned up to kiss her lips. "You don't have to answer if you don't want to."

"My dad," she started, but Quinn kissed her again, cutting her off. "Hates it here, too. Said it smelled awful, and there were too many bugs."

"City boy?"

"Through and through. He and my mom developed the travel bug a few years back after my dad retired. They call every once in a while, but mostly they're off somewhere seeing the country. He'd probably like you though, because—"

"His daughter likes me?"

"That, and you can do all the things he wishes he could. He's never been able to tell a flat head from a Phillips, and he sure couldn't name a breed of horse." She closed her eyes as his fingers gently raked through her hair. "Quinn," she whispered.

"Uh huh?"

"I'm hungry," she said with a smile. "You can stay out here with Joe, or you can help me make breakfast."

Suddenly feeling famished, he offered his help in the kitchen. "I can whip up some eggs or a nice omelet."

"Omelets sound good." They walked to the kitchen followed by Joe. "Pancakes or waffles?" she asked him, grabbing the towel she left by the door to dry Joe with.

"Waffles."

They fell into a comfortable rhythm working alongside each other while they cooked, grazing arms and caressing backs when reaching for ingredients or a forgotten spoon, out of reach on the far counter. Gerti stole glances at Quinn's back while he whipped the eggs, allowing the way his muscles flexed with each move he made to distract her. Quinn kept an eye on the tie holding her robe closed, trying to will it to fall open for him.

"You know my aunt WillaMae would've had a fit if she saw me in the kitchen without a shirt. It was one of her rules." He poured the eggs into the skillet, listening to the sizzle it made to make sure it wasn't too hot. "You don't have a rule like that, do you?" She shook her head no then turned towards the counter, trying to concentrate on making sure all the flour mixed into the batter correctly. She was about to consider it done when she felt Quinn's strong arms wrap around her waist, pulling her back into his strong chest.

"I'd hate to do something you don't like." With his hands on her hips, he turned her to face him, then used his tongue to trace the line separating her lips. Their tongues met in a slow sensual dance to the soundtrack of Gerti's soft moans. The clatter of utensils falling to the floor kept them from going any further. Gerti placed both hands on Quinn's chest and pushed him back, screaming in her head at how strong it felt.

"Listen here, Quinn Garland, get back over there and stop distracting me." Stepping away from him, she went to the drawer to get another spoon to replace the one she dropped. "I like omelets, and if you burn mine, that's something I won't like." Her smile through the whole speech only added fuel to the flames they'd already ignited.

"Good to know."

They ate almost an hour later. A few more distractions delayed them, but they were finally sitting down to eat the omelets Quinn made, plus the bacon and waffles topped with blackberries and whipped cream Gerti made. Quinn poured orange juice for both of them as they sat out on the back porch, the scents of rain and wet grass mixing with the aroma of their breakfast.

"Who taught you how to cook?" Gerti asked after taking a bite of the omelet, filled with cheese, tomatoes, spinach, and onions. "I could eat this every day."

"My aunt WillaMae mostly, but I've lived on my own for a while, so what I didn't pick up from her, I learned on my own. Can't keep this body eating out all the time." She knew he said that on purpose to make her look at his bare shoulders and arms again. "I can't believe you made this." Quinn swiped his finger across the homemade whipped cream.

"You were standing right..." She lost her train of thought when he stuck his tongue out to lick it off.

"You were saying?" His flirtatious grin was hard to defend against.

"Just finish eating."

"So, this is what you do on Sundays?" Quinn asked after breakfast was finished, both of them full and content to sit out on the porch for the time being. The rain had stopped altogether, ushering in the sunshine and the mugginess that came with it. Sitting across from each other while they ate was about all Quinn could handle, so as soon as she was done, he pulled her back onto his lap.

"Pretty much. It's the one day I get to do whatever I want and as little as possible. Wash my hair, paint my toenails," she stuck out her foot and wiggled her toes, "laundry, and let Joe roll around in the grass until his heart's content." Quinn held her leg by her calf, having to stop himself from thinking about how her ankles felt wrapped around his back last night. His hand took a slow route up her right leg, inching past her knee before being stopped at her thigh by Gerti's hand again.

"Why do you keep doing that?" He looked up at her face. "Stopping my hand?" The small tremble in her fingers gave him pause. "I'm not trying to upset you, Ole Fashion."

Taking a deep breath and smiling at her new nickname, she closed her eyes then let go of his hand. She moved her robe aside so he could see the scar that ran the length of her thigh. She felt his thumb move over the jagged raised skin and did her best not to cry out from him touching her. The injury, although healed many years ago, still held pain and discomfort that went deeper than how touching it made her feel.

At thirteen years old, Gerti watched her big sister

Rose get ready for a party at her friend's house. A lot of Rose's friends were back for the summer after being away at their first year of college, so Rose was excited to see them all. Their parents even lifted Rose's curfew for the night, allowing her to stay out as long as she wanted. They weren't strict, but with her not going off to college right after high school like they wanted her to and living under their roof, they still had plenty of rules for her to follow. Gerti watched her do her hair and put on a cute purple outfit she stressed about all week.

"Rose dragged me to five stores to find the perfect shoes to go with it. I remember whining the entire time, begging her to take me to the party. She waved me off and said it wasn't a place for little girls. Then she grabbed her jacket and took off. It made me so mad she called me a little girl. Then she left me standing there in the middle of her room." Quinn smiled, picturing a young Gerti and her mad face. He was sure it mirrored the one she used on Sam. "So, I waited until my parents went to sleep and snuck out to find that party."

Gerti wanted her to either apologize or invite her to join in on the fun, so she set out to find her. She walked until she saw a bunch of cars and heard loud music. To get to the main road from the neighborhood she lived in, Gerti had to cut through a grassy area that hadn't been developed yet and walk for about a mile, then climb over an old wooden fence. She'd made that walk a dozen times with Rose, but always during the day where everything could easily be seen. That night there was enough moonlight in the sky for her to see, but only what was just in front of her. When she got to the fence, she climbed up and over, then hopped down, but landed wrong and rolled her ankle.

"Fell flat on my face. I was mad all over again." So mad, she didn't feel the nail pierce her thigh. "I thought I fell on a stick or something, but when I moved my leg, the pain got worse. It was an old rusty nail stuck in a piece of the fence that had fallen off. I landed right on it. Sliced right up my leg about eleven inches." She screamed out in pain, but there was no one around to hear her.

"How'd you get back home?"

"I mustered up all the strength I had and pulled it out of my leg. I think it took me fifteen minutes to get back over the fence, but it took me a good hour to limp back home. I was a crying, bleeding, snotty mess when I finally got back home to my room. I peeled my jeans off as carefully as I could without screaming to the high heavens."

"You didn't wake your parents and tell them?"

"I couldn't," she shook her head quickly. "Too scared." Gerti knew telling her parents about her leg also meant telling them about sneaking out, and that punishment seemed worse than the nail in her leg. "I figured I could clean it up; put a few band-aids on it, and no one would be the wiser."

"Didn't work out that way?" He continued to run his thumb along the scar as she spoke. Quinn could feel her heartbeat against him. Steady, but not racing as fast as before.

"I couldn't hide the fever I got two days later. When I went to stand up so they could take me to the emergency room, I collapsed on the floor. Woke up the next day in a hospital bed."

"Infection?"

"Oh yeah. Almost septic. I left a week later with ninety-three stitches."

"Damn."

"I know. Rose didn't take it very well. She kept blaming herself, even though it was all my fault." Rose didn't get back home until the afternoon after the party. Too exhausted to check on her little sister, she went straight to her room and slept for hours. She didn't find out about Gerti until after she'd been taken to the hospital. Gerti went quiet, and Quinn allowed her time to reflect on her thoughts for as long as she needed to. "Anyway, it took me a while to figure out how to do the things I loved again. I found out wearing pants just irritated the scar, so I wore skirts and dresses instead."

"Does it hurt when I touch it?"

"No. Your touch doesn't hurt. It's a strange sensation." Gerti inhaled again as Quinn's thumb continued to brush the length of the scar. "I can handle the feel of your touch."

"That's good to know." He placed a kiss on her lips for her bravery. "What happened to Rose?"

"She got to a point in her life where nothing she did made her happy. She kept looking for the solution to a problem in everything she did, but it never happened."

For months, Rose talked about leaving but never told anyone where she was going. It wasn't until Gerti found her lying in her bed that all the dots began to connect. The goodbye Rose had given her the day before wouldn't be followed by a hello.

Gerti shrugged as her eyes watered. "She died about fifteen years ago."

"I'm sorry," Quinn said sincerely. He wrapped his arms tighter around her waist and squeezed her gently. Her nails raking through the back of his hair let him know she would be okay.

"Suicide," she whispered.

After Rose's funeral, Gerti became restless. Nowhere she went ever felt like it was for her. The guilt she felt from not seeing the signs kept her from living the way she should. She was apprehensive about planning for a future because she wasn't sure if a future would happen.

She went quiet again and let herself get lost in her thoughts by staring at Joe rolling around on the ground. She still hadn't shed a tear for Rose, and although it made her feel guilty, she couldn't bring the tears on, and she didn't plan on starting today. Taking a deep breath, she focused her eyes on Quinn, who stared up at her. Giving him a reassuring smile, she touched his scruffy cheek with her hand.

"When you want to talk more about it, I'll be here."

"Thank you. You're a sweet man, ya know."

"What every man wants to hear." Hopping off his lap, Gerti grabbed Quinn by the hands.

"Come on."

"Where are we going?"

"It's time to change the sheets and make the bed." She pulled him through the house to her bedroom.

"Why?"

"My grandmother always said, a bed that's made is a bed that'll make you happy."

"I know how to make you happy." He pulled her into him, pressing his hardness into her back. "I don't know why we're making the bed since we're just gonna mess it up again."

"Oh no, we're not. You're out of condoms, remember?"

"Shit." He forgot. "Damn Terrence." She stepped out of his arms, laughing at him. Leaning up, she kissed him, then pushed him down on the bed.

"I've got an idea." Untying her robe, she let it fall to the ground and stood there in front of him, scar and all. "Now that you can see, let me show you how I keep it warm. Take off your pants."

"Yes, ma'am."

Chapter FOURTEEN

A month later, the sweltering humid heat of June was in full swing. Like every other summer before, everyone forgot how hot it got until the temperature hit triple digits. Today, despite the heat, the annual Juneteenth celebration was being held at the ranch. He never sent out invitations; people heard by word of mouth. That meant there were always more and more people each year. It got so big, a few years back Quincy started charging five dollars a ticket to get in. The money covered the cost of the meats he provided, but he always sent half of the money to a local charity.

"Hurry up, girl, we're gonna be late." Gerti tried to rush Cora along to no avail. They were half an hour late because Cora had gone through four dresses to find the right one. She came over to Gerti's and modeled the dresses while Gerti finished making a covered dish to take to the ranch. She didn't want to wait any longer.

She hadn't seen Quinn since yesterday since he had to help get the ranch ready, and as he put it, nothing gets ready when he's around her.

"It's a barbecue, Gerti. How can we be late?" Cora took one last look in the mirror then grabbed her purse. "Besides, Quinn's not going anywhere."

"What are you talking about, Cora?"

"You two think you're being slick, but you're not. That bright ass Garland Landscaping truck parked at your house overnight gives y'all away, you know."

Pulling up to the ranch felt more like pulling into a circus this year. There were people everywhere, and horses being ridden by both adults and kids. Some were racing while others were being shown off and admired. Cora and Gerti heard four-wheelers being driven somewhere in the distance and assumed the teenagers of the county were having a good time on them. When they got out of the car, they could smell the smoke from Quincy's many smokers that had been going all night. It seemed like most of the people in the county were at Honeybells to celebrate Juneteenth this year.

"Cora, it's about time. Please do something with Ms. Faye's potato salad. She won't let me near it."

"I thought you were gonna tell her not to bring any this year." Cora smiled, knowing Jordyn or anyone else didn't have the gall to tell Ms. Faye not to bring any food. Her eyesight started going bad about five years ago, but she refused to wear her glasses, especially when it came to cooking. That meant sugar got mixed up with salt, often. It was always a gamble to eat her cooking, and the stakes were always too high for anyone to chance it.

"I did... I mean, I tried. She still brought a big ass bowl of it." Jordyn turned to Gerti and smiled through her frown. "The two of you can do it. One can distract her, and the other can hide it," Jordyn pleaded.

"We'll see what we can do," Cora told a stressed-out Jordyn. "Your hair looks good today," Cora added of Jordyn's long beaded braids.

"Thank you. I'll be swinging them on the dancefloor later. I'll tell Quinn you're here, Gerti." Before she could feign offense, Jordyn walked away in the other direction with a soft chuckle and the ting of her bracelets sounding quietly as she left.

In the kitchen, Cora and Gerti found Ms. Faye standing by the fridge in defense mode. She wasn't allowing anyone near it without a reasonable explanation of why they needed to be. Gerti walked in, holding a large foil-covered plastic bowl, and headed towards Ms. Faye, who promptly stopped her.

"What you got there, Gerti?" the older woman questioned.

"Black-eyed pea salad." Gerti held the bowl up, and the smell of onions and rice wine vinegar met Ms. Faye's approval.

"I've always loved the way you make yours. Did Gloria teach you how to make it?"

"Yes, ma'am, she did. The key is..." Gerti walked over to the counter in hopes Ms. Faye would follow, and she did. "Cut everything the same size." She plucked a plastic fork out of a Styrofoam cup on the counter as Quinn walked in. Cora got his attention with a hand wave and motioned him to stand behind the ornery old woman to block her view while Cora rid the fridge of her potato salad. "See, the tomatoes are the same size as the onions. And you have to use the right amount of salt. Sprinkle, don't shake. That's what my grandmother used to say." Ms. Faye nodded with a smile, patted Gerti's arm, and turned to go back to her post in front of the fridge, but she ran into Quinn's chest instead.

"Quinn Garland, when did you get in here?" Before he could answer, she asked, "And what the hell are you doing standing right behind me?"

"I'm sorry, Ms. Faye, I'm listening to Gerti the same way you were. Can't wait to taste it." He looked over to Gerti as she tried to hide a smile before her dimples gave away her embarrassment from his double entendre.

"Well, I'm sure she'll give you some."

"I sure hope so." He kept his eyes on Gerti and licked his lips, so he didn't see Ms. Faye trying to get around him.

"Get out of my way." She pushed passed him in a huff.

"Yes, ma'am." Cora came up behind Gerti. Not wanting to fuss with Ms. Faye about being able to put food in the refrigerator, she took the bowl then walked it down to one of the coolers on the other side of the kitchen.

"Quinn Garland," Gerti said in the sternest voice she could muster without laughing out loud.

"What? Did I lie?" He stepped closer to her, looking around before rubbing a hand up and down her bare arm. The sleeveless white dress she wore made the creaminess of her brown skin even more appealing than usual.

"Get a room, you two." Quinn looked up as Cora passed by with a wave.

The heat did nothing to combat the goosebumps Quinn's hand created on her arm. "Yeah, she says we're not fooling anybody."

"Did she now?" he asked with raised brows and a smile. "So, I can do this." Leaning in, he gave her a gentle kiss on the lips before pulling her into a hug.

"Take all that out of here away from the food!" Ms. Faye shouted from her post.

Taking her hand in his, Quinn led Gerti out of the kitchen and outside where the tables and chairs were being set up under tents to shade from the heat. Gerti and Quinn walked the grounds of Honeybells, stopping to talk and catch up with the people they came across, everyone giving them approving smiles seeing them linked by their pinkies.

"Yo, Q!" Terrence called out, running up to them. "Hey, Ms. G, nice to see you out." He noticed their closeness and asked, "He's not asking for my peanut clusters, is he?"

"No. Your treats are safe, Terrence."

"Good. I'll be by next week to pick some up." Without thinking, Quinn pulled Gerti into him with an arm around her waist, circling her hip with his hand. "Oh, I see. Look at you, Q," Terrence said, giving a nod of approval. "I need a partner for the bones tournament."

"Do you know how to play?" Quinn asked, still holding onto Gerti.

"Man, of course I do. I would've won last year, but Freddy can't count. Come on, man." Terrence pleaded.

"Alright, but if you embarrass me, I'll make sure you work so hard next week, you won't be able to think about peanut clusters, let alone go to The Shop to get some.

What time does it start?"

"In ten minutes. Get your kiss for luck so we can walk away with this trophy."

Two hours later, Quinn and Terrence walked away with the second-place ribbon, losing to Ms. Edith and Freddy. It might not have been so bad if they could have walked away and sulked in peace, but Quincy insisted on having their picture taken for the newsletter. Quinn schooled his face when he heard Charles and Anthony laughing off to the side with Gerti nowhere in sight to make it all better.

"I didn't know she could play like that," Terrence cried. "She's just a little old lady." He pushed his chair in and walked away from the table as Quinn glared at him. "Maybe next year, Q."

"Next year, get a new partner," yelled Quinn to his back.

"Tough break, man," Charles said, patting him on the shoulder. "But you should've known you were gonna lose. Remember who taught you how to play?" Quinn looked over at the smug smiling Ms. Edith. She'd taught him and Charles to play the summer before fourth grade. Her lessons involved lots of fussing and a few tears, but she never let them win. It was a hard lesson learning the best wins were earned, but they'd carried it with them since they were nine years old. "Let's go get some food before all the old guys eat it all."

When Charles and Quinn got in line to get their food, they were surprised by how fast the long line moved. And they saw why once they got up to the tables. Usually, Quincy served the food buffet-style, with the elder women spooning food onto every plate shoved at them. But this year, Gerti, Cora, and a few of the younger women, including Shelbi Lynn, were spooning food onto everyone's plates.

"What are y'all doing?" Quinn asked, taking a plate from Cora. He felt a bit irritated they were behind the tables.

"Starving and serving up food, like good little women," she answered sarcastically. "Apparently, it's our turn." The older women of the county had appointed them as food servers for the year. Quinn looked behind him down the line to see who else needed to eat. It didn't look good if the ladies were going to eat too.

"Give me another plate." With two plates in hand, he moved down the line getting food for him and Gerti. He declined the coleslaw but made sure her plate got some. When the plates were full, he told the ladies to put down the spoons and let the rest of the line fend for themselves. Happy and hungry, they complied. He walked with Gerti, carrying their plates while they looked for a table.

"Say, Quinn," Freddy said, coming up to him. "You got a smoke? Dumbass Reggie got mine all wet, pouring water on me after that bones victory." They noticed the huge wet stain on the front of his shirt.

"Sorry, man, I left 'em in my truck," Quinn answered. The desperation in Freddy's eyes was one Quinn knew all too well when nicotine came calling. He gave in. "Gerti, reach in my pocket and get him the keys." To get him back for what he said earlier in the kitchen, she moved her hand in slow motion, feeling around in the front pocket of his jeans even after she already had the keys in her hand.

"Here ya go," she said, handing the keys to Freddy. She didn't take her eyes off of Quinn as Freddy grabbed them from her, already running to Quinn's truck.

"You're gonna pay for that," Quinn warned. Gerti gave him a smile over her shoulder as she walked ahead, telling him she was counting on it.

After the sun went down, the real party started. The zydeco band jammed out, keeping everyone moving and sweating on the dancefloor. A proud Quincy looked on as his guests stepped in time to the beat of the drums, fiddle, and bass guitar, working off all the food they ate earlier. The flashing red, yellow and blue lights sweeping over the crowd looked sharp against the white attire that became a tradition ten years ago when Honeybells Ranch got a new logo and shirts for members to wear. As the song wound down, they could hear only the sound of the bass as the lead singer, wearing a vest frottoir, talked to the crowd.

"Y'all know what time it is. Time for you ladies to get your pretty asses off the dancefloor. Let the men show y'all how it's done."

There were faux grumbles from the women as they started leaving, but they knew this was coming. They sauntered off the dancefloor, walking off to the side, leaving only the white Stetson hat-wearing men on the floor to get in position for the line dance. The women looked on from the side, catcalling and teasing their respective mates as the band started back up, and the men went through the steps, each of them adding their own special flair and wobble to each one.

Jordyn watched Charles, who stood between Quinn and Terrence, while Gerti kept her eyes on Quinn as he stepped, turned, and bent his knees, throwing in a sexy shimmy of his shoulders to make her laugh. A couple of times, he caught her watching him, throwing her a wink without missing a step.

During the middle of the second song, Jordyn walked up to Gerti and handed her a beer. At the end of the song, the changing of the guard always took place. This was tradition. Whenever the men were done dancing, their dates handed them a beer, then ushered them off the dancefloor. This would be Gerti's first time taking part, and she was beyond excited. She held the beer in her hand and listened for the cue from the lead singer.

"You fellas did alright, but I'm tired of looking at y'all. Let the ladies on the floor so I can see something pretty." The unattached men left the floor first, leaving the rest of the men waiting for the women to usher them off. Charles held his hand out for Jordyn to hand him his beer, then placed his cowboy hat on her head and a kiss on her lips.

Everyone looked over at Terrence, who beamed as the older Angel handed him a sweaty brown bottle of his own. Gerti walked up to Quinn and handed him the beer like the other ladies, then took his hat and placed it on her head. Laughing at the smugness on her face, he gave her a chuckle before grabbing the beer out of Terrence's hand then turning back to Gerti.

"Let's see what you got, Ole Fashion." With that, he walked off behind a hatless Charles to stand and watch the women do their thing.

With the dancefloor filled with women in white dresses, white skirts, or white jeans, the band played. They were as uniform as the men, but their shimmies were a lot sexier and their dips a lot lower. The men watching whistled and yelled their approval, bringing smiles to the women's faces. Sipping his beer, Quinn kept his eyes on Gerti with an impressed gaze as she danced with her back to him. Four taps to the side with her left foot, then a step to turn her in his direction. She gave him a smile then stepped with her right foot to the side before bringing her foot forward to do a shuffle hop. Quinn thought she looked exceptionally good wearing his hat and let his mind drift to how she'd look wearing nothing but his Stetson.

"She's pretty good, for a first-timer." Charles interrupted his thoughts, noticing how focused his friend was on his lady.

"Yeah, she is," Quinn agreed as Gerti bent her knees and did a slow swivel of her hips before repeating the shuffle of her feet again.

"You ready?" Charles asked Quinn, draining the last of his beer and setting it down onto a nearby table.

"Yeah, I am."

It was that time of the dance where the men interrupted to take back their hats and dance with the ladies that had put on such a good show for them. They stepped onto the dancefloor, each of them walking to the beat of the music to stand in front of his wife, girlfriend, or significant other.

Once Quinn stood in front of Gerti, he took her right hand in his left then lifted it to give her a twirl. When they faced each other again, he brought her hand to the back of his head, where she slid it down his shoulder to his arm while he took his hat back and placed it back on top of his head. Quincy looked on, proud, and once again awed by the smooth transition that happened so flawlessly every year.

Chapter FIFTEEN

The sun felt good on Gerti's face riding in the passenger seat of Quinn's old Cornet convertible. He'd finally fixed it up enough for it to run, and Gerti was the first person he wanted to show it off to. She closed her eyes and listened to the wind as it whipped past her ears and let the song playing from the radio ease her mind on this hot Sunday afternoon. Not too long ago, she'd been at home braiding her locs when Quinn drove up, honking the horn and coaxing her with kisses to go for a drive with him. He knew he risked his life by interrupting her Sunday, but the kisses worked.

"Where are you taking me, Quinn Garland?" He drove onto Honeybells but detoured off the driveway towards a grove of trees to the west.

"You'll see in a minute." He grabbed her hand and placed a kiss to the back, his smile reassuring and mischievous, leaving Gerti wondering what his motives were.

They finally came to a stop near an old wooden fence. The trees were thick, with the grass left untamed. She saw a few squirrels scurrying through the branches and heard birds chirping nearby.

"What are we doing out here?" She looked around to see how far from the house they were. It was quite a distance. "This is the setting for half the horror movies made, you know?" She looked around again as he turned off the car. "Woman follows the handsome, mysterious man into the woods, and he chops her into small bite-sized pieces."

"You think I'm handsome?" he asked. Wearing faded jeans that seemed to have been made for his thick thighs and ass, plus a simple orange tee-shirt and his ever-present cowboy boots, Gerti thought he looked extremely handsome, but she wasn't going to tell him.

"That's what you got from that?" Quinn chuckled and nodded his cap-covered head before taking a small wicker basket from the backseat. "What am I gonna do with you?" He gave her a look, hoping it involved her having her way with him. "Get out of the car, Quinn."

"Yes, ma'am." Opening the door, he came over to her side and took her hand, eyeing the boots she wore with her dress. "Interesting outfit you have on today."

"I was working in the garden earlier. These are my gardening boots." She lifted a foot so he could get a better look at the yellow and green butterflies covering the white waterproof material. In her rush to get out the door, she'd grabbed the first thing she saw, which were her boots. "You like?"

"I do." He kissed her hand again, tucking it in his arm

to lead her closer to the old fence. "You smell that?" Taking a deep inhale of the air around them, she grinned, looking up at him. "Honeysuckles?"

"Yeah, this part of the property is covered in them." He allowed her to enter through the gap in the fence where a gate used to hang long ago but was now an empty space. "I haven't seen any since I lived here. Not too many growing on the tracks, you know?" Gerti watched him walk over to the vines, plentiful and full of the sweet-smelling white and yellow flowers, and pull a few off, his large rough hands such a contrast to the small delicate flower he handed her. She pinched the bottom before pulling out the stamen and sucking at the small bit of nectar it offered. Quinn did the same and then handed her another one. "I talked to Sam the other day." She went still and waited, not giving anything away. "Saw him at the gas station with a jar of honey he picked up on the road." Quinn tossed some petals on the ground. "I really don't like him. Said a sweet girl like you deserves it—for some cake you make." His gaze remained steady as he looked into her eyes. The light cognac flecks of brown dotting her irises shimmered each time the sun peeked through the small openings in the canopy of trees overhead.

"My honey butter cake." She couldn't make it because Mrs. Clark's bees hadn't been producing like they should. She watched Quinn toss a few more flowers in the basket then she hid her smile. "Quinn Garland, are you jealous of Sam Franklin?"

He ignored the question but handed her another flower to taste. "Figured I'd show you where you could get a better option."

"Thank you," she said sincerely. Her grandmother used to make honeysuckle ice cream when she'd come for the summers. The light flavor of the flower brought back memories of the two of them in the kitchen together. Quinn watched the smile spread on her face, but the way her tongue looked as she licked the nectar off the stem held his attention more.

He shook his head out of his Gerti daze and looked somewhere over her shoulder to focus and gather his words. "My aunt WillaMae used to make a syrup with these all the time and use it for tea."

"Did she teach you how to make it?

"No. It's a process, if I remember correctly, and I didn't have the patience to sit still long enough to learn."

"You know, I've always preferred the taste of honeysuckle to honey, anyway." She saw him trying to hide his smile, but the way his beard moved as his cheeks rose gave him away. He walked towards another bountiful vine and started filling the basket.

"I'll let Sam know you won't be needing anything from him." Gerti thought it might be better coming from her and told him as much. Quinn raised one shoulder to let her know he didn't care, as long as he was told.

He gestured with his head for her to have a seat on the fence while he filled the basket. "Too bad you don't wear jeans. I don't want any critters crawling up that pretty dress of yours." Quinn watched as she lifted herself up on the top of the fence rail to sit. She pulled down the hem of her jade green dress, making sure her knees were covered, and settled her boot-covered feet on the middle rail.

"Believe it or not, growing up, I was a tomboy. Then

after I hurt my leg, I had to learn how to do everything in a dress. It was uncomfortable at first, but I figured it out."

"I'd say you did. I like your skirts and dresses." Walking up to her, he fit himself between her legs, rubbing her bottom lip with the honeysuckle, then licked it off before she could do it herself. Leaning her head back, she focused her eyes on his lips and prepared herself for more, but when he leaned in, he bypassed her mouth, placing his lips at the base of her neck. For Quinn, it was closer to her heart, and the place he wanted to be most. "Let's head back to the car."

The more time he spent with Gerti, the more time he wanted to spend with her. The cracks in the fling plan they'd agreed on earlier were getting harder to ignore. It would have been easy if she'd been just a warm body to him, but she was so much more. She was Gerti. The woman made him earn every small piece of her guarded, protective heart, and that both scared and excited Quinn.

"How long has this ranch been in your family?" They were sitting in the Cornet, Quinn in the backseat and Gerti sitting above him on the trunk, the basket of honeysuckles sitting at her feet. "How am I supposed to make syrup if you eat them all?" He laughed, not feeling guilty, and touched a stem to his tongue, making a show of sucking on it.

"It's been in the Garland family for five generations. When Badge's great-grandfather Quinten had enough money, he bought up as much land as he could afford. These thirty acres might not be much for some, but for him, it was way more than enough to secure a future for his family."

Quinn told Gerti the land used to be farmed when Quinten lived on it. Rows of vegetables and bales of hay sustained the ranch for years. "There's never been a single cow at Honeybells."

"You Garlands aren't into big animals, huh?"

"Not unless it's a horse. Badge found his success outside the ranch, anyway. He's always said you appreciate home more when you don't expect it to feed you."

"Where did the name Honeybells come from?

"When Quinten and his wife Elizabeth were deciding on where to build their house, he left it up to her, and she found a group of hostas so pretty, she wanted them right out near her front door. So that's what he did. He built her a house around a bunch of plants." When Quinn first heard the story from Quincy, he didn't think much of it. He kind of thought it laughable to let a bunch of leaves dictate where you live, but now, telling it to Gerti, he fully understood.

"Honeybells hostas? I've seen those before." Gerti said. "They're beautiful. Do they still grow around here?"

"I've never seen any around. I think only the room Badge sleeps in is original. The rest has been added over the years. He built that big ass wrap-around porch for Aunt WillaMae as an anniversary gift. Maybe they're somewhere under there."

"Quite a gift."

"He lived by the saying, happy wife, happy life."

"I've always known him to be a smart man." Quinn gave her a shrug then reached for the water bottle in the front console. He took a sip of the water then handed it to her.

"Thank you. When did your aunt pass?"

"I was seventeen when she first got sick." Quinn looked over to the stand of trees where the honeysuckles were growing. Thoughts of that time always made him sad. "They tried to keep it from me, but two months later, she passed. Badge had to sit me down and explain her cancer." Quinn had taken his aunt's death hard. She'd raised him and had been the only constant woman in his life for such a long time. Her suddenly not being on the ranch hurt in a way that he thought he'd forgotten about. "Ms. Edith stepped in, always coming around to make sure I was okay." He went quiet for a long time, thinking about his life and the people who seemed to come and go whether he asked them to or not. Looking over at Gerti, he took a sharp inhale, letting her face be his anchor, bringing him back to the present. "So that's the story of Honeybells Ranch. Not very exciting, is it?"

When she first heard the name Honeybells Ranch, it brought a smile to her face. Even before she'd stepped foot on the property, she felt a connection. "It's kind of romantic." Gerti enjoyed learning about his family. Getting to know where he came from, and what made him Quinn. He didn't talk about his parents at all, but when he spoke of Quincy, his eyes always lit up. She and him were the same in that way. Only giving out bits and pieces of themselves until they felt the person they were giving them to could handle the full picture and not run away. There'd be no running away this time, but they could both see the end near.

"You ever gonna paint this car?"

Quinn relaxed at the change of subject. "Steel grey

not your thing?" The old Cornet had been painted and stripped so many times, no one knew the original color. Right now, it sported an ugly grey until Quinn could decide.

"No," Gerti shook her head. "You need something flashy for this car."

"I can't pick a color the way you pick nail polish." Quinn grabbed her boots and slid them off her feet. She wiggled her toes once they were free, causing the bubblegum pink shade on her toenails to shimmer in the sun. "If I choose the wrong one, I can't just remove it and start over." He ran a finger along the arch of her foot, then held it when she tried to move her ticklish foot away. "I want to make the right decision the first time, and my mind changes every Sunday."

Gerti smiled at the mention of her Sunday ritual. "I guess that makes sense, it is a big decision."

"It is. It might take a while." He lifted her foot to his lips, pressing a kiss to the bottom. "I can tell you pink is at the top of my list today." Gerti tried to hide her blush but failed. Still holding her foot, he moved his kisses higher up her leg until he was on his knees in front of her, lifting her skirt higher to place his lips on her thighs. He knew by her jagged breaths she still wasn't comfortable showing her scar, even to him.

"Quinn..."

"I'll stop if you tell me to," Quinn whispered. His voice barely ranged above the songs of the birds in the nearby trees. He licked his way up and down the outside of her thigh, focusing on her scar to show her he wasn't the least bit put off by it. Not hearing her voice his need to stop, he explored the texture of her skin with the tip of his tongue, mapping her scar until she couldn't call it a flaw anymore but perfect like he saw it.

He asked with a gentle touch, and Gerti granted permission by leaning back on her elbows and parting her legs to allow him to settle between them. He placed his right hand on her hip, then started edging her dress higher up her legs, growing more excited as inch by inch of her brown skin came into view. He'd had his hands all over her legs before, but in the darkness of her bedroom, not in the light of day surrounded by the trees of Honeybells Ranch. Gerti inhaled when the pads of his thumbs reached the cotton triangle at the front of her panties. Quinn kept his eyes on hers, wanting to watch her face while he played, making her bite her lip and move her hips in time with his teasing thumbs.

"What if someone sees us?" She looked around, worried, but her fears were quickly forgotten when Quinn removed her panties.

"It's just us and God, Ole Fashion." The feel of his scruffy beard scratching the smooth skin of the inside of her thighs made her want to laugh, but she sighed instead when Quinn's tongue pressed firmly on her clit, coaxing it out so he could greet it properly with flicks, circles, and caresses.

Gerti lost herself within the focused attention Quinn paid to her as he enjoyed himself tasting her while he memorized the pitch and sound of her moans as he licked and sucked. Her hips moved on their own accord, and when he inserted two fingers into her snugness, her arms stopped working to hold her up, and her back fell flat on the trunk of the car. Quinn dove deeper, alternating his tongue and fingers in a sensual dance that had Gerti on the brink of crumbling all around him.

"Quinn... mmm." His name, a pleading whisper, floated past his ears, disappearing into the air.

"It's just me, baby, let it go."

So she did, breaking into a million pieces Quinn happily put back together with the slow sweep of his greedy tongue, lapping up all she offered. Soon after, they were both undressed in the place of sunshine and honeysuckles. Quinn wasn't content with one, so when his thick length replaced his fingers, and he felt her slick walls tighten around him, he didn't let up until his name soared loudly from her lips.

They put on a show, a rousing performance leaving them both breathless and spent, nothing left untouched, kissed, licked, sucked or fucked. When they were done, Gerti and Quinn bowed to their audience of trees, grass, and sky, then nature applauded them with a cool breeze begging for an encore.

Chapter SIXTEEN

"**W**ell, look who's here."

"Funny." Quinn shut the door to the truck then turned to Charles, who smiled at him. Quinn looked around the parking lot of The Shop, surprised by the number of cars he saw. He figured most people would be gone already. He hadn't seen Charles in a few weeks. Between Garland Landscaping, Charles' job, and Gerti and Jordyn, the two of them hadn't found a lot of time to get together. "Jordyn let you out for a little bit?"

"Just a little bit," Charles answered, looking down to see what Quinn was holding. "What's in the bag?"

"Cherries."

Understanding Quinn wasn't going to elaborate his one-word answer, Charles pulled out a cigarette and offered one to Quinn. "You don't have your own parking spot by now? Thought there were perks to being with the owner."

"Being with the owner?" Quinn asked, taking the

lighter from Charles.

"I don't know what to call it," Charles said, blowing out smoke. When it came to women, Quinn kept a lot to himself. He didn't kiss and tell, or even sit around talking about how much someone meant to him. "Dating, courting like our grandmothers used to call it, or fu..."

"Watch it, Charles," Quinn warned. Charles put his hands up in surrender. Quinn had never been that guy. If he ever talked about the women in his life, he was very particular about the words he used.

"Just trying to figure it all out." They were both standing with their backs leaned against their trucks, Quinn in a defensive stance with his arms crossed. "I mean, you got her, and you got Shelbi Lynn sniffing around, too. Aren't you getting too old for all this?" He hadn't thought about Shelbi Lynn since he'd seen her at the Juneteenth celebration. She'd tried to talk to him a few times, but she was so far off his radar he ignored her.

"I don't have Shelbi Lynn. I can't help that she... comes around a lot. I wish she didn't." He looked over to the front door he wished he was walking through and saw the subject of their conversation. Shelbi Lynn turned to them and offered a wave before walking into The Shop. "Shit," Quinn whispered.

"She's always coming around for something." Charles stared at Quinn, thinking of a reason. "Did you fuck her?"

"Hell no!" Charles knew he'd offended Quinn, but with nothing else to go on, he didn't know what to think. He'd seen them leave together at the end of the night after his wedding and noticed the way she'd watch Quinn when they were in the same space. She looked at him as if he was her salvation. "I ran into her at the wedding.

We had a dance, and I walked her back to her room."

"And?" Charles asked, knowing there had to be more.

"And nothing. That was it. I didn't go in. She asked me to, but I didn't." Quinn threw his half-smoked cigarette to the ground, feeling too upset to smoke it any longer.

"Why? She's been after you since junior year," Charles smiled, genuinely curious. Everyone knew for Shelbi Lynn, Quinn was her weakness. She was used to getting what she wanted whenever she asked. Blame it on her father, who spoiled her rotten after her mother died at a young age. He never wanted to see her unhappy and did everything in his power so he wouldn't. Not being able to get Quinn irked her to no end, but also made her the perfect person for Quinn to have whenever he wanted. "She's a sure thing."

"A sure thing I don't need or want."

"And Gerti?" Charles asked. He'd seen the two of them together and didn't miss the way they looked at each other, as if time wasn't a factor. "Y'all discuss what happens when you leave?" Quinn's silence gave him his answer. "Hey, y'all are grown," he shook his head, relenting. "I'll let you do you. Remember, when you leave, I'll be the one here having to deal with everything. By everything, I mean Jordyn and Cora's mouth about you leaving their friend heartbroken."

"There won't be any broken hearts," Quinn said with guilty eyes, not sure if that included his own heart.

"What can I get you?" Cora asked, without a smile.

"I'll take some tea." Cora was about to walk off when Shelbi Lynn added, "And a slice of pound cake."

"Coming right up," Cora told her, looking over at Gerti, who was filling coffee mugs at the front of The Shop.

"Well, hey, Gerti, you're looking nice today." Shelbi Lynn gave her a fake smile when she got behind the counter. Gerti gave her a blank stare.

Counting to ten in her head, she finally spoke. "Thank you. Is Cora getting you something?"

"Yes, I had a craving for some tea and thought I'd stop by. Seems this is the place to be these days." Gerti didn't reply. Instead, she tried to figure out Shelbi Lynn's angle. She had only been in The Shop a handful of times, always with her nose in the air. "So, how's Quinn?" Shelbi Lynn asked. "You two seem to be attached at the hip these days."

"She's not his keeper, Shelbi Lynn," Cora said, placing her tea in front of her. She looked out the window to where she'd seen her brother and Quinn talking before. "He's right out there," she pointed. "Get it from the source if you want to know so bad." The glare Shelbi Lynn sent her way could have frozen boiling water if Cora was anyone else, but true to form, she didn't back down. Turning to Gerti, Cora asked, "Did Quinn ever tell you Shelbi Lynn's been in love with him since junior year?"

He hadn't mentioned it, but thinking back on the way Shelbi Lynn acted towards her, it made perfect sense. "Actually, she never comes up when we're together," Geri answered, looking from Cora to Shelbi Lynn.

"Hmm. You hear that, Shelbi Lynn? You don't come up." Staring her straight in the eyes, she added, "I bet something else does, though." Cora's eyes moved to the door where she waved bye to a couple of men leaving, not caring that Shelbi Lynn looked a bit flustered.

She took a sip of her tea to calm herself. "You have

nothing else to do but be crass, do you, Cora?"

"Oh, I've got plenty to do." She wanted to add so did Quinn, but the look Gerti gave her made her swallow down the comeback. "See you tomorrow, Mr. Sanders!" Cora yelled out instead. Since Shelbi Lynn entered, The Shop had cleared out because of the time. There were only a few people left so close to closing. "You should hurry and drink that, we won't be open for much longer." Walking off to go clean tables, she left Gerti and Shelbi Lynn by themselves.

Before Gerti could walk off too, Shelbi Lynn asked, "Does he still do that thing where he kisses you on the cheek and then the forehead? Probably so." She didn't allow Gerti the time to answer. "It's like a signature of his or something. It's very sweet." Taking another sip of her tea, Shelbi Lynn reached into her purse to pull out some money. She left a few bills on the counter next to her half-empty glass and untouched pound cake, then walked to the jukebox on the wall. Looking around, she didn't see anyone left in The Shop but her, Cora, and Gerti, making the sound of her quarters dropping to the bottom of the coin slot extra loud. She pressed two buttons to make her selection, then turned and said, "I love this song." Gerti and Cora heard the first notes of Dr. Feelgood play then watched Shelbi Lynn walk out.

"Hey, Quinn," Shelbi Lynn happily said as he walked up to her on his way into The Shop.

"Shelbi Lynn." He nodded once then continued to walk past her.

She spoke again, making him stop. "Quinn, when are

we gonna stop dancing around each other and get together?" It was a bold move, but she needed to know. He looked at her, stunned by her question. "I mean, I thought after the wedding, we could be headed towards the path we were always meant to be on."

Quinn thought it best to be quiet and let her get it all off her chest. His memories of that night were a lot different from what she remembered. He couldn't think of anything that would make her believe they could have anything more than a so-called friendship. "Then next thing I know, you're all over Ms. COGIC in there."

"Ms. Who?" he asked, annoyed and offended. Keeping quiet ended with that statement.

"Like you don't see it? The skirts and dresses below her knees, hair always up," she pointed out. "She dresses like she's ready for a revival to happen. What does Miss Modesty have that I don't?" Shelbi Lynn's voice rose in agitation with her question.

"I—" Quinn realized he didn't owe her an explanation of his feelings for Gerti. He didn't like being the bad guy, but he needed to make sure he left nothing unsaid, and there was nothing confusing. "Look, Shelbi Lynn, there couldn't have been anything between us. I never saw you as anything more than a friend, and that was twenty years ago. If I did anything to make you think differently, I apologize, but whatever you and I don't have has nothing to do with Gerti. You got it?"

Shelbi Lynn could only stand there, floored by his words. For once in her life, she didn't know what to say. Quinn was right. The reason they'd never explored anything between the two of them was because there never was. But being the stubborn girl she'd always been, if she couldn't have Quinn, she would have the last word. "It's not like you gave us a chance."

"A chance isn't a guarantee, Shelbi Lynn."

Looking out into the distance, she watched the tops of the trees blow in the wind as a few birds sought shade. She was quiet for a long time before finally speaking. "But it's still a chance."

Gerti had her back to the door, refilling the sugar dispensers, trying to figure out why she let what Shelbi Lynn said to her about Quinn's signature kiss get to her the way it did. The light stomp of Quinn's boots on the tile announced his entrance, giving Gerti no reason to turn around to see who had entered The Shop. A few steps later, she felt the heat of his body at her back as he stood behind her, hands wide on the countertop so she couldn't go anywhere. He'd had a long day, and all he wanted was to see her, but he kept getting interrupted.

"I've been missing you something bad, Ole Fashion." With a slight push forward with his hips, he brought on the laugh he'd been waiting to hear all day. He gave her a kiss on the neck then let her finish her task without moving from his spot at her back. "You didn't pick up your phone when I called earlier."

That morning, she'd taken her time deciding what to wear. Trying on multiple combinations of skirts and shirts with Quinn in mind, she'd finally settled on the second thing she tried on once she noticed the time and the pile of clothes on her bed. She was thirty minutes late getting to The Shop.

"I left it at the house."

"How was your day?" He gave her another kiss on the neck.

"My day was fine." A little sugar landed on the counter when Quinn's tongue ran the length of her neck. She let out a quiet moan.

"You're making a mess, Ole Fashion." Turning to face him, she pressed a kiss to his lips then pushed him away.

"Go over there and sit down. And be good."

"Yes, ma'am." Leaving the bag of cherries on the counter, he found a chair and was content to watch her work. She wore a black skirt with a black-and-white striped tee-shirt today. He had no idea how she made something so simple look so sexy. He was realizing struggling against what was happening between them was doing him no good. He was powerless to her smile, her laugh, and the touch of her hands.

Looking at her, he felt as if overnight, she'd become a thief, and his heart was the most expensive heist of her life. Not accustomed to these feelings, he wasn't sure what to do, but talking about it wasn't an option. If his second interview went well, he'd have a job to go back to. They'd both known going into this there was an expiration date, but that hadn't stopped him from falling.

"I've got some peanut clusters for you to take to Terrence."

"I'm not giving Terrence shit. He's the reason I'm late getting over here." Quinn cursed the nineteen-year-old under his breath. "Every day he asks thirty questions. Thirty different questions while he takes his time cleaning up. No matter how much I yell, it's always like his feet are made of lead."

"He looks up to you, you know. It's obvious he values your opinion, or he wouldn't ask you anything." Quinn shrugged, not wanting to admit she was right. He focused his attention on Gerti's back, and how her ass moved with every step she took.

Twenty-five minutes later, Quinn looked up at the clock on the wall. "How much longer am I gonna have to wait? I'm dying here, Gerti."

"You're such a baby," she laughed, looking at him. His cap was in his hand as he scratched the top of his head. His long jean-covered legs stretched out in front of him, one crossed over the other, with part of the bottom of his jeans tucked into his boots. "You can wait ten more minutes. I think I've spoiled you."

"You have, that's why I'm impatient." Going around the counter to put away the sugar and get the rag to wipe off the mess Quinn made her make, she thought back to the first time they met, and how quickly he went from just a guy sitting at one of her tables for the very first time to almost being a staple at The Shop. People asked about him every day, and she would miss him when he left.

"You want something to drink while you're waiting?"

"I'll take some water when you finish." He didn't want her to take up any more time finishing than she had to.

Finally done after twenty more long minutes, Gerti stood in front of the counter with a glass of ice water in her hand, looking at an anxious Quinn. He started to get up, but a slow shake of her head stilled him and kept him in his seat. She reached inside the bag and pulled out a long-stemmed cherry, wrapping her lips around it. He couldn't do anything but laugh as she strolled towards him, sucking on the cherry. She untied her apron with one hand behind her back, still holding the water with the other.

Even though they were alone, Quinn still looked around to make sure no one else was there. Positive it was only them, he reached out for her when she was close enough and sat her on his lap, thrilled by the weight of her as she straddled him. He took the water and set it on the table, no longer thirsty for it but for her and her smile.

"I thought you wanted water." Gerti smiled around the pit in her mouth, then tried not to laugh too loud when Quinn put his hand under her mouth for her to spit it out.

"Changed my mind." Gerti felt his hands wrap around her thigh under her skirt. Used to feeling his fingertips touch her scar, every time he did, it felt like he was telling her it was okay to be happy even if her body held the mark saying otherwise. It was okay to lean on him and be held by such strong arms, arms that wanted her to feel secure in her own skin. He made her feel she could let herself be weak if only for a moment.

He buried his face in her neck and took a deep inhale of her warm skin. "You smell good." He looked at her for permission to take her headwrap off. He wanted to take all her clothes off but would settle for uncovering her locs for now. With a single nod, he untucked a corner, and her locs fell down her back.

"I think you're biased. I smell like I've been working all day." Quinn threaded his fingers through the back of her hair, pulling gently to tilt her head back, giving him an unobstructed view of the smooth brown skin of her neck. One long lick from clavicle to ear lobe was all she needed to know about what he thought of the way she smelled. Her skin held her entire day. Sweet from baking, fragrant from gardening, and still hot from the summer sun. She was his own personal flavor made up of all the things she loved, mixed just right for him to taste.

"How 'bout you come home with me, and I'll show you you smell good enough to eat."

"Quinn Garland." The throbbing between her thighs intensified with the seriousness of his eyes and the deep timbre of his voice. Standing up with her still in his arms, he let her slide down his body until she was firmly on her feet.

He placed his cap back on his head and said, "Hurry, before you end up on this table."

Chapter SEVENTEEN

*A*fter leaving The Shop, they barely made it through the front door before he started undressing her, leaving a trail of clothes along the hallway. He'd been so pent-up, the first one became a quick and dirty prequel for the rest of the night. When they got to his room, he bent her over the dresser and worked her until her legs could barely hold her up. They had the house to themselves with Quincy out of town for a few days. Quinn made sure he kept Gerti satisfied until he had nothing left to give.

When she fell asleep beside him, he expected to be right behind her, but sleep never came. He listened to her breathe, feeling the rise and fall of each slumbered exhale on his chest while his hand splayed out on her belly. The steady evenness of her breathing should have lulled him to sleep like it always did, but tonight, he had too much on his mind. He carefully eased out of bed, pulling on his jeans he'd tossed over the back of a chair. Turning, he checked to make sure Gerti hadn't stirred. He contemplated whether or not he was making the right decision by leaving her alone in the bed. Her soft naked body under the wrinkled sheet seemed too inviting, but he needed to think, so he left the room and walked to the kitchen.

The sound of the coffee dripping and Joe's snoring as he lay at Quinn's feet eased some of the tension of the silent house. Quinn ate the last slice of chocolate cake left on the cake stand while it dripped and filled up the glass container. Too restless to sit, he walked around, taking bites of the cake and looking around the old square kitchen. He walked to the back door to look through the screen at the land he was starting to see with new eyes.

When he first got to the ranch, the vastness and all the green he saw overwhelmed him. He couldn't believe someone could own so much and do whatever they wanted to do with it. He had learned to appreciate the ranch and the value it held for his uncle. But something deep down inside made Quinn believe he didn't deserve the same thing. That was the reason he left, and guilt made him stay away for so long.

He settled down in one of the red rocking chairs on the porch and took a small sip of his coffee. Black tonight, since he didn't know how to make it as good as Gerti's. Putting his mug down, he spied the glowing eyes of a few rabbits out in the distance then pulled out his cigarettes from the back pocket of his jeans.

The sun had set long ago, taking with it some of the unbearable heat from summer. Even as night turned into the early hours of the next day, the air felt thick with heat. Quinn sat in the old wooden rocker looking out into the darkness from the back porch. The light from the kitchen provided his only source of light, allowing him to see the coffee mug, and his uncle's old record player; a staple on the old porch. The music playing wasn't loud, but low enough to help him think and ensure Gerti continued to sleep peacefully. An hour ago, he'd been right beside her in bed, snuggled up to her body, her skin still damp from their lovemaking.

With a lit cigarette and the sounds of Otis Redding, Quinn looked out into the night. He listened to the sounds of the ranch, the quiet rustling of the trees made by the breeze, even a few birds singing their night song. He missed this part the most. Being able to sit outside and be with his thoughts in the night's quiet, to work out what troubled him. His drive back to Kansas popped into his head. All the miles that would separate him from Honeybells. The excitement of his new job came next. He mentally counted the ties he owned and wondered what a life of wearing one every day would feel like. He hoped his cowboy boots would be dressy enough for the position, because if not, there might be a problem. They were his most comfortable shoes. The job was offered to him last week, and he'd eagerly accepted. He'd felt as if his life had been in limbo since being laid off, but now with a job to go back to, he felt as if he had a purpose.

He took another sip of coffee then leaned his head back on the rocker to take a drag of his cigarette. He could feel the wood of the chair digging into his skin, and beads of sweat ran down his back. Without his shirt, there was nothing he could do about it. At least the mosquitoes weren't out. Quinn closed his eyes and thought about how many more days of sweltering heat there would be. Fall had always been his favorite season. Temperatures cooled down, and football season started. He had to remember to buy some authentic gear from his favorite team before he left town.

Fifteen minutes later, he turned his head to the sound of footsteps, smiling when her scent invaded the air and cut through the smell of his cigarette. "You're supposed to be asleep."

Gerti stood on the other side of the screen door, watching the puffs of smoke disappear into the air. "I rolled over and reached for that beard of yours, but it wasn't there. I had to come find out where you went."

"Couldn't sleep," he told her, motioning with his head for her to join him. She stepped out onto the porch, and the door slammed closed, interrupting the quiet for a second.

"Sorry," she said, sitting in the seat on the other side of the table. She rocked slowly, getting accustomed to the thickness in the air. He noticed she was wearing the tee-shirt he had on earlier. She must have picked it up in the hallway because he didn't make it to the bedroom wearing it. He loved the way it clung to his favorite parts of her body and fell right below her ass.

"Always making an entrance." She picked up the warm coffee and took a sip, making a face at the bitter flavor, then set it back down. Quinn chuckled, feeling bad she put herself through drinking his horrible attempt. "It's nothing like the way you like yours, but I wasn't going to wake you up to make me coffee."

"The way that tastes, you should have." They both went quiet, looking out into the night.

"You want to talk about it?"

He turned to her and asked, "About what?"

"Why you can't sleep?" She took a drag of the cigarette and waited for his answer.

"Got a lot on my mind, I guess. It's too hot to sleep, anyway." He turned to her and smiled. "That hot little body of yours puts out a lot of heat."

"Maybe you should stop heating it up, then."

"Bring your smart ass over here." Gerti laughed as she got up to sit on his lap. Quinn gave her a kiss when she'd settled in, then rubbed his hand up and down her thigh. "Didn't mean to worry you."

"I wasn't worried. I knew you couldn't have gotten too far." She figured leaving soon had him up so late. She was genuinely happy for him and didn't want to show anything different, so she avoided the topic altogether. She let out a yawn, covering her mouth when she realized how big it was. "I don't think I've ever been up this late, or is it early?" She shrugged and reached for the coffee mug on the table.

"Thought you didn't like it."

"I've definitely had better, but right now, I want the caffeine." Gerti swallowed down the coffee, hoping it worked soon because she wasn't sure if she could handle another sip.

"It's not so bad," Quinn said, knowing different.

"It's not so good, either, but it'll have to do for right now." She felt his hand on her back under the shirt she wore. The warmth gave her goosebumps. She ran her nails back and forth through his hair, scratching his scalp the way he liked. "So, what's on your mind, Quinn Garland?"

"Oh, just thinking about when I first got here for the wedding. Charles dragged me all over the city, then we ended up at your shop. I didn't know what to expect when he said we were dropping by. I wasn't in the mood for cake, that's for sure."

"But you liked it."

"I did." Quinn picked up her hand and kissed her fingertips. "These hands are magical."

"Thank you." Gerti busied herself by looking over the tattoos on his arm under the faint light from the kitchen. "What made you get these?" She'd seen a few on the older men in the county when they came into The Shop. Most were from their days in the military, but none of them had an arm full like Quinn.

"Bored one night," he answered. "Walked into a shop I'd driven past a few times and started talking to the owner." She traced one of the many inked-on gears and fuses, trying to ignore the feel of his muscles under her fingertip. "You like 'em?"

"I do. They represent you very well." Even though he'd glossed over them, each image on his arm represented something personal to him. Time, his job, the ranch —even a heart, camouflaged to look like the moon. "I think I like this one the best." She pointed to the components of a car engine. "There's so much detail. How long did it take?"

"A while, actually, since I was on call. I'd go when I was in town. When I knew I wouldn't be needed at work the next day." He went quiet when the first notes of the next song played. "Hop up." He patted her ass, and she stood to her feet, followed by him. "Dance with me." He took her hand and held it to his chest then pulled her close, swaying with her as the song played. "This is my favorite song." She let him lead as Otis sang of cigarettes and drinking coffee at three in the morning. It was the soundtrack to their early morning, and Gerti could see why he liked it. When the song ended, Quinn tilted Gerti's head to his and kissed her lips. "Gerti," he said sweetly, drawing her name out the way he did when he wanted something.

"Yes?"

"Can you make more coffee, please?" He punctuated his question by nuzzling his nose against her neck. "I can't handle another sip of whatever it is I made."

"Come on," she laughed, then turned to go into the kitchen, receiving another soft swat to her ass for her kindness. "You're so spoiled." Grabbing his hands, she pulled him with her. "Let me show you how to do it."

Quinn leaned against the counter watching Gerti, but he never saw her spoon three scoops of coffee grounds into the filter then pour the right amount of water in the machine before pressing the start button. The jiggle of her breasts as she moved around the kitchen and the way her nipples pressed hard against the fabric of his shirt interested him more.

"Did you get all of that?" Bringing his eyes up to her face, he licked his lips instead of telling her the truth. "You are unbelievable, Quinn Garland." She walked to him, intending to hit him on the arm, but when he grabbed her right hand and then her left, lifting them both and fitting her arms around his neck, she forgot the reason she was pretending to be mad and gave him a wide grin.

"You can't blame me for being distracted." He snaked his hands around her waist. Taking advantage of the shirt being raised, he went lower to fill his hands with her bare ass before kissing her forehead. Her smile fell, and she couldn't believe Shelbi Lynn's words popped in her head at that moment. The single forehead kiss Quinn gave her had her wondering if what she'd said was true. "What's that face for, Ole Fashion?"

Stepping out of his arms, Gerti looked to the floor, too embarrassed to look at him. "Um—the last time Shelbi Lynn came by at The Shop...she mentioned..."

"Mentioned what?" he asked, agitated, especially since her name was being brought up right now. There really was no telling what Shelbi Lynn would say if it meant she got what she wanted.

"That you have this thing where you give a kiss on the cheek and then one on the forehead." Quinn looked at her, waiting for her to get to the part that made her mood change so quickly. "She called it your signature." Gerti took a deep breath. "But you've never done that to me," she whispered.

"Kissed you on the cheek?" He leaned his head down, trying to see her eyes.

She shrugged, knowing how silly it sounded. "Yeah, I guess."

"Look, baby. I don't really care what Shelbi Lynn has to say." Quinn took a step towards her. "But if it makes you feel any better," he took another step, stopping when they were toe-to-toe, "I'll kiss you anywhere you want me to." No longer thinking about Shelbi Lynn, Gerti started to speak, but Quinn continued. "And before your smart mouth tells me to kiss your ass—I plan on it. With the biggest smile on my face. Then... I'll kiss all the surrounding areas until you beg me to stop." This time her hand landed on his chest, trying to push him away, but his strong body didn't move. He pulled her into him and kissed her on the lips.

When they parted, Quinn took so long to stare at her beautiful face that Gerti got worried. "What are you thinking about?" she asked.

"If I knew you'd say yes, I'd ask you to marry me right now, and we'd say "I do" right out there in the yard under the stars and the moon." Gerti didn't know what to say. She hadn't allowed herself to think about them beyond his time here. She had a business, and he had a dream job to get to. There was no point in wanting something that would never be.

"I'm gonna miss you, Quinn Garland."

"I'll miss you too," he said back genuinely. "But first —" Swooping down, he picked her up, flinging her over his shoulder, and carried her out of the kitchen and down the hall to his bedroom, kissing her ass the whole way there.

"What are you gonna do without me?" Gerti asked, facing Quinn in the bed. The sun had come up an hour ago, bringing with it rising temperatures and making the sheet they had earlier of no use to them, especially since it got tossed somewhere on the floor. Quinn outlined the shape of Gerti's body with his hand starting from her shoulder, down her arm then rested his palm on her hip.

"I'm sure I'll be miserable until I can learn to live without you." He squeezed her hip with a smile, downplaying the truth of his answer.

"Good. That's what you get for turning my world upside down."

"Why did you let me?" It'd been a question he wondered about since their first kiss.

She wasn't sure if she had let him, or if she even had control over it. "I think it's because you aren't staying." Taking a loc between his fingers, he brought it to her nipple and brushed it across her skin until it pebbled and hardened.

His tongue replaced the loc against her nipple. "So, you were just using me?"

"No," she whispered. "I can't focus when you do that." Quinn stopped when she moaned, much to Gerti's disappointment.

"Sorry, go on." The space between them was larger than he liked, so he pulled her closer, bringing her leg on top of his.

"One of the reasons I moved here was because people kept staring at me in my hometown." Everybody knew about her sister and the scar on her leg. After a while, Gerti got tired of everyone's pitiful looks. She had nowhere to run, and the boys kept trying to get under her skirt to take a peek. Like her mom, she went off to college far away from home. Once she graduated, she'd taken the first job that offered travel and gone from place to place all over the world until she tired of it.

"So, you get here?"

"I get here and find out my grandmother's property is available and I move out here, where no one remembers me or knows me."

"You could fade into the background?"

"Yes, but then..."

"The men started coming around."

"Yes." She swatted his arm for not letting her finish her sentences. "I was flattered, but not ready to open up to anyone in Bellbush."

"So why me?"

"Because you're leaving." At least, that's what she told herself and hoped he believed her. Maybe that was the reason she said yes when he said he wanted to kiss her, but it didn't really explain why he fit so easily in her life. "I've told you all my secrets, and now I don't have to watch the pity in your eyes when you realize how fucked up I am."

"We're all kinda fucked up." Quinn leaned down and kissed her softly on the lips. "Thank you for trusting me with your secrets." Another kiss. "How are we supposed to do this?"

"You mean when you leave?" Quinn nodded.

"Well, we can either try the cold turkey route, or we can ease into it. See each other a little less each day."

"I hate both of those."

"Well, we have to decide on something. You'll be leaving soon."

"I'll think on it later." He ran his hand along her leg and hip, stopping when her plump ass filled his hand. "After you put some clothes on. I can't think straight with you like this."

"Oh, yeah?" Gerti reached down and wrapped her hand around his thick length. "I like what you do when I'm like this."

Rolling her over on her back, Quinn widened her legs, fitting his body between them, then slowly slid inside of her wetness. "That's good to know."

Chapter EIGHTEEN

"So, you're really leaving us, Q?"

"Yeah, signed my contract the other day," Quinn said with a smile. "Time to get back on the road. Back to my house, my bed." Quinn had been thinking about what pulling into his driveway would be like. How he'd be walking into a quiet home surrounded by the sounds of the city.

"This is a big-time gig, huh?" Terrence asked, brushing down a black-and-white spotted saddle mare in the stables. The rest of the crew had already left, leaving Terrence to ask his questions by himself. "You're gonna be making good money, too?"

Quinn ignored the second question but answered the first. "Yeah, it's a big gig." The trainer position came with a level of clout Quinn didn't get as a mechanic. Even though they did the heavy lifting, they never got the accolades the suits got. "I'm ready for a change."

"You're gonna miss us, aren't you?" Quinn chuckled

instead of giving Terrence an answer. His silly crew of teenagers had grown into men over the few months he'd been with them, growing on him in the process despite his efforts to keep them at arm's length. Even with the many annoying questions they asked him daily, he still looked forward to seeing each of them every morning. He wondered how his days would go without seeing and working with them five days a week. "Aww, Q, you know you will. It's okay to admit it. You've seen us every day for months. What would you do without us?"

"I'd have a lot less stress and more money, that's for sure." Quinn rubbed his beard. "And less greys."

"I think you came to town with those grey hairs, don't blame us. And I said I'd pay you back." Quinn knew he shouldn't hold his breath waiting for Terrence to pay him back for all the condoms he'd begged for every Friday and Saturday when Angel came calling, or all the cigarettes he'd given to Freddy, who seemed to turn into a chain smoker when he wasn't paying for them. They were both always conveniently out, patting down their pockets to show they were empty. Quinn, finally tired of giving his things away, bought Freddy his own carton and gave Terrence a value pack of rubbers.

"You get that application in, and we'll call it even, alright?"

For the last month, Terrence had been wrestling with the decision to go to school. After graduating high school a year ago, he wasn't doing anything with his life he would be proud to tell anyone about. This summer spent talking to Quinn made Terrence realize there was more to life than the small country town he lived in, and Quinn made him believe he was smarter than he thought, even teaching him to help with payroll and equipment orders for Garland Landscaping. It seemed to build his confidence so much, he took and passed the college entrance exam. Now he could start applying to schools, but he was hesitant.

"We got a deal?" Quinn asked, seeing the indecision on his face.

"Yeah... I guess I can do that."

"Terrence..."

"Okay, I'll do it," he corrected with more enthusiasm. "Besides, when I went to take the test, there were a few fine ladies giving me the eye. I think I'll like college. Maybe I'll get a leather backpack and some glasses. Girls dig guys with glasses."

"Girls dig guys with their shit together, Terrence. Don't be up there acting up." Terrence knew he was being serious, so he filed Quinn's words away. Quinn might not have known it, but all the guys looked up to him and respected him as a father figure. There weren't many men Quinn's age around, so it was hard for them to take advice from old men with old-school mentalities. Quinn said things in a way that made it easy to understand and didn't patronize.

"So with you gone, that'll leave more peanut clusters for us, huh? I went there the other day, and Ms. G said you ate the last ones. You did that shit on purpose, didn't you?" Gerti hadn't stopped spoiling the crew with her candies. She'd started putting some away to the side for them, no longer bothering with what was leftover.

"She offered," Quinn said, tapping the heel of his boot on the toe of his other one to get some dirt and dust off of it. "Besides, I'm sure she gave you something else, anyway." Terrence smiled, making Quinn shake his head.

"She did. She let me taste-test some caramels she made. They were really good. I need to see if she has more. Angel's pretty much allergic to anything that has to do with a stove."

Quinn laughed. Terrence came running every time Angel called, but left feeling empty in more than one way afterwards. "Don't let me hear about you in The Shop every day bothering Gerti, you hear?"

"But she likes me, I wouldn't be a bother." Terrence gave him a nonchalant look. "Plus, I'll need the fuel for all the late-night studying I'll be doing."

"Go buy a coffee maker."

"Coffee?" Terrence looked up, picturing a big mug of steaming coffee. "She sells coffee too, right?"

"Terrence."

"I'm kidding. I won't go by The Shop every day. Can I at least go twice a week?"

After giving it a little thought, Quinn nodded his head. "That's fair."

Terrence quieted for a few moments while he finished up the horse, brushing her down to ensure her coat shined. "You excited about leaving?" Quinn didn't respond, so Terrence took his silence as a no. "Why not stay?"

"It's not that I'm not excited. I've gotten used to all of y'all." He knew it would be hard driving away, it already was. But he was also ready for this new chapter in his life. Terrence could see the happiness in his eyes and was happy for him, but he could also see a small glimmer of trepidation about walking away from a life he'd created. Even if only for the summer, it was still a life Quinn had grown to love.

"Did y'all plan for this?"

"Plan for what?" Quinn asked, having an inkling of what he was talking about. He had barely talked about this with Charles, his best friend, so he wasn't sure how deep he could get with Terrence.

"I mean, I ain't never heard of old people fooling around for the summer." Terrence sat down and crossed his arms over his chest, waiting for Quinn to answer.

"Old?"

"Yes. It ain't like y'all are... my age. You're pushing forty, right?" Terrence paused to allow Quinn to correct him, but he never did. "I mean, I've asked a few girls for something like that, but mostly because they were ugly and I didn't want anyone at school to find out about it."

"Terrence."

"What? I got a rep to uphold." He brushed some dust off of his jeans then looked at Quinn. "Anyway, for an older woman, Gerti's fine. Even my young ass can see that." Terrence pointed to Quinn and laughed, "You know what, maybe it is better if you leave." Ducking out of the way, he barely missed being hit by the water bottle Quinn threw at his head. Terrence let out another laugh that brought on a smile from Quinn. "You know I'm playing, Q."

"You better be." Quinn grabbed the horse by the reins and walked her away.

"You're done, right?"

"Yeah."

"Good, I got things to do."

"Didn't expect to see you here," Quincy said after walking into the kitchen to see Quinn sitting at the table. Seeing his nephew after the sun went down was rare these days. They might see each other in the mornings to talk about landscaping or run into each other at The Shop, but after sunset, Quinn was usually with Gerti, so it surprised him that he was at the ranch now.

Quincy set his hat on the counter then filled a glass with water from the tap, taking a big gulp before looking over at Quinn's solemn face. He turned a short tumbler in circles between his hands, seemingly content to watch the swish and wave of the bourbon as it went around the glass. "You alright, son?"

Nodding slowly, Quinn answered, "I guess I will be."

"You feel like talking about it?" Quincy wasn't sure how he'd answer. Quinn was more like him than he cared to admit sometimes. For both of them, it seemed easier to keep things to themselves than bare their souls to anyone. They hadn't had a man-to-man talk for a long time, and although Quinn hadn't lived at the ranch in many years, he still knew talking about his feelings wasn't something his nephew did often. When he did, it was because he'd run out of conversations to have with himself.

"I guess I'm worrying myself with starting this new job."

"You're ready for it, aren't you?"

"I am," Quinn answered with conviction.

"Then you'll be fine." Quinn smiled at Quincy's simple answer for something Quinn thought so complicated. It was just a job. The job he wanted. It wasn't like he'd be going off to war. Quincy came to sit with Quinn at the table, moving the bottle of bourbon out of his reach.

"Keep in mind the reason you want it."

"I know. I..."

Understanding what Quinn was having such a hard time saying, Quincy said, "Sounds like you have a decision to make."

"Decision's already made; I start my new job in two weeks." Quinn sighed, then took a sip of his drink. "I'm excited, Badge, I really am. I'm gonna miss things around here, is all. I didn't think it was gonna be like this. I was supposed to only come here for the wedding, hang out for a while, and then go back to where I came from." Leaving the first time had been no problem. He'd packed up and left. He hadn't felt like he had any ties to keep him at Honeybells. "Now, it's different."

"That's understandable, son. You've been here for quite a while; a lot longer than I thought you'd be." When Quinn called and told him he'd be down for the wedding, Quincy was excited to get to see him but didn't let it settle in too deep because he knew he'd be leaving soon after. "You've helped me out a great deal while you've been here. Don't know how I'm gonna wrangle those boys without you." Quincy looked at Quinn's face, so much like his mother's. "You met a new friend." Quincy smiled at the way Quinn looked at him when he called Gerti his friend.

"Yes, I did."

"Not that I don't like you being here, but shouldn't you be with her right about now, not here in this kitchen looking all sad?"

"We... She thought it would be best if we go through something like a... trial separation." Quinn took another sip of his drink, wincing at the burn and the twinge of anger welling up inside of him when he thought about the talk he'd had with Gerti before he'd left her place to start his day that morning. With him leaving soon, the cold turkey route won out since neither of them were into long goodbyes. He kissed her at the door after they talked. Quinn kept quiet as she rattled on about how they shouldn't see each other after that, saying how much easier it would be on both of them if they let that be the last time. Quinn agreed, but he didn't like it.

"What the hell does that mean?"

"It means it's over. I'm headed back up the highway soon, and she'll be here." Quinn knocked back the last of his drink then reached over to grab the bottle of bourbon from Quincy, pouring more into his glass.

"So you're gonna drink it away?" Seeing Quinn so downtrodden over a woman was new for Quincy. Even in his younger years, he'd always been so sure of himself. He'd left Texas and figured out how to live on his own. He didn't call one time asking for money or a ticket back home.

"I'm trying my damnedest," Quinn responded. He knew it wouldn't help, but right now, he'd rather feel the burn in his chest than the ache in his heart.

"If leaving is making you so miserable, then stay."

"It's not that simple, Badge." Quinn had wanted this job for a long time, and he was finally getting a chance to do it. "I've got a whole damn house back in Kansas. A life." He sighed, wishing the drink in his glass was stronger. "Plus, we agreed this was the way it was gonna be when we started this thing. No attachments."

"Then what's the problem?"

Quinn knew the problem with leaving this time was

it didn't feel like it did last time. He didn't have that antsy feeling, that pull to run. But he had responsibilities and commitments to uphold. "I guess...I've changed my mind."

Quincy got up and grabbed his own tumbler. He hated to see someone drinking alone, especially if they were miserable, and Quinn fit the bill to a tee tonight. "You know, I held you in my arms when you were two weeks old." Quinn looked over at Quincy, surprised because he'd never heard that before. "Your mother called me out of the blue and told me she'd had a baby boy. She left here two years before, and that was the first time she'd called. I rushed out to where she lived to see you. You were this little brown bundle wrapped in a white blanket. When she told me she'd named you after me, I almost fell over. All the names in the world, and she picked mine."

"I had some big shoes to fill. Once I realized what a great man you were, I got nervous I'd disappoint you."

"You filled them just fine. I remember I left that day thinking of all the things I wanted to teach you. I didn't know who your daddy was, but I doubted he knew anything about ranching with the way your mother left out of here." Quincy gave Quinn a sad smile. "I was prepared to step in and give you what he couldn't." WillaMae and Quincy were never blessed with children. They had a couple of pregnancies, but none of them stuck. So when she found out about Quinn, she was over the moon. "Your mother even brought you to the ranch once. You were maybe one, walking around the stables and pulling up the flowers. WillaMae had a fit." He laughed, then filled his glass again. "But then your mother disappeared and took you with her. We couldn't find y'all or anyone who knew y'all. It was a hard time for both of us." Quincy took a big gulp of his drink, thinking about the tears his wife shed when they couldn't find Quinn. "Then when we'd given up on seeing you again, there you were on the front porch."

"Looking sad and confused." Quinn laughed sadly. Things hadn't changed much.

"Yeah, you did. You cried for a week straight. Then Charles came around one day, and you two were inseparable. I'll always be grateful to him. Then Greg and Anthony were here too, eating all our food, keeping the house full of laughter. If it wasn't for them, you might have run away sooner."

"I wasn't running away, Badge. I just...I needed to find my place in the world. A place I decided on and not one I was dropped off into."

Quincy understood how important it was for a man to find his place and make his own way. He'd been there before, and was happy Quinn had figured it out and didn't let his past trap him in a place he couldn't get out of. He wanted him to hold on to his fears, and let them drive him, make him an even better man.

"Were you mad at me for leaving?"

"At first, because you up and left. No note, no goodbye. But once you called, I relaxed. I needed to know you were alright and not in a ditch somewhere." Quinn poured more bourbon into his glass then offered some to Quincy, but he refused. "Then you started calling every week." Quinn laughed because their standing Thursday night conversations were the one constant in his life, no matter where his job took him. "You go on to Kansas and be great at that job. I'll be fine. I'm real proud of you, Quinn."

"Thank you, Badge."

Chapter NINETEEN

Quinn knew he shouldn't be walking up onto her porch. Knew he wasn't supposed to be knocking on her door, but he didn't care. Last week, a storm came through and damaged parts of the county pretty badly. The heavy rains caused flooding, and the strong winds knocked down trees and power lines. Luckily, East Rock wasn't hit bad, but an old friend of Quincy's called Garland Landscaping to help with the damage on his two hundred and fifty-acre ranch, so for the last four days, Quinn and five other men had been on the cleanup crew. They worked from sunup to sundown, wearing themselves out until they were too tired to drive back home. Then they slept on cots in a hot muggy trailer, too drained to complain about how uncomfortable they were.

Even though he was exhausted and weary, Quinn still had to leave for Kansas tomorrow. But not without seeing

Gerti one last time. To hell with the agreement, he needed what only she could provide—one last time.

He opened the screen door then rapped his knuckles on the shiny fuchsia front door. He let the screen close then shoved his hands in his pockets while he waited for her to answer.

Gerti stood on the other side of the door and counted to ten before opening it. Her reaction to seeing Quinn through the peephole surprised her. She didn't realize how much she'd missed him until that very moment.

"Hey," Quinn said when the door opened. Joe stood at her feet wagging his butt. The huge rottweiler had missed him too. Quinn wore his favorite camo cap pulled low on his head even though the sun had gone down hours ago. His jeans were muddy, and the tee-shirt he had on was spotted with dirt, sawdust, and bits of leaves.

"You just get back?"

"Yeah, not too long ago. I went by the ranch and grabbed my things before heading over here. I know what we said, but I didn't want to leave without seeing you."

"Come on in." She pushed open the screen door for Quinn to walk in then closed the door behind him. "Is everything okay out there?" She hoped her voice didn't sound as shaky as she felt.

"It's getting there. The other guys will be out there a few more days." He took his hands out of his pockets, wanting to touch her. "Thanks for sending the food the other day. We really appreciated it." His hands went back in his pockets, not knowing what to do with them if he couldn't touch her.

"You're welcome." The tension between them was so

thick, even Joe could feel it. They weren't sure what to say but knew the silence sounded too loud. "How are you?"

"Tired, but I'm good," he answered. "Better now."

"Did you eat yet?" She could see how worn out he looked, and knowing him the way she did, he probably hadn't taken a break to eat the way he should.

"No." He took off his cap to stuff it in his back pocket. "I didn't come begging for food, Ole Fashion."

"I know," she smiled shyly, and his heart skipped a beat at the sight of her dimples. "Go hop in the shower, and I'll have a plate ready when you get out." Quinn hid his slight embarrassment at her nice way of saying he didn't smell well, but he followed her directions.

After getting his bag from his truck, he went into the bathroom and took a good look at himself in the mirror. It surprised him Gerti had let him in with the way he looked. Quinn rested his hands on the edge of the sink, feeling like he needed to talk himself out of being there, wrestling with what he needed. He needed a haircut, and his beard trimmed, and he could stand for at least twenty-four hours of uninterrupted sleep, but mostly, he needed her.

Under the spray of the shower, Quinn leaned forward with his hand on the white tile to hold himself up. He let the water cascade down the back of his neck, washing away the aches and dreariness that settled into his tired body three days ago.

He started paying attention to the droplets of water as they fell from his face, through his beard then down the drain. The hot water felt so good on his skin, he ignored the time, aware he was taking longer than usual. The shower made him feel lighter, but he knew once he turned it off, and he stepped out, the real clock would begin.

He found Joe waiting for him, lying across the floor when he stepped out of the bathroom. Quinn gave him a scratch, and they walked to the kitchen together. The only thing he found was his plate, no Gerti, so he sat down and ate. Joe lay at Quinn's feet as he listened to the sound of his own chewing against Gerti's rustling down the hall behind her closed bedroom door. He guessed she was probably fluffing the too many pillows she kept on her bed and brooding about Joe choosing him over her.

When he finished, he gulped down a glass of water then washed his plate before turning out the light and walking down the hall. He didn't bother knocking. He turned the knob before a protest could be uttered, closing the door softly after seeing her sitting by the window. The scents of cherry and jasmine filled the dimly lit room from the stick of incense in a holder on her dresser. The trail of thin grey smoke crept across the room, disappearing into the darkness of the corner.

"Before you say anything... I had to come. I couldn't leave without seeing you."

Truth be told, she wanted to see him too. He'd been away for the past four days, but she couldn't call him up in the middle of cutting down trees to tell him she needed to see his face. Wanted him to rub his beard between her hands or needed to look at his tattoos one more time. Not after she'd said they should have a clean break and not see each other anymore.

Getting up, she walked to where he stood at the side of her bed. He didn't speak. He reached out for her hand, pulling her into him. His other hand went to her locs as he leaned down to kiss her, letting her know how much he'd missed her. More than even he knew.

Waking up without her had been the lowest part of his days since they made their agreement. Her warmth so far away from him had kept him chilled to the bone despite the heat outside. The kiss intensified, and Gerti gripped the sides of his shirt, needing to hold on to something, feeling lightheaded with the way his lips felt against hers. The fabric twisted within her fists as she moved closer, moaning when his hand slid down her back, stopping to rest at her waist. The sound made him pull back to catch his breath and breathe her in.

Quinn filled his eyes with her kiss-swollen lips, committing them to memory because he knew there'd be a time when he might need it in the future. He leaned down for another kiss. Chaste this time, a whisper as he decided tonight, he was going slow. He'd do whatever he needed to keep tomorrow from showing itself too soon.

On his way down to sit on the bed, Gerti felt his lips on her forehead, her nose, her chin. His lips pressed to the hollow of her throat, then the soft, smooth space above her breasts. He could feel the pounding of her heart against his lips. Quinn touched his forehead to her stomach, and the coolness of the fabric from the navy wrap dress she wore felt good across his brow. Moving his head from side to side, he contemplated where he wanted to start. Gerti's nails scratched along the back of his head, and he exhaled, quivering at her touch. Finally, looking up at her, his eyes asked permission to undress her. She answered by deliberately pulling the long ties herself. Quinn's hands were opening her dress as soon as he could, separating the two halves to reveal the smooth brown skin he'd been yearning for since the last time they were together.

Her eyes closed when she felt his lips, his tongue, kissing her, licking her skin as he made his way down to the thin band of her black cotton panties. The arms of her dress were tugged down, then she felt the cool fabric slide past her calves as it pooled at her feet. Getting up, Quinn stood behind her to unclasp her bra, adding it to the pile with her dress. He moved her hair to one side, kissing her sweet-smelling neck while filling his hands with her ample breasts, her nipples hard against his palms.

Turning her around, his lips touched hers again softly, slowly. Using his strong body, he backed her up against the edge of the bed, laying her down to look at her, taking in all the parts of her he'd miss when he left. He looked at everything.

The shadows of the room changed with the moving of the clouds, revealing the bright moon in the sky that illuminated her body, casting a silver hue on her skin. Kneeling at her feet, he spread her legs, kissing her right knee then her left, licking his way up her thighs, stopping to nibble and suck on the fleshy parts of the inside of both, making sure she felt the scratch of his beard on her skin. She let out a quiet giggle, so he did it again to hear the sound one more time.

The scent of her arousal was getting stronger the closer he got to her center, still covered in her black panties. He pressed his fingers to the smooth fabric, feeling her clit already making its appearance, ready to be paid tribute. Flattening his tongue, Quinn slowly licked his way up to her waiting clit, sucking it through the fabric until Gerti's breathing turned ragged, and her legs shook. Dragging her panties down, he worked his way from the top down this time, kissing her shaved mound once, then again before making contact with that warm nerve-filled bundle he liked to tease so much. He kissed it with a closed mouth, then with parted lips, then last, as the French would, adding his tongue, sweeping it across her clit until her hips rose from the bed.

Moving down, he savored what flowed so freely from her, humming when the taste hit his tongue. Slowly, Quinn began the ultimate tease. He never pressed as hard as she wished he would. He kept his touch light, the pressure agonizing. He used his tongue to toy with her wet delicate skin, lapping, sucking, and savoring until she was trembling with desire.

Gerti's head rolled to the side, losing herself to the meticulous attention Quinn was giving her. She watched the long curves of the incense smoke as it floated through the air. Her hands clutched the quilt underneath her while Quinn's tongue penned a farewell letter, telling her all the things he couldn't verbalize. The tip of his tongue moved to write each word perfectly, punctuating the end of each sentence with his whole tongue for emphasis. He had a lot to say and left nothing out, even as she was rocked with a well-earned orgasm, her legs closing around his head to keep the immense sensation of pleasure in. He didn't stop; he kept writing. Using his shoulders to widen her thighs, he continued, making sure nothing was left unwritten on her silky wetness.

He moved his tongue faster, inserting his fingers so they could work in tandem to keep her rocketing as his letter came to a close. Finally finished, he signed his full name.

Still soaring, Gerti felt no need to come down. She knew what that meant, and she wanted this to last for as long as it could. She welcomed the dip of the bed under his weight when he climbed on top of her, his latex-covered length brushing against her thigh. Eyes still closed, she felt the heat of his hot tongue as it swept over her mouth, but he didn't linger there, finding her nipples more enticing at the moment. Quinn flicked, sucked, and nibbled, making sure he'd never forget the taste and texture of her dark skin or the soft moans that fell from her mouth when his tongue swirled around their hardness, such an exquisite contrast to the softness he slowly slid himself into.

Gerti focused on the way his arm flexed under her hand, knowing he was forcing himself to go slow, reveling in her tightness as much as she was concentrating on the way he stretched and filled her so deliciously. Aware of every single inch as he moved deeper inside her, pulling out when he reached his target, only to repeat it again.

Quinn kept his eyes on her face and knew she was grabbing the sheets with her left hand like she always did, trying to hold on to something, anything as he treated her to his slow torturous strokes. She felt too good, too snug around him, as if she was made for him. Curved to him, fitting around him like he was meant to be inside of her. She knew just when to tighten her walls around him to make him rapturous and when to let go so he could breathe again.

Bringing his body closer, Quinn reached over to grab her hand, threading his fingers between hers, gripping her hand as much as she gripped his, almost as if the desperation of the act they were sharing was the only thing keeping them alive. Quinn wanted her to hold him tighter, so he pressed his body even closer. She loved the feel of his weight on her. He went deeper. She whispered to him how good it felt, how close she was.

Despite his long slow strokes, she was close. He wanted to get her there, feel her tremble beneath him, squeeze her thighs tight around his waist, so he gave her a reason to, reaching deeper, higher, filling her up so much the only thing she could do was cling to him as she fell over the edge. And fall she did. Little by little, that tiny tingle started deep in her belly, radiating throughout her body, touching her toes at the same time as it touched her hair follicles before she exploded all around him.

Like all the other times before, Quinn's strokes continued as he fucked her through the orgasm coursing through her body. He didn't stop, even as the sound of her wetness filled the air, joining her moans and soft gasps in an erotic melody only the two of them could create.

Gerti was well aware of the power he had over her body. He was gravity, controlling her like the tides, making her rise and fall at his command, swelling and rising until she crashed again, bathing him in her ocean.

The sound of her moans made holding out no longer an option for Quinn. She was too slick, too tight, the pulsing of her walls around him too strong to ignore. Reaching his limit, he finally sped up his pace, unable to go any other speed but hard and fast. Raising her hips,

Quinn stroked a spot left untouched, unleashing another round of deep satisfying sighs from her mouth. Feeling his body on the verge of release, Quinn leaned down to kiss the lips he would miss so much. He brushed, pressed, and bit, all while moving in and out of the best place he'd ever known. Moving his bites and kisses to her neck, Quinn went deep one last time, muffling the sound of his release into her skin.

Overwhelmed and spent, they both found themselves unable to move, grasping at the last bit of pulsing their bodies were going through as their hearts beat at a steady rapid pace together. Gerti felt Quinn's lips again, kissing her neck, her jaw, her cheek, her chin. She felt the wetness on her face from the tears she couldn't hold back any longer and knew they were mixed with his. Quinn reluctantly withdrew, fitting himself behind her before pulling her close to him one last time. Then with a kiss to her hair, Quinn fell asleep, followed shortly after by Gerti, both too tired for anything else, especially tomorrow.

Chapter TWENTY

Quinn looked around his classroom as his students finished taking their tests. He couldn't believe it was already the middle of the term. As mixed as his emotions were when he started, he had grown to love the position with every passing day. Getting up to put on a tie was a lot different from his Garland Landscaping shirt, but he enjoyed picking one out every day, matching his tie to his dress shirt, and figuring out if they went with his cowboy boots. Today, he looked very professional in his dark green shirt with a yellow and grey plaid tie.

Teaching came easy to him. Badge insisted he was a natural leader, but Quinn knew it was his time over the summer keeping his crew wrangled. The guys taught him a lot about patience and laughing when things don't go as planned. He missed his hardheaded crew and thought of them often throughout the day. There were a few students in his classroom that reminded him of Terrence and Freddy. He had to keep from laughing when they asked for things like pencils or even folders to take papers home in.

After the last test was handed in, Quinn spent the next few hours reading over the answers and grading them while he ate his lunch. He never thought he'd be a man who'd input grades into a grade book, but here he sat, typing numbers in little boxes his students would see in a few days that would tell them if they passed onto the next term or needed to find a new line of work.

"Mr. Garland, you have a call on line two."

"Thank you, Annette."

"Quinn, why she always act like she don't like me?"

"She doesn't even know you, Charles." Quinn held in his laugh because Annette was like that with everyone. She came to work to do her job; she wasn't there to make friends.

"It's the way she says 'Please hold.' It's always with an attitude."

"I've told you to call me on my cell. I'll pick up if I'm not in class." Charles called quite a bit, and unless he was teaching, Quinn picked up, and they'd talk and catch up. Charles would fill him in on the things going on in Bellbush, but he'd always leave one person out, and Quinn was grateful for that.

"You're always in class, Mr. Teacher. Plus, I kinda like fucking with her. I want to know which call will have her going off on me."

"Please don't annoy my assistant. She's nice."

"But does she look nice, is the real question? You're living out a lot of men's fantasies, I'd hate to think she's ugly."

"Don't you have a whole wife to fulfill all your fantasies?"

"Yeah, I do." Quinn could tell Charles had started thinking about Jordyn. Probably had one of those goofy smiles he always got when she crossed his mind. "Anyway, when you coming back down here? It's not the same without you."

"I know, man, but I don't know when I'll be back, Charles. This job is kinda kicking my ass... in a good way." There were already meetings scheduled for after the term ended. Quinn had even talked to the department chair the other day about attending the annual conference.

"You wear a suit and tie every day and teach in an air-conditioned classroom. What's so hard about that?" The cool building he got to walk into every day was a bonus, but sometimes he missed the sporadic cool Texas breeze. The kind that dropped your temperature a few degrees with the sweat on your body but was never quite long enough.

"I'm not saying it's hard. It's just a lot of work, making sure these kids know what they're doing. I'm grading papers and shit now. It's definitely not the same as slinging a hammer every day."

"I bet it isn't," Charles laughed. "Are your arms all flabby now?"

"Not even close. I joined a damn gym. I get up at four thirty every morning to go lift weights."

"A gym? Damn, Quinn, you really are big-time now. Paying for a gym membership and shit. Next thing you know, you'll have one of those coffee shop punch cards."

Quinn remembered the first week on the job, Annette brought him one of those fancy coffees in a Styrofoam cup with a cardboard ring around it. He tried to drink it, but he wasn't into the flavor or the extra shot of whatever they put in it.

"No, believe it or not, I make my own coffee now."

"I'm impressed." Quinn gave a quiet grunt and tried not to think of the person who taught him how.

"How's my car?"

"Good. I saw Quincy driving it around last week."

"Damn it, I told him to stay away from her." Quinn took a bite of his lunch, strips of grilled chicken, steamed green beans, and rice. "He's gonna blow the transmission. His foot is too heavy."

"It really is, because all I saw was a grey blur blowing by." Charles heard Quinn curse under his breath. That car needed work, and with the way Quincy drove, it would need more. "You still eat those healthy meal things for lunch?"

"Yeah," Quinn answered. "Can't eat junk every day like you." Even though Quinn joked, Charles still looked down at his burger and fries lunch and kind of agreed.

When he got back to Kansas, he had a week before his job started. As much as he'd missed his house when he first got to Bellbush, he felt restless and cramped after a few hours at home. It was too loud, and the noises were different. He'd forgotten what the sound of the city was like. Quinn had turned on some music and cleaned his house from top to bottom, deciding lemon-fresh was better than stale dust. He even went out and bought two extra pillows for his bed, and a new rug for his living room. When he needed something else to do, he made his way to the grocery store, buying enough food to meal prep lunches for a week. He steamed everything.

"They're good," Quinn added. "Enough to keep me full until I get home."

Quinn opened his desk drawer to look at the five packs of candy he had stashed away. It'd been fifty-six days since his last cigarette. The candy helped with the cravings, giving his mouth something to do. He kept it everywhere, in his truck, his classroom, and at home. The three candy dishes in his living room made him laugh because he never knew anyone with a candy dish except Ms. Edith. "The cravings aren't so bad anymore," Quinn said to Charles. He'd stopped smoking to give himself something else to focus on besides who he'd left back in Bellbush.

"I'm proud of you, man. Maybe I'll try quitting one day, too. Not today, but one day."

"Yeah, come join me on team no smoke break. How's Jordyn?"

"Same as always. Ms. Edith keeps talking about dreaming of fish, and it's giving her baby fever. She went out and bought one of those tests, wants to do it tonight, thinks she might be pregnant."

Quinn beamed with excitement. "Wow, a baby Charles?"

"Yeah, can you imagine, me, somebody's daddy?"

"Are y'all ready for all that?" Quinn hadn't been around a lot of babies, but the kids he'd seen running around Honeybells during the Juneteenth celebration had made him tired just watching them with their non-stop talking, laughing and playing.

"According to her mama, no one is ever ready, so I guess we are. You ready to be an uncle?"

"Hell no," Quinn answered quickly. "But I guess it's

not up to me." He looked at his watch and saw his lunch hour was winding down. "Look, man, I gotta go, second class is about to start."

"Alright. I gotta go too." Quinn could hear the rustling of papers in the background and Charles walking around. The first time they talked after Quinn came back home was hard for him. Having to hear about what went on in Bellbush and not being there took a while to get used to. He would hang up feeling worse than when he picked up the phone. Now, after all the days of being away, it was easy. He could hang up with a smile. "Talk to you later, man."

For the next few weeks, Quinn kept so busy his days ran into his nights sometimes. He tried to keep a very strict schedule that didn't leave much room for idleness or allow him to sit around and think about how much he missed her. He'd get up, get dressed, head to the gym to work out, shower, go to work, teach, then go home, shower, watch TV, and get into bed hoping to fall asleep quickly so he could do it all over again.

He threw himself into his work, and it showed when both classes passed their first two exams. That brought praise his way from his colleagues, and even an after-work drink or two. He loved his job and teaching what he knew to other people.

Quincy could hear it in Quinn's voice when they'd talk every week. Quinn couldn't wait to catch him up on what he'd been doing for the week, and he loved to hear about what was going on in Bellbush.

Most days you could catch him smiling, but there were a few days, every once in a while, where thoughts of Gerti had him playing his favorite song on repeat, and drinking Old Fashioneds until he couldn't see straight. Little things would make him think of her. A sunflower on a painting in the hallway, the smell of vanilla late at night when he drove past the coffee shop. Even the sight of his beard in the morning with its sprinkling of grey hairs made him think of being between her legs.

He lost track of how many times he wanted to call her up to tell her how much he loved his new job. Tell her he had enough ties hanging in his closet to give three to every customer who came through her shop on bacon cinnamon roll day. He wanted to tell her that his assistant Annette stayed on one of those no-sugar diets and didn't understand why he always carried around candy. How she even tried to get him to eat sugar-free mints once. They were still in his desk. He wanted to call and say he missed her.

One particular night, he had to talk himself out of calling her. He remembered the day she put her number in his phone. How her hand felt when she placed it on his chest to give it back to him. It would be so easy to send a short message saying hi. His phone was in his hand getting ready to, but where would that lead? He didn't know if he could handle her ignoring him or even her replying, so he put the phone down and had another drink.

When he climbed into bed, he wished for a sleepless night. One where he tossed and turned, because that was better than dreaming about her. If he was lucky, he'd get a few hours of sleep that would leave him feeling tired in the morning, but without the heartache of seeing her in his dreams, and waking up with her not there. But he wasn't lucky. He hadn't been lucky in days. Not since seeing a basket of cherries at the store.

He dreamt she sauntered towards him wearing a floral apron and a wide grin, her dimples set deep in her cheeks as her locs swayed behind her with each step. Even in his dreams, she felt warm and soft.

The moans he'd memorized the last time they were together were always the soundtrack to his dreams, the erotic explicitness as vivid as if they were really happening, her face in the throes of passion, eyes closed, biting her lip while she gripped his back, tightening around him. It was his favorite part of the dream, but also the worst because they would always cut away to him lying next to her, reaching for her to pull her close, only for her to disappear, leaving him empty-handed, waking up hard in a cold sweat.

A few days before the end of the term of the training class, Quinn was going over the files of his students to determine which ones would move on to the next part of the training course with a new instructor. He was told only the students that met the GPA requirement would get to move on. He smiled as he counted eighteen files that would be moving on out of the twenty he had in his hand.

"Mr. Garland, you have a call on line one."

"Thank you, Annette, send it through."

"Yo, Q, what's up? Charles told me to call this number instead of your cell. Hope you don't mind." Quinn held in his laughter at the fact Charles still tried to annoy Annette even when he wasn't the one calling. "Guess who got offered an academic scholarship?" Terrence's smile could be heard in his voice. "They like ya boy."

"That's alright. Congratulations, Terrence." When Quinn first heard his voice, he'd intended to fuss at him for calling about something trivial like he'd done before, but this news was a pleasant surprise. "You worked hard for it, Terrence. I'm proud of you."

"Thanks, Q. My mama's gonna flip."

"You haven't told her yet?"

"I wanted to tell you first. You believed in me when no one else did." Terrence exhaled through his nose, which could be heard through the phone. He could hear his voice shaking and wanted to rein in his emotions before they got out of hand. "I'm grateful for that, Q."

"You're welcome, Terrence, but you did all the work." Quinn rubbed his forehead with his finger, trying to hold back his tears. "Call your mama and tell her."

"Alright. I'll talk to you later, Q."

"Yeah." Quinn hung up the phone with mixed emotions. Hearing Terrence's news made him proud, excited. He never could have imagined the inquisitive kid that used to call shotgun every day and ask him question after question until Quinn was out of answers would be the Terrence of today, excelling in school and planning for his future.

The fact he'd called him first before anyone else brought a smile to his face. He wished he had the same luxury. Wished he could pick up the phone and tell Gerti all his news. Decompress his day with her late at night. Listen as she told him everything she did at The Shop.

She was always the first person he thought of telling when anything good happened to him. And the realization that he didn't have her to share those things with was getting harder to come to grips with.

The end of the term meant Quinn got to go home a little earlier than usual. With less to do around the office and in his classroom, he told Annette to head home for the day, and he did the same. It was a rare occasion he got to leave with the sun still out, but today he was treated to a spectacular sunset. The colors reminded him of Gerti and sitting on her back porch, talking while the lightning bugs began making their appearance.

Like so many other times before, he picked up his phone to call her, but then set it down after thinking it through. Ten minutes later, as Quinn pulled into his driveway, his phone rang. He picked it up and laughed at Charles's name across the screen.

"Annette might be mad she wasn't able to tell you to please hold." Quinn laughed, but then quieted when he didn't hear Charles laughing with him. "What's up, Charles? You alright, man?"

"Quinn..." The shakiness in his voice made his heart pound. It was bad news, and every scenario ran through his mind of what it might be.

"Just... just tell me."

"Quincy died."

Chapter TWENTY-ONE

ead. That one word shook Quinn to his core. He could feel as each of his limbs went numb. It started with his fingertips while he gripped the steering wheel, needing to hold on to something. His knees were next, followed by his toes and calves. He would have sat in his truck all night, listening to it idle, the vibration a soothing distraction to the outside world. Quinn would have been satisfied to sit in his truck forever if the throbbing in his head hadn't become so persistent or the rolling in his stomach so overwhelming.

He staggered into his house, in search of answers or anything to make the news of Quincy's death make sense. He made it as far as his couch, collapsing facedown with a soundless cry. For hours, he laid in the dark thinking about what a world without Quincy would be like. He thought over their times together, the phone calls they'd shared, and the last time they hugged right before Quinn left for Kansas. He'd never thought of him in terms of age. He'd been all he had for so long, and Quinn wasn't sure what he would do without him.

It took a week to get everything in order. Annette proved to be the consummate professional, helping him fill out paperwork and even giving him a small bag of candy full of sugar, the way he liked. During the day, he was on the phone with the funeral home, making arrangements, then at night, he'd talk to Charles, who'd call to check on him, making sure Quinn was holding up alright.

Finally, when he couldn't do any more from home, he got in his truck and drove the eight hours to Texas by himself. This drive was unlike any other he'd made before. He knew the route, just not where he was headed.

With his phone off, he switched between music and talk radio, never truly listening to any of it. When the voices got too obnoxious, he turned it off completely, opting for silence and the sound of the tires as they rolled along the asphalt.

When he drove onto Honeybells, the first thing he saw was the new landscaping truck Quincy bought last month parked over by the barn. Next to it sat Quincy's old Dodge he painted white a few years ago to give it an update from the ugly gold it had been most of Quinn's life. Driving closer to the house, he saw a car parked in the drive near the house, then Ms. Edith sitting on the porch. He didn't feel like talking, but he would never deny her anything, so he took a deep breath and got out to find out what she wanted.

"Ms. Edith," Quinn said sadly with a single nod of his head. She came up to stand in front of him, looking over his weary face. She opened her arms wide to embrace him. Only just realizing how much he needed it, he stepped into her arms, leaning down to accommodate her height, and received her tight hug with gratitude.

"Oh, Quinn, I'm so sorry."

"Thank you."

Looking past her, he spotted a large cooler on the porch where she was sitting. "I brought you some food. I didn't think you'd feel like cooking after such a long drive, but you've got to eat something. Come on." With a hand on his back, she walked with him to the door. Quinn grabbed the cooler on their way into the house.

He looked around at the walls, trying not to become overwhelmed by the unfamiliar space, new to him now that Quincy was no longer there. He noticed how loud his boots sounded on the wooden floor, how much larger the rooms seemed to feel. Having lived here since he was a boy, nothing had prepared him for this.

Quinn sat while Ms. Edith fixed him a plate. She moved around the kitchen with a familiarity that showed she'd been there many times. She and Quincy were close friends and became even closer after WillaMae died. She had done what she was doing now, making sure he ate and giving him someone to lean on.

She handed him a beer from the refrigerator, then grabbed some water for herself. "Your uncle always kept beer in the house," Ms. Edith said, shaking her head. "I tried to get him to drink something else with his supper, but only beer would do." Quinn twisted off the cap and took a big swig, hoping to keep the tears from falling. "I told him he needed to grow hops, but he laughed at that idea."

Swallowing hard, Quinn cleared his throat. "He talked about y'all's dinners a lot."

"We tried to do them weekly. I never liked him out on this ranch all by himself night after night. Especially after you left."

"He had his poker nights."

"Yeah, he did. But every other night, it was him out here alone. I started coming by, bringing him food, and we'd talk to the wee hours of the night, and then I'd head on home." She sat a plate in front of him and then sat in front of her own plate. Bowing her head, she waited a few moments for Quinn to do the same, then she blessed the food.

For a long time, the only sounds were the scraping of their forks and the soft thud of Quinn's beer bottle on the table. It felt odd for Quinn to be eating while hurting so much. He didn't know what kept him from folding into a ball on the floor, but he suspected it was the food. Ms. Edith knew he needed to do something else besides stew in his grief.

When was the last time you saw him?" Quinn pushed his plate away, grateful for the food, but full after eating only half of it.

"About two weeks ago," she answered. "I made us a pot of oxtails, and he told me some story about you and Charles running from some goats when y'all were little boys." That made Quinn smile. He instantly went to that afternoon on Mr. Derricks' farm. They thought they were helping by feeding the goats, but the goats didn't think they were working fast enough and started chasing after them, trying to get to the feed sacks around their necks.

"We'd never run that fast in all our lives." Quinn

laughed, thinking about how they had to jump on top of an old rusted out car Mr. Derricks kept in his yard. "We didn't have enough sense to throw the food down and let them have at it."

"Quincy said he laughed for a whole week over y'all. Even considered getting goats of his own. Lucky for you and Charles, your Aunt WillaMae put her foot down and said no."

"She was always the smarter one."

Quinn remembered Badge laughing at him and Charles. He didn't even try to hide it. He was loud and in their faces, laughing until his eyes watered. Then he started telling goat jokes. They were the worst, and he and Mr. Derricks were the only ones who thought they were funny. He couldn't wait to go back to school, to get away from those God-awful jokes. Quinn went quiet, twisting the half-empty beer bottle between his hands, thinking to himself.

"We talked about you a lot," Ms. Edith told him.

"He said he was proud of me," Quinn whispered. "But I still feel like I disappointed him."

"No, child." Ms. Edith reached over and touched his hand. "He was very proud of you. He always spoke with a smile when he mentioned your name."

"But I left him." Quinn stood up and walked around the kitchen, opening and closing drawers. He wasn't looking for anything, but the added sound cut some of the silence in the house. He hoped Ms. Edith didn't see his tears falling. "The first chance I got, I left him. After all he'd done for me. I left. Just like my mom."

"That's not the same thing at all. You left because you needed to find out something about yourself. You didn't abandon a scared little boy." Ms. Edith watched him open another drawer, then close it slowly. "He didn't care about you leaving. He sort of expected it. He was happy you were finding your own way. He might have been disappointed you didn't talk it over with him first, but he understood."

Quinn felt guilty he never got a chance to thank Quincy for all he'd done for him. He didn't have to take him in, but he did, and he'd always be grateful. Tired of messing with the drawers, he leaned on the counter and took a sip of his beer, turning up his lips at its warmth. He thought back to when his mother left him at Honeybells, how he didn't understand why she'd leave him with a stranger. "It took me a lot of years to figure out she made the right decision by leaving me here with him and aunt WillaMae. They gave me the family she couldn't. The love that..." He didn't finish, but Ms. Edith knew.

"He let me know every time y'all talked. 'I talked to Quinn yesterday', he'd say. He really admired how you stepped out on your own and made something out of yourself. You didn't allow the way you came to him to determine your path in life. You got to do what he never did." Ms. Edith cleared the table, taking their dishes to the sink.

"What's that?" Quinn asked as the water ran.

"Travel. You've been all over this country with that job of yours, seeing things he never got to." Quinn thought back to the conversations he had with his uncle. Quincy always seemed so interested in where he'd been and where he'd be next. He had a china cabinet full of souvenirs Quinn sent him from different places all over the country. "Yeah, he was real proud of you. The only thing he talked about more than you and your job was wishing you'd settle down and have a family one day."

Quinn looked at her with a confused grin on his face. "He did? He said nothing to me about it."

"Didn't want to scare you, I'm guessing. Can't have you rushing into something you weren't ready for, just to please him." Ms. Edith studied his face as he stared at the tiles on the floor.

"It is kind of scary. I don't even know who my father is, and my mother left me on the porch," he pointed to the front of the house, "with a goodbye and a be good." He'd become a great mechanic by watching Badge as he worked on this truck. Trial and error played a big part, but watching helped him the most. How does a man learn to be a great father when he doesn't have one? "What if I'm not cut out for it?"

"You've been thinking about this a lot, haven't you?"

Quinn nodded. "Not much to do when you're sitting at home by yourself." He really didn't want to have this conversation, so he changed the subject. "Where are the dogs?"

"I left them at The Shop." Shit, Quinn said to himself. He'd tried to avoid talking about anything having to do with Gerti. "When they all get together, it's complete chaos." Ms. Edith laughed then pushed off the counter to go sit back at the table. "Actually, I left them with Cora. Gerti wasn't there when I went by. She almost had a fit trying to wrangle all those dogs."

"Where did Gerti go?" Quinn asked with concern before he could stop himself. He'd never known her to go anywhere but The Shop during business hours.

Waving him off, Ms. Edith answered, "Who knows? She's taken a few days off this past month."

"Has she been... alright?"

"As far as I know." She stared at him for a while, studying his face, noticing the pained way his eyes darted across the room, not focusing on anything in particular. "Do the phones not work in Kansas?" He met her snark with silence. "That's what I thought. You know, for two grown ass adults, y'all sure are acting immature. Call her."

"We agreed we wouldn't." Quinn closed his eyes, thinking about how foolish their plan sounded when he said it out loud. "When we started this... thing. It was supposed to be for the summer, while I was here." Quinn looked up at Ms. Edith, who waited for him to continue. "It's what we agreed on."

"But?" Ms. Edith urged him to continue. Quinn shrugged, afraid to confess aloud what his heart had been trying to tell him for a while. She filled in the blanks for him. "Like the song says, you fucked around and fell in love."

Surprised by her language, he let out a loud laugh. "I don't think that's how it goes, Ms. Edith."

"Close enough," she shrugged. "So, are you gonna call her or not?"

"I don't know. I thought the distance would be enough." Rubbing his forehead with his fingers, he blew out a breath. "But it wasn't. At least not for me." Looking into her face again, he asked, "How do I know she hasn't moved on?"

He walked to the sink to dump out his beer then went to the fridge for another one. He drank half of it down as Ms. Edith watched him. She wanted to tell him Gerti was in the same place as him, except she knew how to hide it better. She masked her sadness in shadowed happiness. She'd smile and laugh, but deep down, her broken heart kept her from enjoying it.

"There's only one way to find out." With that, she got up, patted his arm and left.

Alone, Quinn went through the house, turning on all the lights and walking through each room, looking at them as if he'd never seen them before. As a boy, when he first came to the ranch, all these rooms seemed unnecessary. He and his mom had lived in a small apartment and shared a bed.

He cried for weeks every night after getting to Honeybells, not because his mother left him, but because he was in a room by himself for the first time. Sleeping in a bed too big with too much space to be comfortable kept him up at night. The shadows were unfamiliar, and the sounds from outside were too quiet to keep his eyes closed long enough for him to fall asleep.

It took years and the help of his friends for him to overcome the change. The rooms were repurposed and became the perfect place for a game of Hide and Seek. He discovered the shadows weren't as scary during a sleepover.

Quinn hesitated at the door of Quincy's bedroom, letting his hand hover over the knob before touching it. Anytime he'd ever been through this door, Quincy was always in there. This was where he'd taught him how to tie a tie and shine his shoes. He'd told him stories about his mother growing up, and how although he never expected to have his sister's child dropped off at his doorstep, he'd been glad it happened.

Walking around the room now, Quinn chuckled at the huge bed made the way Aunt WillaMae liked. The dresser was impeccable, only holding an antique jewelry box, an old bible, and a few colognes Quincy liked to wear. They were all sitting on top of a long, yellowed doily that probably used to be pristine white when it was first made after his aunt and uncle's wedding.

Yawning, he suddenly felt the eight-hour drive, and the couple of beers he'd had, but he had a lot to do before tomorrow. Being the next of kin out of state, everything had been done over the phone. Now he had to meet with the funeral home tomorrow, and he needed to find a suit for Quincy to be buried in.

He opened the door to the closet, pulling the long chain to turn on the light, squinting at the brightness. He didn't have much to look through; most of his clothes were folded in the dresser, but he did always keep three suits on hand at all times. A dark navy one, a grey one, and a heavy black one for the colder months. Pulling out the grey suit, Quinn picked a white shirt and matching tie to go with it. He looked down at the shiny dress shoes lined up on the floor but left them there, figuring his ranch-owning uncle would rather be buried in his cowboy boots.

Down the hall in his room, Quinn toed off his boots and unpacked his bag. He turned on his phone to check for messages. He'd turned it off before he left Kansas, wanting to be alone with his thoughts instead of hearing people's condolences. He'd hear enough of them at the funeral in two days. Looking through all of them, he replied to the most important; Charles to tell him he'd made it, and Terrence, who'd sent a text to see if he could do anything for him.

Not able to stand the day much longer, Quinn showered and got ready for bed. He did one last walkthrough of the house, turning off the lights as he went. When he got back to his room, he looked at his phone and contemplated calling her. He wanted to hear her voice instead of the quiet of the ranch, but it was late, and he had a lot to do in the morning. So, he turned off the final light and let himself be surrounded by darkness.

Chapter TWENTY-TWO

The morning of the funeral started with grey skies and drizzle. Quinn rolled over in the bed, slinging his arm over his eyes. The extra darkness would help to get his mind right for today. Or as close to right as it could get to say his final goodbyes and watch his uncle be lowered into the ground. Hoping a few more minutes in bed would help clear his mind, he groaned as his phone vibrated from across the room. He'd left it on the dresser before he went to bed, forgetting to turn it back off. For ten minutes, he listened to the phone and a rooster crowing off in the distance.

Unable to take the noise any longer, he kicked off his covers and put his feet on the wool rug, taking time to notice how it felt under the soles of each foot. The greens, oranges, and browns wove together to make such an intricate pattern, it kept his attention for longer than it should have. This rug had been under his bed since he was fifteen years old. Quinn never truly appreciated the beauty of it until today, but his damn phone wouldn't give him any peace. Pushing off the bed, he snatched the phone off the dresser, unlocking it as the doorbell rang. Cursing to himself, he looked to the heavens for strength then stomped to the front door.

"What!"

Gerti stood at the door, wide-eyed in shock. She hadn't been expecting an angry Quinn so early in the morning. Seeing the door yanked open so suddenly made her think it might have been a bad idea for her to come. "I'm sorry," she stammered out. "I didn't mean to..."

"Shit, Gerti, I'm sorry. Come in." The dreary morning also brought a cooler temperature that he felt when he opened the door for her to pass through. A small chill ran down his spine when she brushed past him.

Gerti tried not to stare, but Quinn only wore a pair of blue shorts. She looked down at her white dress, feeling overdressed and bad for getting him out of bed. "I didn't mean to wake you up."

Quinn didn't know who he'd been expecting or who might have deserved such a hostile reaction from him, but it surely wasn't Gerti. He closed the door softly, wishing he could rewind and greet her properly. Taking a cleansing breath, he looked at her from head to toe, noticing she'd dressed for the funeral. He started over.

"Good morning."

"Good morning," she replied softly. She brought a hand to her belly to feel the breath she held release slowly as she exhaled. "How are you?"

"Been better," Quinn answered truthfully.

"I didn't mean to barge in like this." She pointed to

his phone. "I had Cora call, but she didn't get an answer, so I decided to come by." He nodded, suddenly feeling bad about ignoring his early morning calls. "I'm sorry about Quincy."

"Thank you." He looked her over again, wishing he had the energy to smile at how even though she was dressed in Quincy's requested white attire, she still looked as beautiful as she did the night of Ms. Edith's party. "I need to get dressed. I have to be at the church in a little while."

"Okay." She took a step back, keeping her head down. Gerti didn't know what made her drive over to Honeybells, but the sudden urge to make sure Quinn was alright had settled into the deepest parts of her and wouldn't let her rest until she saw him. "I'll see you...at the church." Moving towards the door, feeling dejected and silly for coming over, she shook her head, determined not to cry, which seemed impossible these days.

"No," he said, stopping her. "Please stay." Quinn's shaky voice made her pause her steps. "You're the only person I want here." Taking her hand in his, he bent his knees to mirror her height. "Stay."

"Okay."

He led her by the hand to his bedroom, sitting her on the bed before kissing her on the forehead. "Thank you."

Having her there made him feel more relaxed than he'd been all week. Since receiving the call, he'd been on edge, not knowing up from down, but with Gerti near, he could tell the sky from the ground. She had a calming presence about her Quinn had always admired. Even when she tried so desperately to deny her feelings for him, she still gave him a serene peace no one ever had.

After showering, he peeked in on Gerti to make sure she was where he left her. He found her still sitting on his bed that she'd made while she waited. She'd been reading the bible he kept in his nightstand but placed it next to his pillow when she noticed him standing there. He could smell the coffee from the kitchen, and his first genuine smile in a week brightened his face.

When he was ready to get dressed, changing in front of Gerti stood at the forefront of his mind. He wasn't sure if he should stay in the room or go into the bathroom. They'd seen each other naked enough times he could describe every inch of her from memory, but their time apart had shifted the dynamic between them. Couples changed in front of each other, but what were they? What had they been?

"I'll go check on the coffee." Gerti kept her eyes on the floor and not the towel wrapped around Quinn's waist. She walked out of his room and down the hall, praying her legs wouldn't give out on her.

He sat down on the bed, rubbing his hands up and down his thighs, reminding himself to breathe and focus on the moment, not the funeral happening in a few hours. Looking to his left, he picked up the bible Gerti was reading, left open to the last page she'd been on. Skimming through Matthew, he stopped and read, Blessed are they that mourn: for they shall be comforted. He hoped that rang true today.

Quinn took his time getting dressed, counting every button as he slipped them through the holes. He made sure the crease in his pants laid right, and the buckle on his belt lined up the way it was supposed to. He'd finished shining his boots to perfection when he heard cabinets being opened and closed in the kitchen. Taking one last look in the mirror, he decided coffee would be next.

Leaning on the wall, he found Gerti spooning sugar into her mug. She stirred it in slowly, watching the whirl of the dark liquid as it went around. Quinn cleared his throat to let her know he was there before walking closer to stand next to her. She handed him his coffee, and they drank in silence while Quinn decided on what he wanted to say first.

"Do you mind... if I lean on you a little today?"

Gerti placed a comforting hand in his as a response. It felt warm and soothing and full of her promise to be there for him through one of the hardest days of his life. He kept her near, not letting her go more than an arm's length away from him the entire day.

He drove them to the church in his truck, holding her hand throughout their silent ride. She sat close beside him in the pew, thigh to thigh even though there was plenty of room for them to spread out. He held her hand and busied himself with the way the color of her nails contrasted against his skin, trying not to look around the room at all the somber faces staring at him. The women were dressed in white, and the men wore their starched Honeybells shirts and white cowboy hats. They looked good even through their sadness. Quinn thought his uncle would be proud.

They buried Quincy in the family plot on the south side of the ranch next to his late wife WillaMae, his parents, and a handful of other family members. Surrounded by friends, most close enough to him to be called family, he was silently lowered into the ground as tears fell amongst the mourners.

The house buzzed with people as Quincy tried to make his way through it, being stopped countless times for someone to say, "Did I ever tell you about the time—" before they'd launch into a story about Quincy anywhere from forty years to a month ago. Not that the stories were uninteresting or boring, he just didn't have the energy to listen the way they wanted him to. Quinn stood behind Gerti, nodding and giving a smile when he thought it necessary so he wouldn't offend anyone. The stories went on for what seemed like hours. Every time someone would finish, Quinn and Gerti would walk away, only to be stopped by the next person.

"I'm really sorry about Quincy. He's gonna be missed around here."

"Thank you, Shelbi Lynn," Quinn said, still standing behind Gerti. He was surprised she came and spoke to him after the way their last conversation ended. He'd noticed her at the church, but she'd kept her distance, only smiling at a few people and avoiding eye contact with Gerti. "I know the pain of not having someone you... love in your life anymore. It hurts, but it gets better when you have someone special to help bear the pain." She looked at Gerti and took her hand. "Take good care of him." With that, she turned and walked out the door.

Wrapping his arm around Gerti's waist, Quinn used his thumb to rub circles on her belly. The feel of the fabric of her dress relaxed him, her warmth a balm, a solace. So, while Mr. Vern told his story of when Quincy got up one winter morning to find out one of his outbuildings had collapsed, then spent the rest of the day and night rebuilding it in only a tee-shirt and jeans, Quincy heard nothing, too interested in the way Gerti felt against him, fit against him. He tried to decide if she felt the same or if their time apart made her feel better. Ignoring Mr. Vern's story, Quinn softly brushed his lips against Gerti's neck, whispering his thanks in her ear. She closed her eyes and squeezed his hand, accepting his praise.

Chapter TWENTY-THREE

Two hours later, Quinn stood by himself in front of Charles, shooting the shit about nothing of consequence. Charles knew he needed to talk about anything but Quincy. Treading lightly, he started with work, then moved on to the weather, and the crops some ranchers said they would lose with the soil so dry. Ms. Edith had pulled Gerti away from him an hour ago, insisting she eat and sit for a bit. She told Quinn the same thing, but he declined, feeling bad for monopolizing Gerti the way he'd done.

Quinn saw her from across the room, giving a small smile to someone as she walked past them, and he decided then that he'd had enough of being away from her. He crossed the room in a few long strides, rushing Gerti off to his room to get away from everything. Closing the door, Quinn was thankful the lock would keep everyone out.

He walked Gerti to the bed and sat down so he could look up at her, feasting his eyes on her face for what seemed like the first time that day. "I missed you," he said, rubbing the back of her hands with the pads of his thumbs. "I should have called." He felt guilty, even though they'd agreed. Still, he could have called and asked about her day. Found out what color she painted her nails, or even if Joe was alright. "Should've done something, anything but what I did."

"You didn't do anything."

"That's what I'm talking about." He pulled her towards him, circling his arms around her waist, breathing in her scent. "I didn't do as good as I thought I would—away from you."

The last night they were together, even though he knew leaving would be the hardest thing he'd ever done, he went to her anyway. He went to her because she was the only one who could talk him out of leaving, but then he woke up alone. Gerti knew if she stayed, he'd wrestle with not going back, so she made the decision for him. She'd left the bed extra early that morning, as quietly as she could. She'd dressed and left the house because seeing him as he left would probably break her, and she didn't know if the pieces could be put back together again.

She raked her nails over his hair while he hummed into the fabric of her dress. "Thank you for making the bed." She could smile about it now. After she left the house, she didn't go back home until the sun went down. She drove Brownie and Joe out of the county, finally stopping when she felt she'd put a good amount of distance between them not to turn back and see Quinn drive away.

When she got back home, Joe barged into the house first, sniffing through all the rooms, looking for any sign of Quinn. Gerti took her time, not wanting to see anything reminding her of him but secretly hoping she would. When she got to her room, she found her bed made, the sheets changed, and the old ones washed and hanging on the line in the back.

"Took me a while to get the corners the way you like 'em, but I was determined. Couldn't have you come back home and get into an unhappy bed." She could picture him struggling with the sheets to get them right.

"I would have survived." Stepping back, she moved to the bed and sat down next to him. He watched her as she lowered herself down, noting the way her earrings swung as she adjusted her body to get comfortable. "How's the job going?" She wanted to change the subject, move the conversation on to something that would make him smile.

He took her hand, lacing their fingers together before answering, "I loved it."

The feel of her hand in his distracted him. Quinn liked how warm she felt. She'd always been so warm. Sinking further into the mattress, Gerti had forgotten how comfortable his bed was.

Opening her mouth wide, she let out a big yawn before she could cover her mouth. "Sorry." She didn't want him to think he bored her.

"That's alright." Quinn leaned over, pressing his lips to her temple. "It's been a long day." He thought about his dinner with Ms. Edith the night before. "Ms. Edith said you've been taking days off. Is everything okay?" Gerti nodded through a smile then laid back on the bed.

She watched the ceiling fan whirl around, focusing on the center lights until the blades were a blur in the background. She looked over at him as he lay beside her on the bed, the worry in his eyes clear.

"Everything's fine." She squeezed his hand as her eyes closed. "I'm pregnant."

Quinn sat up quickly, looking at her from her head to her knees bent at the edge of the mattress. "A baby?" His hand instinctively went to her belly, as if he'd be able to feel the life they'd created beneath the fabric of her dress. The life he'd been rubbing on for hours without even knowing. "You're having a baby?"

He saw the tears on her face. "Oh, Ole Fashion, what's wrong?" The kiss he placed on her lips brought on the sob she'd been holding in all day. He held her tight, letting her cry as he moved his lips to her neck. "Are you not happy about this?"

Quinn realized that throughout the day, she'd been keeping him together all the while hiding the fact she'd been falling apart too. She'd smiled and talked and buffered him from unwanted questions and people while holding in a secret so big it brought her to tears.

"I'm... scared, Quinn."

"What's to be scared about? You're having my baby." He smiled wide, showing his undeniable happiness.

"You don't live here, Quinn. You started your dream job a few months ago. I'm not leaving Bellbush."

Lifting his head, he wiped away her tears and kissed her lips again. "That job stopped being a dream a while ago." He looked in her eyes, reacquainting himself with the astonishing way the depth of her brown eyes always hypnotized him. "One night, I walked through the door, and I had to remind myself you weren't there to talk to about my day. There were so many times I wanted to call you. I came real close a few times. Had my phone in my hand, but I couldn't get my fingers to dial the number."

"Because we agreed..."

"Yeah." Quinn's hand splayed over her belly as he tried to feel how much rounder it had become.

"That wasn't a very smart decision," Gerti whispered.

"One of my worst." Although they had agreed, he had no problem with putting all the blame on himself. "I didn't think it would be so hard."

"Me either. I figured I'd throw myself into work, and you'd become a distant memory after enough time."

After fumbling through the first week of work after Quinn left, Gerti stopped trying to pretend things were okay. She smiled and put on a brave face in front of her customers, but behind closed doors or in The Shop's kitchen beside the refrigerator, she allowed herself to break down. Cora found her one day, unable to stop crying, and sent her home.

They ran out of food early that day, but Gerti's wellbeing was more important. The next day, she stayed home and promised herself she'd only allow three more cries. She'd never felt more out of control or lonely as she did that day. It took a couple of weeks, but she learned to get out of bed without thinking of Quinn or looking for his camo cap in the crowd of people at The Shop.

"So, what happened?" Quinn asked.

She gave him a small smile as she thought back to the morning that changed everything. "Cinnamon happened."

"Someone new in town?" Quinn asked confused.

Gerti let out one of those strangled laughs, thick with

snot and unshed tears. Quinn adored the sound. "I was making a honey bun cake one morning, and the smell of the cinnamon sent me racing to the bathroom. It's hard to forget someone when they've left something inside you that refuses to let you make one of your favorite cakes." She smiled and wiped her hand down her face.

Quinn couldn't stop the laugh that came out of him. "Poor kid doesn't like cinnamon, huh?"

"How about poor mama?" She made a weak attempt at swatting his arm, but it turned into a caress instead. "I had to take everything with cinnamon off the menu. You know how many times I've been asked when the bacon cinnamon rolls will be back?" Quinn's muffled laughter shook the bed. "Cora made up a lie I was trying out new recipes."

"Does anyone else know?" He used his finger to draw hearts on her stomach.

"Only Cora and Ms. Edith. And only because I couldn't hide being nauseous around them every day. They've been helpful with deflecting, though." Leaning on his elbow, Quinn looked at her face and took in the deep brown of her eyes, the roundness of her cheeks, the curve of her nose, and the pout of her plump lips. He took his time, silently repeating the route three times. "Why are you staring at me?" she asked. Instead of answering, he leaned down and kissed her, pouring three months' worth of missing her into one kiss.

Looking at her a moment ago, he didn't see the Gerti he left; he saw the Gerti he never wanted to be away from again. The woman carrying his child. His future. His hand traveled from her belly to the warmth between her legs. She moaned softly, aware there were still people in the house on the other side of his bedroom door. "I missed you, Quinn Garland." His fingers brushed along the outside of her panties, and she pressed her lips together to keep from crying out from the way her body responded to the touch she'd missed so much.

"Is this okay?"

"Yes." She used her hand to help guide his fingers to where she wanted him most. Soon, the clothes they were wearing were shed, and they were skin-to-skin with Gerti's legs wrapped around his waist as he filled her with long hard strokes, Quinn covering her mouth with his own to muffle her moans.

He thought back to the last time they were together in this bed and how long that night had been. He couldn't sleep, but he knew he wanted to be with her, try his hardest to get his fill of her before he left. Thinking about it now, that was the night they created another life. Impatience and greed had kept him from reaching for the condoms in his nightstand, neither one of them enough in their right mind to notice. He stroked her deeper, wanting to get her to a place she hadn't been since he left, a place he'd only been in his dreams.

"Quinn..."

"I'm right here," he said against her lips, feeling her tightening around him. "I'm not going anywhere. Let it go."

He watched her close her eyes tight and felt her hand squeeze his arm before her back arched off the bed, causing him to go deeper. Quinn didn't stop, even though he wished he could sit and watch her, the way her body quivered beneath him as she pressed her lips together tight, then slowly opened them, feeling relaxed, letting out a sigh that told Quinn she was ready for the next one.

The clock ticked seven o'clock before they noticed the house was quiet. No one checked on them, and Quinn suspected he owed that to Charles. He'd looked directly at him when he rushed Gerti off down the hall, and his best friend knew what time it was. With his right arm tucked behind his head, Quinn's left hand stroked Gerti's locs as she laid on his chest. They'd been in the same position for almost an hour, unable to leave the bed. Her body pressed against his, making his heart beat faster with every breath she took.

"Gerti," he whispered, cutting into the silence of the room.

"Hmm?"

"Marry me." Quinn could tell his question stunned her because her breathing faltered.

For five seconds, she held her breath before asking on an exhale, "What?"

"Marry me, Gerti."

"And what, watch you leave in a few days to go back to Kansas? I can't..."

"I turned in my resignation two weeks ago. I told you I wasn't going anywhere."

She sat up to look at him. "You did what?" she asked, repeating the word 'resignation' in her head again.

"Should you be moving that fast?" He sat up too, placing both hands at her waist, then had to close his eyes at the sight of her nude body, so warm under his hands.

"Quinn, you quit your job?"

He raised his shoulders in a shrug. "After a while, it didn't mean the same without you." She quietly looked at his face, studying his features. His beard looked a little thicker but still framed his lips so nicely, even more so as they turned up into a smile. "I needed to come back," he sighed, lying back and tucking his arm behind his head again. "Even before Badge died, I knew I'd be coming back. Kansas didn't feel like home anymore."

Running a hand down her bare back, he gently nudged her to lie back down next to him. "You feel like home," he confessed. Fitting himself behind her, he pressed his face into her locs, inhaling the scent of the fruit-smelling oil she used and the sweat she'd worked up earlier. She didn't say no to his proposal, and even though he wanted to hear a yes, he didn't ask again. He knew there would be other times, so he changed the subject. "When did you find out?"

"A little over a month ago." He threaded their fingers together, holding their hands against her belly. "I took three tests at home and still needed a doctor to confirm it," she giggled to herself. "It wasn't the cold I thought it was." Gerti felt the bed shake with his laughter. "I'm about fifteen weeks along. I wanted to call you and tell you."

She remembered that night so clearly. She had the phone in her hand, her finger hovering over the call icon as she looked at his name at the top of her screen. As her finger lowered down to touch the screen, Cora called with news of Quincy's death. She couldn't bring herself to make the call after that.

Quinn understood why she hadn't called. He probably wouldn't have answered in the overwhelming state he'd been in. "Besides nausea, how have you been feeling?"

"Tired and hungry."

"You're around food all day," he said, moving her closer to him.

"Yeah, but I don't want sweets, I want savory. I almost came by here a few weeks ago and asked Quincy for some of his brisket, but I knew if I did, I'd probably end up telling him why I was begging for food, and I wasn't ready." Quinn kissed her temple, letting his lips linger on her skin. "I ended up at Bells Blues, begging Mack for a sandwich instead."

"With slaw?"

"Two scoops."

Chapter TWENTY-FOUR

"Did anyone call while I was...?"

"Peeing? For the fifth time in the past two hours?" Cora smiled at Gerti, watching her adjust her dress over her growing belly. At four and a half months, her belly seemed to get rounder every day as the baby grew.

"I didn't realize you were keeping track." Gerti rolled her eyes then tied her apron back behind her back. "No calls?"

"No, Quinn hasn't called." Cora looked up at the clock on the wall and poured more tea for Ms. Edith. "He said he'd be by as soon as they finished. I'm sure he's trying to make sure everything's perfect." Quinn had been out of town for a few days and called that morning when he got back to let Gerti know he'd made it in and to tell her he'd be by to get her later.

She looked over at the specials board to see what they had left. With closing time near, there were empty chairs but enough customers to eat the remaining desserts. It surprised her to see only the sour cream pound cake and lemon bars left on the board, but by the look of the cake plate, the pound cake would be gone first.

"What happened to the strawberry cake and brownies? Was I in the bathroom for that long?"

Cora nodded. "We sold them while you were in there." She went around the counter and started gathering the sugar dispensers from the empty tables. "Looking at your belly again?" Gerti bit her lip and nodded. She couldn't help it anymore. Every time she walked by a mirror, she had to turn and look at her profile to see how much her belly had grown since the day before.

Gerti tugged on the simple black dress again, pulling it down and then up again when the neckline revealed too much. She looked around to make sure none of the men in The Shop had noticed. "I know I've never been small, but this is getting ridiculous."

"Yeah, you've held out long enough, girl. It's time to buy some maternity clothes." Cora loved shopping, so she'd be more than happy to help Gerti shop for clothes to fit her growing body. "You wear a fourteen, right?"

"Yes," Gerti answered, "and no, you can't wear my clothes while I can't." Gerti stood so she could see her reflection in the window. "This dress didn't use to fit like this."

"No, it didn't," Ms. Edith said around a mouthful of brownie. "But consider yourself blessed to experience such a thing."

"Yes, ma'am," Gerti replied, feeling a bit chastised. It had taken time, but Gerti realized how much of a blessing this baby was. Every pang and flutter she experienced brought on a smile. Quinn had been speechless the first time he felt the baby moving around. He had the proudest smile on his face and went around telling everyone about it.

Cora held in her laugh at Gerti's scolding, then sprinkled a little salt in her wound. "Ms. Edith, do you remember when Gerti and Quinn disappeared on us after the funeral?" The wide-eyed look Gerti threw Cora's way made her laugh out loud.

"I do," Ms. Edith said, nodding her head. "I made her eat, and the next thing I knew, he had rushed her through the house and down the hall." Gerti tilted her head at Cora. The last thing she wanted was a lecture from Ms. Edith about how you don't leave your guests to fend for themselves at your house. "But then I didn't see them anymore after that. I figured they were floating around the house talking to everyone." Ms. Edith looked sternly at Gerti before asking, "Where were you, child?"

"We... went somewhere to talk." Gerti felt her cheeks grow warm with embarrassment.

"Y'all couldn't have talked after everyone left?" Ms. Edith waved off her own question, already knowing the answer. "Never mind."

"I think it's funny Quinn said 'forget all these people, I need to be alone with my woman' and left on out." Cora refilled Ms. Edith's glass then looked up to see everyone had left.

With about ten minutes until close, Gerti noticed too and went to lock the door. She stopped when she saw Sam Franklin pull up. "Sam's here." She waited at the door for him to walk up.

"Huh, haven't seen him in a while," Cora said. "I guess

he's missed his Gertrude."

"Hush, Cora," Ms. Edith warned. She turned in her stool and greeted him once he came inside. "How've you been, Sam?"

"Been fine, ma'am," he said, nodding at all three of them. "Job's got me busy these days." He walked up to the counter then looked over at the specials board, trying to decide what to order. He didn't want to spend a lot of time choosing since he'd come right at closing.

"It's all we have left," Cora told him. They were all wondering why he hadn't spoken to Gerti yet. Her name was usually the first thing out of his mouth. "What can I get you?"

"Let me have the rest of the lemon bars." While Cora went to the back to get what he'd asked for, he turned around and leaned on the counter, watching Gerti clean the tables. Ms. Edith allowed him to look for a few moments before patting his arm and motioning her head for him to talk to her. "Hello, Gertru... Gerti," he corrected. "How have you been?"

"I've been good. You just get back in town?" She rubbed her belly, feeling the baby move. "Haven't seen you in a while."

"Trying to stay out of trouble." He pushed off the table and walked over to her. "I heard about Quincy." She stood still, not sure what he'd say next. "Tell Quinn I'm sorry for his loss." Gerti nodded her head and gave Sam a small smile. "I would have come to the funeral, but I was on the road. I know how it feels to lose someone." Sam's father died when he was ten. He had been his best friend, and without him, he was lost for a long time. He still missed him. "Let him know if he needs anything, don't hesitate to ask."

"Was that him giving up?" Cora asked after Sam had left.

"I think that's him realizing he'll have more success elsewhere." Cora shrugged at the more eloquent way Ms. Edith said it.

Cora and Gerti cleaned up for the night as Joe kept watch with his eyes closed under the window. Sonny and Jack were right beside him doing the same. Gerti kept checking the clock, wondering where Quinn was.

Placing the chairs up on the tables, Cora remembered they never finished their conversation about Quinn and Gerti's disappearing act, so she brought it back up. "So, what all did y'all talk about?"

"When?" Gerti asked, too focused on wiping the table to know what Cora asked.

"When you and Quinn disappeared after the funeral to talk." Cora used finger quotes for emphasis on the word 'talk', then looked over at Ms. Edith, who looked at Gerti for her answer. Sensing she couldn't get out of telling them, she sighed and started from the beginning when he opened the door, then ended the conversation with his proposal. "You mean to tell me he asked you to marry him, and you said no?" Cora asked, surprised.

"I didn't say no, Cora," Gerti shrugged. "I didn't say anything. Besides, he only asked because I'm pregnant."

Ms. Edith scoffed. She saw herself and her late husband in Quinn and Gerti. She would never admit how stubborn she'd been back then. Too scared of how much she loved him, she would have found any excuse to push him away.

"That's not the only reason he asked, and you know it," Cora said, frustrated. She hated when people had all they needed in front of them but refused to see it. Gerti watched her wipe the counter with more force than necessary. "Quinn wants to do more than what's right. He wants you. That baby is a bonus."

"She's a smart girl, Gerti. You should listen to Cora."

"Thank you, Ms. Edith. I'm glad someone finally said it out loud." Cora held her head a little higher after Ms. Edith's comment. "He's got those boys over there every day building—what's he building?"

"I don't know," Gerti answered. "He won't tell me."

"Well, whatever it is, he's building it for you. That's really all that matters."

A few days after the funeral, Quinn called the crew to work on a special project for Gerti. Once they were finished with their landscaping for the day, they'd go work at Honeybells. The sounds of hammering wood and circular saws could be heard all over the ranch. Quinn wouldn't tell Gerti what they were building, but he promised she'd love it.

"What about the job he loved so much?" Gerti still felt guilty he gave up something he loved for her.

"Well, that ship has sailed, girl," Cora said, looking over at Ms. Edith, who nodded in agreement. "Just think about it, okay? Think about how perfect things would be with you as his wife, baby Cora running around the ranch." Ms. Edith laughed, nearly spitting out her tea.

"Who?" Gerti asked, confused.

"Don't tell me you haven't thought about naming the baby after me?" Ms. Edith laughed so loud, all three dogs lifted their heads to find out what was going on.

"Why would we do that?" Gerti asked. Baby names hadn't been a conversation they'd had yet even though they got plenty of suggestions from everyone.

"I'm the reason you and Quinn met."

"How do you figure?" Gerti stopped and placed her hands on her hips to look at Cora. She'd said some outrageous things before, but this one had moved up to the top of the list.

"I'm the one who told Charles to bring him by The Shop to see me the day y'all met." Cora mirrored Gerti's stance and put her hand on her hips too. She'd seen the sparks the first time they laid eyes on each other and had been rooting for them since. "This is all because of me. Baby Cora is the least you could do to thank me."

"And saying yes," Ms. Edith added.

"She say yes yet?"

"No," Quinn answered. He and Charles were sitting on the porch drinking beers, talking about Quinn's next move. "She's...being cautious, I guess."

"Or stubborn, like most of the women around here." The day after the funeral, after Gerti left, Quinn took one call; from Charles. He thanked him for keeping people away and then told him about the baby and the proposal.

"I'm gonna ask her again."

"Wouldn't expect anything less," Charles said, holding up his beer in salute. "Never known you to be someone who gives up easily." He looked out at one of the outbuildings where the Garland Landscaping trucks were parked. He sighed, remembering the summers he'd spent in those trucks, driving from job to job to earn enough money to take Jordyn some place nice. Regret coursed through him because he'd never told Quincy how much that job meant to him. How much being in his life meant to him. Charles had always felt he had time. "You meet with the lawyers today?"

"Yeah, took me an hour and a half to get out to that damn office with all the traffic. Took less time for them to hand everything over and sign all the papers. They could have at least drawn it out and made it worth my gas." In the three weeks since the funeral, Quinn felt like all he'd been doing was running around.

He spent the first two weeks tying up loose ends in both Texas and Kansas. He put his house on the market then had to figure out how to get it packed and sold from Texas since he didn't want to leave Gerti for very long. After she reassured him she'd be fine if he left for a few days, he reluctantly drove back to Kansas, taking Terrence, Freddy, and Leon to make the packing and cleaning go faster. It took them four days to get everything ready, and then they headed home.

"Any surprises?"

Quinn shook his head no. When he met with the lawyers, they told him Quincy had left everything to him, which meant he was now the owner of Garland Landscaping. It was up to him to make sure the landscaping business didn't fall apart.

"This is all mine." Taking a sip of his beer, he marveled at how the events of his life had turned into this day.

"Remember running around this place when we were little? It had the best hiding spots."

Quinn chuckled, thinking back to a time when all they had to do was imagine it and the ranch easily transformed to anything they wanted. "We made Greg hide, and we'd go looking for him. Thought we were

Bass Reeves."

"We were gonna form a posse and ride around the county catching bad guys." Quincy put a stop to their dreams after they lassoed Greg chasing him on their horses. "Too bad it didn't work out," Quinn chuckled.

"You own this place, Quinn. You know what you're gonna do with it?"

On his drive back from the lawyer's office, Quinn thought about every acre of the ranch. What he could grow if he wanted. What he could build. The truth of the matter was, he could do whatever he wanted because he owned it. He thought owning his own house was a big deal, but now he owned a legacy. Honeybells Ranch had been in the family for generations, and now, like his uncle before him, it was up to Quinn to make sure it stayed that way.

Gerti always stayed on his mind when he thought about the future. He wondered if she'd like spending her Sundays on the back porch here, or if the baby would like the grass under his feet.

"From personal experience, it's a pretty good place to raise kids. I haven't really thought farther than that."

"You know, Jordyn's kinda pissed you and Gerti beat us."

"Only by a few weeks." Quinn looked over at Charles, who beamed at the thought of becoming a dad. Jordyn let the news spread like wildfire when she found out. Babies in Bellbush meant growth and the continuation of a way of life some people didn't even know existed. They were a promise for things to come.

Charles smiled to himself as he thought about Jordyn and how she would look in the mirror every day, focusing on her belly button, waiting for it to pop out. "You know, when Cora was a kid, she would always talk about how she and her friend were gonna grow up, get married, and have kids at the same time. I always thought that was the dumbest shit. But now—" Charles looked over at Quinn and couldn't believe all they'd been through. "Now I understand."

Quinn did, too. He held up his beer to offer a toast.

"To sons, because neither of us would know what to do with a daughter."

Chapter TWENTY-FOUR

"**W**here are you taking me now, Quinn Garland?"

"I've got a surprise for you." Gerti looked at him skeptically and wondered what he was up to. She hadn't seen him in a week then, as she'd locked up after Cora and Ms. Edith left, he came walking up with that confident strut of his to take her away. They loaded up Joe in the truck and headed off.

"Did everything go okay?"

He looked over at her, admiring her black dress, then brought his hand down to palm her belly. After not seeing her for a week, all he wanted was to undress her and see what he'd missed while he'd been gone. "Everything went great. Got the house packed, cleaned, and on the market." His smile, although she loved it, made her nervous. He was driving her to Honeybells for a special surprise that had taken nearly a month to finish. He'd kept it well hidden and made everyone keep their mouths shut about it. "Did you miss me?" he asked arrogantly.

"A little bit," she answered shyly. She'd missed him more than she knew how to put into words. As soon as he'd said bye and walked out the door to handle things in Kansas for what he promised to be the last time, she started to miss him. Quinn made sure he said goodbye this time, and Gerti appreciated it, and held onto his promise to return.

Since his return to Bellbush, Quinn spent most nights at Gerti's so she'd be closer to The Shop after being kept up all night. Then he'd drive over to Honeybells to meet the crew and go off to the first job of the day.

It wasn't until Quinn came back that Gerti discovered she didn't like sleeping alone. She liked him sleeping behind her, his arm wrapped over her waist, and his leg slung over her calf. During the night, his hand would alternate between rubbing her thigh, squeezing her hip, and stroking her nipples, but he'd always end up at her belly. "Did you miss me?" Gerti asked.

"I missed y'all like crazy." He gave her belly a small squeeze.

"Then what took you so long?" She took his hand and pressed it where she could feel the baby moving.

Quinn knew he'd never get used to that. The flutter grew stronger every day as if the baby was trying to be heard and join in the conversation. "Had to make sure everything was how it's supposed to be." He pulled into Honeybells, and Gerti looked around for the surprise he talked about but saw nothing.

"Are we going to the house?" Quinn put the truck in park and shook his head when Gerti said, "I really need to use the bathroom."

"The house it is," he laughed. He came around and opened the door for her then let her take the lead up the front steps into the house.

After she finished, he took her hand and led her towards the back door. "I gotta cover your eyes, Ole Fashion." She didn't look pleased, so he had to remind her. "Surprise, remember?"

"Fine." She turned her back and closed her eyes to wait for him to cover them. He kissed the back of her neck first, making her giggle, then shielded her eyes with one hand and placed his other at the small of her back to guide her. "Don't let me fall."

"Never."

Gerti listened for new sounds and used her nose to figure out where he was leading her. She could smell fresh cut wood and the sweet smell of flowers, but nothing to give away the secret. They walked down the steps then about twenty yards away from the house before Quinn told her to step up. She felt a wooden platform under her feet, and then Quinn uncovered her eyes.

"Quinn," she whispered, turning around to take everything in.

"What do you think?" She dropped her head and cried, leaving Quinn not sure what to do. Weeks of hard work had left her crying, and he didn't know why. If she said she hated it, he'd tear it down with his bare hands and start over until she loved it. He wrapped his arms around her in a hug she received and reciprocated. "Why the tears, Ole Fashion?"

"It's beautiful." She looked up at him, and he gave her a kiss on the forehead. "Thank you."

The day Gerti left after the funeral, Quinn decided he wanted to build her a place on Honeybells where she could sit and think like she did at home. Part of his motivation was as long as she was thinking, she might think of becoming his wife.

"Come on and sit down." He walked her over to the high-backed wooden bench that sat at the back of the large wooden pergola he and the crew had built for her. The bench had sunflower cushions and lots of pillows like she liked. A small coffee table and dark brown rocker sat off to the side, easily moved if she needed them. He even had a small footstool for when she painted her toenails.

She looked up and saw two fans hanging from the large beams covering the top, and her eyes sparkled. "Figured you might want a place to sit when you come out here." He knew she would have sat on the old porch without complaint, but he wanted to give her something just for her. "If these fans don't cool you off enough, I'll add more."

Her head moved from side to side, looking at the colorful flowers planted all around the pergola and the few vines climbing the posts. "You planted all these?"

"A few of 'em." Even though he'd worked for and now owned a landscaping company, picking flowers he thought Gerti would like was a daunting task. Usually, the client would request what they wanted, what they liked best. Not being able to ask Gerti, he drew from his memory of what she had at her house and what she wore in her hair. And one surprise he hoped she was ready for. "I put the roses in," he said cautiously. He looked at her to gauge her reaction, hoping the roses weren't too much. She nodded her head while wiping away more tears and smiling.

"I love them." They were blush pink with light yellow along the edges. She thought they represented her sister perfectly. She didn't have any roses at home because she could never bring herself to buy any without getting sad. Having Quinn plant them made it okay to be sad because healing wasn't too far away. "And the honeybells?"

"Those, too." He scooted closer to her and took her hand. "Took me a little while to find them, but I thought the ranch should have some again." He remained silent while she took it all in. Quinn sat and watched her as she looked at everything repeatedly, her eyes darting back and forth, memorizing the fruits of all the labor he and his crew put in. After fifteen minutes of quiet and watching the sun go down, Quinn got nervous. "Talk to me, Ole Fashion."

"I can't believe you did this for me. It's way more than I could have asked for."

"You probably don't remember this, but that day at The Shop, right before Ms. Edith and her dogs jumped in my truck, you smiled at me. One of your real big smiles that shows off your dimples." He watched her give him one of those smiles before continuing. "Nearly knocked me off my feet. Still does. I wasn't expecting you to do that, especially after you yelled at me for mowing on the wrong day."

"I didn't yell," she denied. Her peaceful Sunday had been turned upside down, and she didn't see them ever going back to the way they were.

"You didn't have to." Quinn thought her glare sounded louder than anything he'd heard before. "The way you stared at me was enough." He chuckled and wrapped his arm around her shoulders. "Then after getting to know you, I couldn't believe you could walk around this world... oblivious to the power you had over me. Why do you think I went to The Shop every night?" Her smile had become a magnet to him, pulling him to her every night so he could see how close they could get.

"You were fixing the jukebox."

"I didn't care about that thing. I wanted to be where you were." He turned to her and held her left hand in his, stroking her ring finger with his thumb. "Honestly, Gerti, this is about the least I could have done. Have you ever seen your smile?" She graced him with another one, and he pulled her closer to him on the bench. "You can ask me right now for the moon, and I'll start building a ladder to get it for you." He kissed her hand and looked out into the darkening sky. "You can ask me for anything."

She had helped him in ways he couldn't voice yet. She made it possible for him to find the place he called home, where he needed to be in the world. "Anything?" she asked, testing his declaration.

"Yes," Quinn answered, prepared to build a ladder.

"Can we get married at sunset?"

Chapter TWENTY-FIVE

Four days ago, Gerti's parents arrived in Bellbush. Since meeting Quinn, he and her dad Marcus had been joined at the hip. Seeing them together, getting along the way they did made Gerti happy beyond measure. It also allowed Gerti and her mother Trudy to catch up and talk.

"He's a great guy, Gerti. I don't know how I'm gonna get your father out of Bellbush now."

"That's not so bad, is it? You two staying?"

It had been so long since she'd seen her parents, Gerti just wanted them close for as long as she could.

"Tomorrow, you'll be a wife. No one wants their parents around on their honeymoon. Besides, once the baby's here, we'll be back." Trudy dabbed at her eyes once the tears started again. Seeing Gerti living life the way she wanted in a way that made her truly happy was all she'd ever wanted for her. "I'm so proud of you, Gerti."

"What for?"

"You found a happiness that some people will never experience." Trudy took Gerti's hand and squeezed. "When you first came here, I didn't understand why a young woman your age would want to go live in the sticks. I hated living here. But then you'd call, and I could hear in your voice that you were happy. Not a fake happy like you tried to use after your sister's death." Gerti bit her cheek, unaware her mother could see right through her. "You were truly happy. Today, you are beaming with joy. I don't know how much of that is Quinn or this baby, but I hope you never lose it."

"Me, too."

After her accident, Gerti became a quiet child, not wanting to bring too much attention to herself so she didn't have to answer questions. All Trudy wanted was for her to jump and shout and present herself to the world the same way the sun did every morning. She was almost there, but then Rose died, and her shell was pulled back on. Seeing Gerti now, there wasn't even a faint glimmer of darkness.

"You know, I remember Quincy," Trudy said. "He was always such a nice man. Stern, but always nice." She placed her hand on Gerti's belly, the excitement of becoming a grandmother almost too much for her to handle. "People dying always puts life in perspective. Stop being afraid to leap, baby. You've got Quinn to catch you."

"I swear, Jordyn, if I didn't love you so much, I would have already killed your husband." Cora stomped into the bedroom designated the Bride's Room in a huff and ready to fight.

Jordyn rolled her eyes at her sister-in-law. She and Charles always fussed about something or another these days. She couldn't keep up, and with her pregnancy, she didn't try to. "I would hate for you to kill your brother. What has he done now?" Cora came over to stand beside Jordyn to help with Gerti's hair. For her wedding day, she was wearing it down, braided with flowers and hairpins throughout.

"He won't leave Ray alone," Cora whined, looking in the mirror at her two friends, glowing with pregnancy.

"The guy you brought?" Gerti asked, holding up a pearled hairpin for Jordyn to grab.

"With the grey cowboy hat?" Jordyn added, thinking about the handsome cowboy who'd walked up to the house with Cora on his arm.

"Yes," Cora answered. Raymond Brooks had walked into The Shop one day while Gerti was out, and Cora served him up a cup of coffee and her phone number. They'd been getting to know each other for a few months. She figured the wedding would be a perfect place to introduce him since her brother would be too preoccupied with his wedding duties to bother him. "He's got him cornered in the kitchen, asking him the weirdest questions. Why would Ray know what I like to do first thing in the morning? They even have your dad working with them."

"He's making sure you haven't stayed the night. That he's never seen you too early in the morning and knows how you like your eggs and morning wake up call." Jordyn shrugged it off, knowing how protective Charles could be with all those he loved. "It's what big brothers do." Gerti nodded in agreement. She didn't have a brother, but Charles had become as close to one as she'd ever get, and she knew how he was.

Cora tucked one of Gerti's locs behind her ear and secured it with a hairpin. "Quinn is right there beside him. He's lucky it's his wedding day, and y'all have a baby on the way, or I'd be trying to figure out how to kill him too." Putting her anger aside, Cora allowed herself to look at Gerti for the first time. She wore a little makeup to play up her eyes, and a pretty shade of pink on her lips. "You look beautiful, you know?" Cora sniffed back the tears that had formed in her eyes. Jordyn shook her head at her, finding humor in the fact that Cora's anger at her brother and Quinn had already been forgotten.

"Stop, before you make me cry too," Jordyn said in a shaky voice.

"I'm not crying." Cora's voice cracked, and she dabbed at her eyes with the pads of her fingertips. "It must be all these flowers around here." She would never admit the love story of Quinn and Gerti was one of her favorites.

"Yeah, must be it," Jordyn said, finishing with Gerti's hair. Gerti stood up to get a closer look in the mirror in front of her. She leaned her head forward and ran her hands over her hair, watching the sparkles of her hairpins reflected in the mirror.

"Look at the two of you." Cora eyed Gerti and Jordyn, who stood side by side, their bellies almost matching with the roundness of pregnancy. "I can't believe I'm gonna be an auntie to two cute little babies. I really hope the baby favors you, Jordyn, because no one deserves to look like my brother."

"Be nice, Cora," Gerti said. "Charles is very handsome." She smiled at Jordyn and winked. "Almost as much as

Quinn." Gerti gave Jordyn's belly a gentle rub and offered her a hug. "Thank you for being here with me today. It means a lot." Although the void of Rose would never be filled, Gerti knew the blessings she'd been given by having friends like Cora and Jordyn in her life.

"Don't you dare start with the tears again, Cora," Jordyn warned, fanning her eyes to keep from crying. "Come on, let's get you dressed. It's almost time."

Although Quinn would have been happy going down to the Justice of the Peace the day after Gerti said yes, he also knew she deserved something more formal. They talked it over and decided they wanted Charles to officiate the wedding, then let everyone at The Shop know they'd be having a sunset wedding by writing it on the specials board right under the strawberry cake. Two weeks later, everyone showed up to watch Gerti and Quinn get married.

At 6:30 in the evening, Gerti stood at the edge of the porch, escorted by Marcus, wearing an ivory-colored, ankle-length, off the shoulder chiffon gown with an empire waist to accommodate her belly. It had taken her a whole day to find the dress, using her Monday to shop. With Cora's help, the last dress she tried on ten minutes before the boutique closed turned out to be the perfect fit. Ms. Edith made the bouquet she carried with orange lilies, purple roses, and magnolia flowers. She looked out at the crowd. Her parents and friends were in attendance, and she felt giddy for the first time in her life. Taking a deep breath, she finally looked at Quinn standing in the center of her pergola, waiting impatiently for her.

He didn't think anyone would look at him with Gerti around, but he wore a dress shirt with his jeans anyway. He couldn't sleep last night without Gerti beside him. Cora had made them sleep in separate houses because of tradition, claiming Gerti being pregnant didn't negate the practice. Quinn held his breath when she took her first step off the porch then exhaled slowly after her next steps brought her closer to him. When she'd gotten halfway down the walkway, an anxious Quinn stepped down to walk with her the rest of the way. He hugged Marcus then took Gerti's hand in his.

"Hey, that's not how it works," Terrence yelled out. Everyone laughed, even Gerti, who looked up at Quinn. He kissed her forehead then continued walking together, hand in hand, stopping when they got to the pergola.

Charles stood in his confidence as officiant for the wedding of his best friend and the woman who made him want to settle down and be a family man. He'd written speech after speech trying to come up with the perfect words, but nothing ever seemed right. That afternoon as he drove over to Honeybells, inspiration hit him.

"When Quinn came back to Bellbush for my wedding, he was my best man. Apparently, he thinks he broke the mold because he asked me to work his ceremony instead." Everyone laughed as Charles stood at the center of the pergola, speaking to the guests. "It's a funny thing to look back on your life to see how far you've come. All the growth that had to happen to get you to this point in your life.

When I think about how many times I heard Quinn

say he'd never, ever, ever get married, I have to laugh. He stood his ground for a long time, swore up and down." Charles looked at Quinn, who grinned, thinking about how unwavering his stance had been, but also very wrong. "Then he met the one who made his nevers and evers turn into forever and always." A few amens could be heard from somewhere in the background, and a lot of nodding could be seen from the guests. "So tonight, as the sun is turning day into night, Gertrude Eloise Gordon and Quincy Emerson Garland invite you all to be of witness as they become husband and wife." There were hoots and hollers and lots of clapping when they finally joined Charles in the pergola and turned to each other to recite their vows.

Gerti had attended one wedding in her life, at a hotel she worked for. The beautiful bride wore a gown costing thousands of dollars. She walked down the aisle to a string quartet, and her groom stood there stoic, ready for things to be over. When they said their vows, there was no emotion to them, just a monotone reply to what the minister said. She'd hoped her own wedding felt nothing like theirs.

With watery eyes and a shaky voice, she looked Quinn in the eyes as he held her hand, vowing to love and honor him until death. When it was time, she excitedly said, "I do."

When it was Quinn's turn to do the same, he vowed to protect and love her with all that he was while she wiped at the tears falling from his eyes.

"Y'all don't worry," Charles said, grinning. "Looks like the wind might have blown something into Quinn's eyes." Everyone laughed, and a few wiped at their own tears. "He'll be alright," Charles joked, touching Quinn on the shoulder.

"Get to the kissing part already," Quinn said, focusing on Gerti's lips.

"Now he's impatient," Charles said to the guests. "Then let me take my time and say something to the both of you." He took a deep breath and smiled at Quinn's impatient stare. "Sometimes, when we least expect it, life has a way of giving us what we need even before we knew we wanted for anything. Gerti and Quinn, I want you to remember this exact moment. The feelings you have for each other, and the absolute love that makes you perfect for one another. There will be days you might not feel that love, but you have a host of people here who will remind you if you need us to." There were more amens from the guests. "Gertrude Gordon, you have been perfectly made for Quinn as he has been created to love you."

"Until the end of time," Quinn finished.

"I am honored to present to you, Mr. and Mrs. Quincy Garland." The clapping started off quiet then rose to thunderous applause. "Wait, wait!" Charles yelled. "Before Quinn ends our twenty-five plus years of friendship, let me say, "You may kiss your bride." Quinn wasted no time pulling Gerti into him and pressing his lips to hers. His hand went to the small of her back, and he leaned into her, bending her back slightly, keeping his other hand on her belly. When they finally broke apart, Gerti laughed while Quinn stood staring at the kiss-swollen lips of his wife.

They held the reception in the barn, with lots of dancing and food. This time, Gerti let Quinn kiss her without running away while they danced like no one was watching, swaying, dipping, and turning through half a dozen songs.

After dancing with Marcus, Gerti was pulled away by people wanting to talk to her and see her wedding ring, offering blessings in the process. Before she knew it, an hour had passed, and Quinn was nowhere to be found. Right as she went to look for him, Charles came to tell her where she could find him.

"What are you doing out here, Quinn Garland?" Gerti came up behind him and slid her arm through his. He was standing in the pergola, looking out over the ranch.

"Waiting on you, Mrs. Garland." He pulled her to the front and placed a hand on her belly. He'd walked out there after not being able to get to her while a group of people surrounded her. "I got you something." He motioned with his head to something on the table. She laughed at the jar of lightning bugs blinking against the night sky. "They felt tonight deserved their sacrifice." He kissed her on the forehead. "How are you feeling?"

"Married and very happy."

He laughed. "Me, too." His hands started at her hips, traveling to her waist, then around to caress the tops of her rounded breasts. "You look gorgeous." He leaned down then kissed her neck, licking his way down to the place his hands were, but she stopped him before things went too far. The sad pout on his face made Gerti smile.

"We have a barn full of people over there, Quinn."

"You know I don't care." She kissed him, and he hummed at the softness and warmth of her lips.

"I know, and so does Charles. He's only giving me five minutes to bring you back. He said no disappearing tonight."

Quinn placed his head on her shoulder and groaned. "What does he care?"

"It's time to cut the cake."

"You made a cake?" he asked, lifting his head.

"No, I wasn't allowed." She frowned then laughed. She was happy to hand over the reins this time. "I think Cora made it."

"Well, I hope she's been paying attention to the way you do things." He took her hand, and they started walking towards the house.

"Be nice." She gently squeezed his arm. "And be nice to Ray. Cora says he's a nice guy." Quinn would agree. Ray had held his own against him and Charles, but he had more important things to discuss.

"Don't want to talk about him,"

"What do you want to talk about, then?"

"How long before all these people leave?"

EPILOGUE

"Hey, Quinn, come to check on your girl?"

Quinn gave Cora a sly smile, knowing she already knew the answer to that question. The Shop was closed for the day, and with only one thing on his mind, Quinn looked down at purple toenails, then looked up to a shrugging Cora. "You did this?"

"It's cute, don't you think? Purple is her color."

"I can't believe y'all let her do this." The three dogs he spoke to huffed out their breaths in unison then watched as Quinn lifted out the baby girl they'd been watching over all morning.

"She was almost asleep, Quinn. Gerti's gonna get you for that."

"I can handle Gerti." Quinn nuzzled his nose against the sweet-smelling neck he'd been missing for hours. "Besides, I told Quincy Rose I'd be by to see her before she took her nap. She's been expecting me."

When Quinn and Gerti found out they were having

a girl, Gerti couldn't be happier, but Quinn was nervous. Not only didn't he have much experience with babies, but he sure didn't know anything about raising little girls. Their daughter was born on a warm day in May, just before midnight. She entered the world weighing a healthy nine pounds and seven ounces, which Gerti blamed all on Quinn. The name didn't come to them until after she was born. Gerti's mom Trudy thought she had Rose's eyes, and Ms. Edith swore she had Quincy's.

"She's been too busy being pampered to miss you." Cora still couldn't get over the way Quinn looked at his daughter. Charles was the same way with his daughter Charlotte. The two of them enjoyed being dads so much, they were even considering buying a few goats from a nearby farm. "Where's Terrence? I've got a whole jar of pralines for him."

"Working. The cherry trees are being delivered today." The cherry trees were meant to be a surprise for Gerti. After contemplating what he could grow on the ranch, cherries seemed to be the obvious choice, but he was too excited for them to keep it a secret. Quinn blurted out the news one night after dinner when they sat in her pergola. They decided to plant them where the blooms could be seen from their bedroom.

"Well, if it isn't Mr. Garland. How you doing, Quinn?"

"Just fine. You and Gerti party planning, Ms. Edith?"

She nodded and gave him a wide grin. "This one will be the biggest yet."

"I can only imagine," Quinn said.

"Those dogs didn't give you a hard time, did they? You know they won't let anybody get too close."

"That's what they're supposed to do," Cora said,

laughing. The three Rottweilers were very protective of Quincy Rose. The thick circle of black and brown fur that surrounded her was enough for people to keep their distance and ask Gerti first before touching her. "If you're ready to go, I'll walk you out, Ms. Edith. I don't want to be around when Gerti gets in here. Quinn's got that look in his eyes." He looked at her without trying to deny it.

While Ms. Edith and Cora got ready to leave, Quinn picked a few songs on the jukebox and danced with Quincy Rose, staring into her eyes as they waited for Gerti. Moments later, they were alone, and he didn't even notice the click of the door as it closed. He danced and hummed to the music, lulling Quincy Rose to sleep with the vibration of his chest.

"Will she mind if I cut in?"

Quinn smiled and reached for Gerti, wrapping his arm around her waist. "I don't think she'll say anything," he whispered. Quinn pulled Gerti closer, pressing his lips to her forehead. "How you doing, Ole Fashion?"

"Doing pretty good now." Gerti rested her head on Quinn's chest and rubbed his arm. The part of his arm that now held a rose and cherry tattoo was her favorite. "You're in a good mood."

"I'm blaming you."

The song changed, and Quinn slowly turned all three of them as Otis Redding sang about how strong his love is. Quinn wasn't sure if he could express it as soulfully, but he felt every word. He closed his eyes and thought about the dream he had the night before.

In it, Gerti was sitting under the pergola with him, looking out at the ranch. They were old, with his beard grey and her locs the same. Even with their wrinkles, Gerti was beautiful. Just as the sun went down, eight children came running out from behind them. Then just as Quinn was about to say something to them, they multiplied. Their ages changed, and suddenly, the eight they started became generations of Garlands. Cowboy boots and headwraps as far as he could see. All because of him and Gerti.

"I'll always take the blame if it ends up with us slow dancing."

"I love you, Ole Fashion."

"I love you, too."

"That's good to know."

Acknowledgments

It isn't until you write a book that you realize that they're more than pretty words with nice covers. It's a bunch of hard work. I may have been the only one typing but this was definitely a group effort.

My mom, who made it possible for me to type every single word of this story. You believed I could, so I did. Michael, you understood and never complained about the early mornings or late nights that inspiration claimed. Georgia who gave honest opinions about anything aesthetic wise I had a question about. You have a great eye. Hendrix for asking if they kiss in my book; just a little. My editor Kai. It's hard to trust someone with your book baby, but you took great care of it and returned it with instructions. If only everything was that easy.

None of this would have happened if Juanita hadn't asked me to join a group, just to start another group, who blossomed into something spectacular. To the ladies of WTOWW- If it weren't for your honesty, laughter, tears, and strength I would have quit a long time ago. You've taught me so much and inspired me even more; this is for you.

www.ingramcontent.com/pod-product-compliance
Lightning Source LLC
Chambersburg PA
CBHW021951170626
46808CB00001B/102